LENGTHS

A novel

By: Steph Campbell & Liz Reinhardt

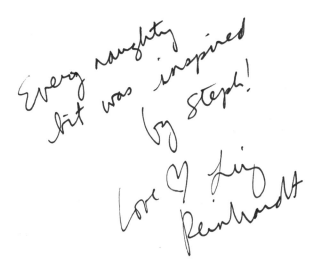

To the gals of the FP.
We'd sink for every one of you, any day.

and,

To Marcus Flutie, Him. Yes. Him.

Published by

Liz Reinhardt and Steph Campbell

Cover design by: Todd Maloy

Cover photo by: Yuri_Arcurs the Photographer

The characters and events portrayed in this book are fictitious. Any similarity to real persons, living or dead is coincidental and not intended by the author.

-One-

Deo

My mom stuffs me with homemade coconut cake she's been making every year for my birthday since I was a little guy, but she's updated it nicely by lacing the icing with dark rum. Last year she gave me diving gear, which I have yet to use. I have plans for it, though. Eventual plans. This year she hands me a name and number on an old scrap of grey recycled paper for my twenty-second birthday, and it's definitely something I can put to immediate use.

"Rocko does fantastic work." She pulls down one shoulder on her flowing purple dress and shows me a bunch of lotus flowers in pinks and whites so perfect, I feel like if I reach out the petals would be smooth under my fingertips. "Tell him I sent you and that this means we're even." She ducks her face down, all her waist-long hair falling forward and hiding her little blush like she's a teenager with some crazy crush.

I shake the paper at her. "C'mon. Tell me you didn't do some fucking booty-call barter to get me a tat."

Her eyes, light brown just like mine, narrow in my direction. "Don't be a creep, Deo. First of all, the lavender I just pressed sold out before I finished bottling it, and I have double orders in for my next harvest. Secondly, my nookie is none of your damn business, but I will voluntarily tell you that I don't use it for barter." Her lecture completely loses its serious tone, and she pokes me with a foot decorated with a dozen silver rings. "Though it's so damn good I could make a killing off of it if I wanted to."

I'd just scooped a mouthful of rummy icing into my mouth, and now I have to resist the urge to vomit it back up. "Too much, Mom. I don't need to know."

"Then stop being a smart-ass and say thank you when your mother gives you a perfectly nice gift."

She holds her cheek out and I kiss it, catching a whiff of the vanilla and jasmine scent she mixes herself in her little hippie-dippie store. It's not my thing, but I'm happy for her. Her weird little cottage full of creepy potions and witchcraft draws every looney hippie from a hundred miles in for all kinds of herbs and oils, and she makes a decent slice for herself. I like that I don't need to worry about her and that she's happy.

And I thank Gaia, or whoever the hell she's praying to nowadays, that she can't hear my thoughts and give me another women's libber speech. My mom thinks it's cool that she doesn't have to rely on a man for her living. Me too. Just, sometimes, I wish she had someone else to lean on when shit gets rough.

"Thank you. It's an awesome gift. You know most moms would have picked up a nice sweater set or a tie or something." I tug on her long hair, red from the henna she puts in it all the time.

She lays a cool hand on my arm. "Really? A tie?" For a minute she squishes her eyebrows down together uncertainly, like maybe she's thinking a tie would have been a good idea.

"I have no clue, actually. We're not most people, right? Let me go get a nice heathenish tattoo to celebrate my youth before it's all gone." Mom likes being edgy except when she thinks I'm behind the curve or losing out.

And considering I'm officially twenty-two, recently fired from my fucktastic full-time job, without a place of my own or reliable transportation, maybe she thinks a tie might have given me some direction.

"Just...get something meaningful, okay? Something you really care about." Her eyes are shiny, probably from tears, but I'm just gonna pretend it's because she's excited.

I grab my hoodie off the back of the old wooden kitchen chair. "So, no severed clown heads?"

A smile tugs on one side of her mouth. "No. Unless you have some spiritual tie to severed clown heads. Don't forget to take a plate of cake for Grandpa." She gives me a too-tight squeeze as I head out the door, the cake she wrapped up balanced on one hand. "Oh! And you got a package."

The smile that was almost a real thing goes wooden and overly wide on her face. I sigh, not knowing what's in the little brown box, but positive about who it's from.

"Dad?" I don't want to even take the fucking thing, but she's holding it out with all this hope, like I'll be able to be super mature and look past his douchiness and be glad he sent something.

Being cool with his fuck-ups is her bag, not mine.

"You know he wanted to be here this summer, Deo. You know that. He's in the Congo. There's no way he could have made it back." She presses the little box my way, and I pull it out of her hands and turn it over in mine, wishing I was badass enough to toss it in the garbage and not give it another glance.

But he's still my dad. He still sent a gift. He still fucking cares, even if it's not as much as he should.

I hold it next to my ear and shake it, long like a pencil case and strangely light. "I'm gonna guess it's a boomerang."

"Did he ever wind up getting you one? You must have asked five or six years in a row." She tucks her hair behind her ears, and it hits me again how much my grown mother can look like a little girl. Maybe it's because she doesn't do the whole makeup thing or because she wears all this jangly jewelry like some teenager, or just because she has this optimistic-but-vulnerable vibe down pat, but she looks so young, it's easy for me to pack up whatever hard shit I'm trying to deal with and put it away where it won't bother her.

"Yeah. The Christmas I was fifteen. Airmail from Sydney." I toss the box and catch it in the hand not balancing the cake. "Thanks for the cake and the number. I'll stop by when I've got some decent ink to show you, alright?"

She leans in the door frame behind the torn screen door I should fix but haven't bothered to yet and smiles at me.

Pissed as I am at my father, I sure as shit managed to pick up some of his crappiest traits. Like being able to leave my mom hanging. Worrying the piss out of her. Dropping more on her shoulders than she needs to deal with.

I slam the door on my Jeep and throw the box into the back, then pull away from my mother's house fast so I don't have to focus on that rolling disappointment, all wishful eyes and sweet, sad smile.

I slide my phone out and unfold the scrap of paper she gave me, dialing with half an eye on the road.

"This is Rocko." The voice is business-crisp.

"Hey. Marigold Beckett gave me your number, told me I should call you for some good ink." I glance at the box from my father in the rearview mirror and wonder what he felt was an appropriate gift for this un-monumental birthday. Last year, for my twenty-first, it was Balkan 176, vodka so strong it knocked me over and out before I could drink enough to get myself in real trouble. My grandpa and my best friend, Cohen, pried it from my drunk fingers and proceeded to help me down the entire bottle over the course of a weekend. We were stupid-drunk as sailors on leave, and it was good times.

Would have been better to have had my dad there for it, but beggars can't be choosers.

"Marigold, eh?" I feel a wave of pissed-offedness at the creepy happiness in this guy's voice when he says my mom's name.

"Yeah, Marigold Beckett. My mother." I make sure the words are clear as a fucking ringing, clanging bell for him.

He clears his throat. "Right. Okay. I'm off of 80, past the Surf Shack. You wanna come by and check out my portfolios, work up some sketches? I have a client scheduled in a few minutes, but once she's done, the night's open."

"I'll stop by." I click off just in time to pull into my grandfather's driveway and honk twice. He swings the door of his tiny-ass house open with a bang.

"What are you honking like that for? You got no manners, you know that? You do that when you pick up girls? Cause if any girl comes when you honk like that, she's a damn floozy!" He has a limp on his left side, but other than that, my grandpa could wrestle a fucking tiger with one arm tied behind his back.

"I only date floozies! They're the most fun!" I yell at him, and he cracks a wide, gap-toothed smile. "I'm just stopping by to tell you I'm going to get a new tattoo, so I won't be around til late. You need a phone you can hear, you deaf son of a bitch! I tried you twice on the way here!"

He leans into the driver-side window, slaps me on the back of the neck twice and says, "More tattoos? Why? You aren't ugly enough yet? You think you're a big man now? I can still put you over my knee and cane you anytime." He pats my shoulder. "Did you bring home some of your mom's cake?"

I pass the piece to him through the window. "Did you eat anything real today? I don't need to come home to you in a diabetic coma."

"Stop clucking around me like a damn mother hen," he gripes, taking a swipe of the icing and eating it off his finger like a little kid. Or like me fifteen minutes ago. "Your mother is an angel. You got a package from that idiot son of mine?"

I jerk my thumb in the back. He raises an eyebrow at me. "I don't want it," I explain.

"Stop pouting like a little girl and open the damn thing," my grandpa snaps.

But I hear the letdown behind his grumpy-ass words. My dad is a professional at letting people down, fucking up, not being where he's needed most, not doing what he should be doing.   When I was a kid, all I could focus on was what that meant to me and how much it fucked up my world. Now that I'm older, it kills me to see how it bites and eats at my grandpa and mom.

"Fine." I reach back with one hand and fish the box off the floor, rip the paper away, and dig through the little box, pulling out three cigars. "The label says 'Gurkha,'" I read and my grandpa chuckles like a kid on Halloween. "Good?"

"Too good for you." Grandpa grabs them in his hand and turns to walk back to the house. "Get home at a decent hour, and we'll have these with the lobsters I caught. Bring that numbskull friend of yours too."

"You made me lobster! Aw, you old sweetie!" I call to him. He waves his hand in disgust, but I catch the laugh that bobs his shoulders up and down.

So Grandpa and I will drag Cohen over, eat some lobster dipped in butter, drink beer, smoke cigars on the porch, and talk about life and everything good while we try to ignore the hole that's always firmly in place when my father's not around. Not the worst end to my birthday.

But first I need to get a little ink.

I find the place, a little neat-looking building, all modern and light with lots of windows and lots more art on the walls. There are the fairly standard pieces that every tourist or eighteen-year-old comes in and wants, no imagination, no real deep thought. Not that I should talk. I have an eagle on one bicep and a heart with 'Mom' through it on the other. So fuck my attempts to keep my tattoos all original and meaningful.

I'm heading to the heavy black portfolio books when a soft, husky voice behind the counter asks, "Did you make an appointment?"

When I look up, I have a feeling I might do even better than some ink and coconut rum cake, lobster and cigars this birthday.

-Two-
Whit

"Hello?" I say, tapping my pen on the counter top to get his attention. "Over here, appointment?"

He likely doesn't have one. No one ever does. They're mostly tourists, who think they need something a little more permanent than a jar of sea shells to remember their trip to Silver Strand. So they come to see Rocko, who never turns anyone away. Which means that this guy, or any other douche that comes in without an appointment, will be here all night deciding which tattoo to get to complement their Affliction or Ed Hardy shirts and Rocko will do it. I'll be stuck here, too, because, though Rocko may be skilled with the tattoo gun, reconciling the register at night is not his speciality. That's what I'm here for.

"Oh, hey, sorry 'bout that," gorgeous surfer-boy finally says. "I don't have an *official* appointment, but I called and talked to Rocko earlier. He said it was cool if I came by."

Sigh.

"Of course he did."

"So, is it alright if I flip through the books?" He points to the heavy leather portfolios, but his eyes stay fixed on me, sexy, friendly, and sparked with that tiny kernel of hungry appreciation I now know as lust. One look from him and a thousand hormonal dominoes tip over and click to every part of my body that can get hot or wet or racing.

"They're over there." I motion to the stack of black books piled on the small table and order my body back under control. Lust is a little bit new for me, but I have to get used to the race and thrill. This guy isn't the first or the last who's going to make me feel this way. And that's definitely a very good thing.

"Thanks." He nods and raises one eyebrow to match his crooked smile. Is he always smiling? He grabs a couple off the top of the stack and plops onto the worn sofa. I cringe a little. Surfer boy may be responsible for keeping me here late, but he definitely isn't bad to look at, and that sofa has seen its share of Rocko's after-hours conquests.

I slide open the top drawer of my desk and pull out my cell phone.

7:05. *Crap*. There's no way I'm going to be out of here in time to make it to Ryan's by 9:00. I send him a quick text telling him I'm going to be late, and toss my phone back into the drawer.

"Hey," I call. "Come here." I wave the appointmentless guy over.

He looks around confused, and presses his hand to his chest as if he's asking, "*Me?*" The front of the store is empty apart from the two of us, so, obviously, I'm talking to him.

"Yes, you, come over here, the weather's fine," I say, rolling my eyes.

He closes the book and walks back over to my desk. He's wearing a plain white t-shirt, nice and tight on his biceps, with a pair of Ray-Bans tucked into the v-neck. Casual. Easy. I like.

"You can sit here," I say, pointing to an extra office chair next to mine.

"You missed me when I was all the way over there? That's seriously flattering." He winks.

"Hardly, just trust me on this one. It's a better option." I wrinkle my nose at the couch and try not to imagine all the diseases crawling around in the cushions like loose change.

"Alright. You have a trustworthy face, you know. Anyone ever tell you that?" He grins and plays along, taking the seat at the end of my desk despite his confusion.

My eyes keep flicking over to him, more often than I should let them. I take in his long frame and taut muscles and pay more attention than I strictly should. I attempt to go back to organizing the day's receipts, but forget what I'm doing long enough to notice the strands of dark hair that are matted together, most likely from the seawater.

"Do you, um, need me to fill something out or something? This looks like a respectable shop that's all about the paper trail." His grin is cocky and laid back all at once.

I blink several times to draw myself out of my lust-induced daze.

"Uh, I just need your name. For the book, I mean." I open the book with jerky, clumsy hands and curse under my breath. I'm not usually this asinine.

He doesn't try to be coy about watching me. "Deo," he says.

"Deo? Is that short for something?" I ask before I can stop

myself. I know how annoying it is to have your name questioned.

"Nope, just Deo. D-e-o," he spells for me. "Last name is Beckett."

"Okay." I write it down even though I don't really need to. Rocko wouldn't care if his name was just Deo. Or Ginger. Or Jesus Christ of Nazareth, as long as he's getting paid. "So, Deo, you came to get a tattoo and you really have no idea what you want?"

He runs his palm across his scruffy cheek and shrugs.

"No, I'm not real sure. I have these two bad boys already," he says. He pulls one shirt sleeve up and reveals a heart with the word "Mom," through it, then, as if it can't get any worse, he turns and does the same to the other arm, showing off an eagle with the flex of his bicep and a low chuckle.

"You have got to be shitting me." He doesn't seem offended in the least when I laugh at him. Actually, his smile is conspiratorial, like we're sharing an inside joke. "How unoriginal can you be?"

He pushes his sleeve back down, and I feel an embarrassing disappointment.

"Trust me, my mom is original enough for the whole damn town. Getting these was like an act of total rebellion."

His big, easy smile is so freakishly white and straight and handsome, it can't possibly be human.

My phone beeps from inside the drawer.

"Excuse me," I say, sliding the drawer out. Because I may be far away from home in this crazy, hippie town, and I may have thrown half my conservative morals to the wind, but I still have some   manners.

No problem. 9pm or 2am,

I'll still be having my way with you.

I feel my cheeks ignite, even though Deo has no idea what the text from Ryan says. This side of me is new, I sometimes feel like everyone, even strangers on the street, know. Not like there's any way they could possibly know that I went from being home by midnight every night so that I could ensure I had plenty of rest before school the next day, to dragging myself into my apartment just long enough to shower and change before running to class. There's technically no way they could know that this person sitting behind the desk at this tattoo shop used to work as a bank teller. And no one would ever come close to guessing that up until three months ago, I had only been with one other guy. And now, well, now I was staying far on the other   side   of   committed.

"Everything okay?" Deo asks. His eyebrows are raised and the glint in his eyes is one hundred percent conspiratorial. He knows.

I slam the phone back into the drawer. "Yep, everything's great. About this tattoo, though?" I wheel my swivel chair over to his side. "Where were you thinking of getting it?" I'm close enough to him now that I can smell him. He smells like a guy, in all the wonderful ways that only guys can smell. Musky and sweaty. But also like the ocean. And something sweet. Vanilla?

"I'm thinking right here." He points to a spot on his forearm. "Maybe. Maybe something that wraps around?" He says it like a question. Like he wants my opinion.

I nod. "That'd be nice, especially with the placement of your others."

Without thinking, I rub my hand across the spot on his forearm. It's tan and smooth and feels warm, like the sand that's been baked by the sun all day. He glances down at my hand on his arm and gives me that freakishly perfect smile, and I pull my hand away in knee-jerk response to it.

"Do you live around here? Or are you just visiting?" I ask to offset the awkward jitters I'm currently trying to control. The answer is obvious from the olive color of his skin and his sun-lightened hair, both side effects of a vast abundance of Vitamin D. I bet there's even sand under his nails.

"Born and raised. Never lived anywhere else. Never wanted to, either." There's something in the way he says it, something behind the simple words. Like he's trying to convince himself more than me that it's true.

"So, is that your only tattoo?" He zeroes in on the place no one has ever noticed before. At least, no one has ever brought it up and asked me about it before.

I reach up and touch the delicate skin behind my left ear, trying to conceal it, even though there's no point now. How did he even notice that?

I   nod.

"A 'W'? Is that for your name? Talk about unoriginal," he teases, bumping my shoulder like we're old surf buddies. "So, what   is   it?   Willow?   Wendy?"

"Whit," I say. "My name is Whit." I leave out the fact that the W behind my ear is not for my name, but for my younger brother,   Wakefield.

"Whit? Is that short for something?" he asks. Just like I knew he   would.

"Whitley. I know, it's odd, but Deo isn't exactly mainstream." I try to preempt the usual questions. My parents had this weird idea that they should use their mothers' maiden names as their children's names, despite the fact that they weren't even all that close   to   either   set   of   their   parents.

"Cool. I gotcha." He doesn't dig for any more information, which is a relief and a disappointment. "So, this tattoo. You got any ideas? I want something with meaning. Something that I won't regret, you know? This one's for my mom, so no more lame   rebellion   ink."

Before I really know what I'm saying, words I never expected to utter are tumbling out of my mouth. "Well, there's this one. I sort of drew it up for myself, but I think I'm done with getting tattoos.   One   is   enough."

I slide a piece of white paper toward him. He turns the paper every which way, trying to read the tiny script I'd written out to look   more   like   a   thin   band   than   actual   letters.

"This is part of me now?" he asks, his golden-brown eyes crinkling at the edges from the smile that takes over his face. The rough skin on his index finger scratches over the paper with a rasp.

"Yep." I'm now regretting showing him the drawing.

"What's it mean?" His eyes lock on mine, and suddenly, that no-worries surfer boy vibe vanishes. It's replaced by something sweet and deep that cuts right through me and clean to the root of my heart, to the place no one can see because it's still too raw and   fucked   up.

"It can mean whatever you want it to mean. Like, maybe it means that you can't change the past. You can't right wrongs. But, I don't know, you can try to make something meaningful of the   future,   you   know?"

I   feel   exposed.

He can see inside of me. He sees that to me, the tattoo actually means that the guilt and the grief are all part of me.

I snatch the paper away from him.

But he's nodding like he gets it. Really, truly gets it. I can see the tendons in his neck stand out when he swallows and his nod   is   tense.

"Sold," he says, plucking the piece of paper back from my hands.

-Three-

Deo

Rocko isn't half bad for a guy with a soul patch and these ironic hipster tortoiseshell glasses. Even if he does have the hots for my mother.

Or maybe I'm high off all the endorphins the relentless prick of the tattoo gun always releases in me.

Or maybe, just maybe, that girl at the reception desk with all the right curves and her mysterious tattoo and her fucking irritating phone and saucy-as-hell, biting attitude is making this whole experience something way more meaningful than even my mom anticipated.

Whit. I like her name. I like the way her hips sway in her tight little skirt when she marches around in those hot heels, putting things in order with this sexy military precision. I like the way her eyes flick over to me, once, twice, a third time, and how her cheeks go pink when she realizes I'm still watching.

"So Whit designed this one?" Rocko clears away some blood and excess ink from my rib and I curl my damn toes so I won't wince, on the off chance she's stealing a look my way. This is a tearing, open flesh wound on the raw skin and muscle of my ribs and it's been the most agonizing half hour of my life. I thought I was tough-nuts because my arms were no big deal, but

I didn't know what it felt like to have the gun shooting straight pain onto my goddamn bones.

"Yeah." I watch her tuck a shiny piece of the dark hair that just reaches her chin behind her ear. The tattooless ear. She bites her lip and I have to suck my next breath through my teeth. I always thought girls only did that to flirt, but she's narrowing her eyes at some receipts that are screwing with her, and that bite is all real, sexy frustration, and I want a nip bad. I focus on Rocko, the pain, anything that will keep the threat of a raging boner at bay. "I thought it would be cool on my forearm, but something this badass needs to go where it hurts."

"It's a good spot for it. She's got an awesome eye for detail, among her hundreds of other talents. I hope she decides to get her PhD somewhere in the area, because I seriously don't know what I'd do without her." He glances up and catches sight of the clock on the wall, one of those black cats with a tail pendulum. My grandpa has one like it in his office and thinks it's the funniest shit. He raises his voice and calls in her direction, "Whit, I'm sorry, babe. You know you can say the word if I go over. It's late as hell. Go, have some fun. Get." He waves her away, and I make a frantic attempt to look down at my tattoo. It's six tiny-ass words. What's taking so damn long? If this girl leaves before I get her number, there will definitely be more tats in my immediate future.

She's got this little uptight walk, like she's at some debutante ball, all straight-backed with these careful, graceful steps. But those hips…they're hypnotizing, and no stiff-spined walk can stop the pure sexiness of those gorgeous hips. "Rocko, it's fine. Last time I left you alone, we had to call the lady to come in and fix the register."

Relief floods through me, and then something hotter and better. She dips her head and looks at the ink on my skin, her dark eyes squinted while she studies it.

"This one's on the house, nothing to ring up. Go ahead. A beautiful girl on a Thursday night in this college town? C'mon, I know you must have plans. Enjoy your youth." Rocko notices Whit's concentrated stare and switches gears, which is good, because the idea of her going out and enjoying her gorgeous, wild youth without me there to help her out is making my vision blur red. "First time you've seen your own design in ink?" She nods, and it's weirdly shy for a girl so in-charge. "It's a gorgeous design, Whit. Simple, elegant. You've got a real eye for this."

"Glad to know my art elective is good for something practical." The shy sweetness vanishes and she goes all iron-spined again. "So, you're sure you don't need me?"

"Much as I love and adore everything you do, I promise I can close the shop up on my own. Fun. You. Now." When she hesitates and wrings her little hands, he pulls the gun away and says, "Look. I'm all done. Now Deo can be a gentleman and walk you to your car, and you don't need to worry about the shop falling down around my ears. Okay?"

I hop off the table and inspect the black lines, almost too graceful and neat, but just jagged enough to be bad-ass. And meaningful.

"Thanks, man." I try a simple shake, but Rocko walks me through a whole complicated hand gesture thing that leaves me trying to hide my smile at his corniness. He's a good egg. A dope, but a good egg. "You gonna snap a shot for your portfolio?"

"Good idea." Rocko looks around, confusion all over his face.

The soft footfall of Whit's steps contrasts with her jangly laugh. "I got this, Rocko. Stop before you hurt yourself." She comes back with a camera and says, "Say 'cheese.'"

She's got a mouth that makes me think dirty thoughts, all pouty, deep pink lips that can't completely manage to look stern or serious no matter what expression she has on her face. Right now she's trying to look all business, but that mouth and those sexy dark eyes and her perfect curves are all conspiring to drive me out-of-my-damn-mind insane.

To the point where I'm standing to get a picture done of my new ink, but I don't bother to show my new ink. I scramble to turn in the right direction when she raises a dark eyebrow.

She sighs, trying to look irritated, but her mouth curls up in a soft smile. She reaches a hand out and lays it on my hip, her fingers warm on my skin. She slides her hand along my back and shoulder, and follows the line through, propping my arm up, letting the tips of her fingers skim the inside of my wrist and along my palm. Swallowing, blinking, breathing, all suddenly become very difficult.

She snaps a few pictures, says, "Let me do the bandage for you," and I'm positive this girl will wind up in my bed tonight.

I slide back onto the table and watch her collect the little pot of Udder Butter, the gauze, and tape. I can do this all myself, but I'm not about to point that out. "Thanks for the tat inspiration." I look at her from under my upheld arm, her hair all glossy, and when I lean closer and take a breath in, she smells like something citrus and something clean, crushed leaves or spring or something I can't quite put my finger on. "I feel like I kind of stole a piece of your soul."

Her eyes flick up at me, and I can see the panic she's wrestling to control. Her voice slices out cold and mean. "It's just a tattoo. I sketch designs constantly. It helps pass the time."

"Alright." Her fingers dip into the ointment and she spreads it over my torn-up skin gently, even though her features have gone ice-hard. "I guess it's a part of me now whether you like it or not." It's a joke. It's clearly a joke, said in my joking voice, but she doesn't brush it off or roll her eyes or chuckle along. She blinks back tears and works like mad to get her shaking hands under control enough to twist the lid back on the Udder Butter.

"It's not a joke." Her eyes meet mine, and they're flashing with some kind of pain that goes right down to her fucking marrow. It's raw and pissed-as-hell. She slaps the gauze on with more force than is strictly necessary, and I wince around her roughness as she rips the tape in rushed, angry jerks.

I want to make it better, tell her I know the pain of no one understanding a damn thing, tell her that jokes or drinks or pointless, shallow fun bury it for the moment, but that only makes it hurt more when it rips through and rears its ugly ass head again when you least expect it.

"Hey!" I call. She's stomping away, throwing things back in their rightful drawers. "Hey, Whit?" I slide off the table and curl a hand around her shoulder. "I was being a dick, alright?" For a second she goes stiff, then relaxes under my touch. She turns her head and looks over her shoulder at me, just slightly.

"I think what I was trying to say but being an asshole about is 'thank you.' So, hear me out for a minute, alright? I've been going through some shit, and I wasn't planning on getting anything done tonight because I wanted to make my mom happy, but I knew there wasn't gonna be anything here that could have any real meaning for me. Then here you are, and here's this tattoo that, I don't really know why, but it honestly feels like you reached into my head and pulled out the one thing that could possibly make any sense of all the craziness I've been feeling. So thank you." I hold my hands up in surrender. "That's all. Thank you."

She turns around slowly, so close she's in my arms and I can move less than a handful of inches and have my mouth on hers.

"You're welcome." The words slip out quick and rigid. The next words are slightly more relaxed. "Sorry. It's been a really long day." She twirls out of my arms and away from me and gathers her purse and that annoying phone I want to smash into a thousand pieces, suddenly in a rush to leave. Me. She waves to Rocko, and turns to me as I'm pulling my hoodie over my head. "Well, it was cool meeting you."

I ignore her attempt at a sendoff and push the door open with one hand so she can walk out in front of me. She tucks her hair behind her ears and heads right to a white Chrysler LeBaron that's kinda pimp. She leans against the driver's side door and smiles, but it's not a real one. It's too angular, too polite, there's too much thought in it. I want to see a smile that rips out of somewhere deep and changes the shape and shine of her eyes.

"Thanks for walking me to my car. So, um, I guess I'll see you around." She pops the door open and leans in, setting her bag on the passenger seat neatly, then looks back at me with expectation clear on her face. Only it's like she's expecting me to go, which I'm not about to do. She's definitely not expecting me to step closer, run my thumb over those sexy lips, watch while her eyes widen with shock then burn with sexy desire, and kiss her. But that's exactly what I do anyway.

It's a good as all hell kiss. I hook my arm around her waist and pull her so her body is locked close to mine. She leans her head back, and I put my lips on the curve of her neck and kiss up under her jaw, right where the crushed leaf smell meets that perfect clean-girl skin smell. I pull back and look at her parted lips, closed eyes, dark, curved eyebrows pressed almost together like she's overthinking this. Before she can change her mind, I press my mouth to hers.

She opens her lips, and I'm a little shocked by the hungry slide of her tongue and the low moan that echos from her mouth to mine. I pull my hands down to her hips and squeeze tight, wanting to feel her skin under my fingers. She turns her head and deepens the kiss, her hands cupping the back of my neck with a possessive need that makes me hard and blots out all thoughts other than her and the clawing desire to get her in the backseat as quickly as possible and peel back everything until it's just the two of us and what we want bared between us.

I nip that bottom lip, exactly the way I'd been wanting to since I saw her bite it in the shop, and she lets out a tight sigh from somewhere deep in her throat. She pulls me closer and licks at me with a tongue so soft, my mind reels and crashes before it can imagine everything that tongue might be capable of doing. I press my hands under her shirt, just grazing the soft skin of her stomach and start moving up for more when she tears her lips away.

She's breathing fast and heavy, her face is pink, her eyes are shiny, she has no idea where she should look or what she should say, and I want to capitalize on her uncertainty by kissing her again, hard and fast, but she ducks out of the way and shakes her head slightly.

"It's my birthday today." I pull my fingers down her arm and take her hand. "My grandpa is making some lobster and we're going to smoke some mind-blowing crazy cigars my dad sent from God knows where. We could pick up some beers. Or some wine or whatever else you want. His place is right by the bay. You can see every star from the dock."

She pulls her hand out of my grasp and presses her palms down along the front of her skirt, shaking her head like she's trying to get her bearings. "Happy birthday, Deo. I'd like to come by, but I...I really can't. I gotta go." The buzz of her constantly-irritating phone interrupts her last words, and she glances down at the screen. Her eyes go wide for one split second, and then she looks flustered and embarrassed before she sends a quick reply.

She's sexting. With someone who isn't me.

It's fine. Or it should be fine. I've known this girl for just over an hour. We kissed one time. It's not like she's wearing my varsity jacket or whatever. So why am I so royally pissed the hell off?

"Look, it's cool, right? Do what you gotta do. I'll see you around, maybe?" I want...more. I want enough to make the tattoo scalding my ribs and that sweet as hell kiss burned in my memory mean something more than they do. But she's not available, and this is probably a good thing. Whit isn't the kind of girl I need right now. Way too uptight. Way too control-freak. The 'W' inked behind her ear is just an anomaly. I know this girl is probably type-A, high-maintenance, high drama, and that's not my thing. At all.

"Deo?" I turn and look at her, hands in my hoodie pocket. She takes a few tentative steps my way. "You have a phone?" She nabs her lip between her teeth again, like she's about to do something she knows she shouldn't, and it makes me feel this wild surge of triumph. I have a feeling her worst instincts are leading her straight to me whether she likes it or not.

And I'm betting she doesn't like it much at all.

Yet.

I dig my phone out of my pocket and hold it out to her. She crushes it in her hand, closes her eyes, and sweeps her thumb over the keys rapidly before she shoves it back my way. "Call me. If you want. If not, it's okay."

She turns on her heel, clips back to her sensible LeBaron and fumbles with the door handle before she slides in and backs out, a little too fast.

I'm left standing in the parking lot, phone in my hand, the screen still bright with her name and number, and I can't stomp the goofy smile off my face. My brain flips through a million scenarios involving me, Whit, and that sweet little mouth of hers, and they melt my mind so completely, I almost manage to forget the painful sting on my ribs, part of me, and a decent part her. Whether she likes it or not.

-Four-

Whit

Ryan smiles as he pulls the door to his apartment open for me. His eyes are droopy, like he just woke up, and his hair is a crazy mess. But no matter what, he's hot, and right now, that's all that matters. I know it seems skeezy that I just kissed Deo and here I am, meeting Ryan for a little action, but it wasn't planned. Deo just snuck up on me.

I barely take a step through the door when he closes it behind me and presses my back against the cool wood. His lips pry mine open and his tongue gets right down to exploring the landscape of my mouth before we even say hello. I can feel him already hard against me, which would be difficult to conceal, since he's not wearing anything other than a pair of boxers. Ryan doesn't bother dressing up. It's all going to end up scattered across the apartment, anyway. But that's why I'm here, right? No strings. Just fun. *No conversation. No lobster dinners.*

"Well, you're not wasting any time tonight, huh?" I ask, pulling away.

He moans. "What's the point? We both know what this is, Whit. And I have an early class."

"I didn't have to come," I say.

I tuck my short hair back behind my ears and fight the urge to bail. I want him. It's not a secret. That's why I'm here night after night. Ryan is nice enough. He doesn't make me feel like this relationship, or arrangement, is shady, he treats me right when we're together, and, good lord, the boy is a god in the sack.

"I *always* want you to come. Let me prove it." His voice is low and sexy in my ears.

He smiles and pulls me back in, running his hands up the back of my shirt and unhooking the red lace bra that I put on this morning, obviously with him in mind. His lips crush into mine as he pushes me back onto the sofa, and Ryan makes good on his promise.

This is always the most awkward part of our arrangement. When the sex is over and Ryan is passed out and I've got to scrounge around the apartment in the dark, hunting for my clothes. I tiptoe to the refrigerator and pull it open, letting the light filter through the front rooms.

"Gotcha," I say. I smile because I've managed to find the next-to-nothing thong Ryan had peeled off of me and flung across the apartment earlier. It's wrapped around the leg of an end table. I sort of thought it was a goner. "Well done, Whit." I mentally pat myself on the back and then move on to tracking down the killer heels I wore over. There's no way in the world I'm leaving without those.

I know I should feel some form of shame that I'm in this situation. That I regularly put myself in this situation. But I don't. I've learned the hard way recently that life is too fucking short, and I'll be damned if I'm going to take a second of it for granted. I'm living doubly hard from now on. I owe Wakefield that much after all he sacrificed. No one should have to leave this earth at eighteen. No matter how honorable their death is. And since he can't be around anymore to live it up, I'll do it for him.

I slide the black pencil skirt over my hips and zip it up. Even the noise of the zipper cuts through the silence in the apartment, and I feel like a first-rate asshole, because what I want least in life right now is to wake Ryan up. Goodbyes are never any good, and really, who wants to say 'thank you' to their fuck-buddy for getting them off? It goes against the no-strings-attached beauty of our arrangement. I hold my gorgeous shoes in my hand as I crawl around the front of the apartment trying to put my hands on the small purse I'd tossed aside when Ryan met me at the door.

Out of nowhere, Ryan's quiet apartment turns into a fucking big band concert when my stupid phone starts ringing. *Shit.* *Shit.* *Shit.*

I easily find my purse now that it's illuminating the room with each note my phone plays from the inside.

"Whit?" Ryan calls groggily from the sofa.

"Sorry!" I squeak. "I'll shut it off and get out of here."

"Thanks for a good time." His voice trails off at the end. I cringe. Exactly what I was trying to avoid.

"I'll call you," I promise guiltily. He mumbles something that's so full of sleep I can't understand it, just as I silence my phone. I pull out my car keys and sprint down the stairs to my car. It isn't until I'm outside in the fresh air that I feel like I can breathe again. I check my missed calls as I walk to the LeBaron. I don't recognize the number.

Perfect.

A wrong number at this hour.

I settle into the car and rub my eyes. It's nearly 3 A.M. I have to be in class at 8. I turn onto PCH and my ringtone screams through the quiet of the night again. I hit the speakerphone button and toss my phone into my lap, because wearing a Bluetooth is never going to happen.

"Hello?" The windows are down and the car is full of salty, damp air. It feels magnificent, but, damn, it makes it hard to hear.

"Whit? Is that you?" a slurring male voice asks. Great. A drunk dial.

"Indeed it is," I sigh. "Who the hell is this?"

"The dude you didn't eat lobster with." It's like I can hear his adorable-as-all-hell smile over the phone.

I can't help but laugh. I'll cut him some slack for this douchebag move since it's his birthday.

"Sounds like you had a little more than lobster there, Deo."

"Indeed I did. Can I be honest?" His voice is deep and sexy, even in his inebriated state.

"It's your birthday, honesty is practically a requirement."

"I can't stop thinking about you. The way you kissed me tonight—"

"Back up there. *I* kissed you?"

"That's how I remember it," he chuckles. "Anyway, since it is my birthday month—"

"Oh, so now you get a whole damn month?"

"I deserve it," he says. Cocky son-of-a-bitch. Still, I feel my cheeks aching from the grin I've had plastered across my face since I answered the phone.

"Right."

"Like I was saying. I know you had a hot date tonight, and I don't know if it's a serious arrangement or just casual or whatever. And it's not really my business," he says, kind of like he doesn't care. Which he shouldn't, because it isn't any of his business. But the smile that had been making my face ache falls a little. "But I'd like you to give me a shot if that's in the cards. So there. I put it out there on my birthday because I really like you, Whit. Whadda ya say?"

I stare at the red light in front of me, waiting for it to turn green. I'm the only car for miles in every direction.

"What'd you have in mind?" I ask. I know the answer to this already, of course. I saw the way he looked at me tonight. And after that kiss, there's no mistaking what he wants to do.

"I thought I could bring you by the house to meet my mom." His slur has a playful tinge to it. Not what I expected.

"I'm sorry, what?" I spit.

"Lighten up, girl. I'm kidding. I don't know. We can go to the beach. What's your favorite one?"

"Um, I haven't actually been to the beach since I moved here. Or, um, ever." I run my fingers along the steering wheel and try to imagine going to the ocean, listening to the waves, breathing that potent salt air deep into my lungs.

Deo's voice borders on horrified. "You haven't been to the ocean? Really? Never? Well no shit! Then we're going. Tomorrow. I refuse to take no for an answer."

I've got to admit, I'm surprised he didn't outright say he wanted to fuck me. Got to give him a little credit for that.

"Where are you from, anyway?" he asks with frank interest.

My fingers tighten on the steering wheel, and I have to let my foot up off the gas a little. Thinking about the place I left makes me stress-speed. "Pennsylvania," I answer through gritted teeth.

His laugh is loud and loose. "Ah, that explains the stick up your ass."

I could be offended, but there's something easy and fun about Deo, and it makes me relax a little. "Well, we can't all be professional beach bums."

"Who says?" he demands, and I can hear a smile I like picturing on his face curving over his words.

It's weird how this is the first time I've ever been on the phone with Deo, but we have an easy back and forth like we've been chumming around for years. "You're obviously drunk, and

I have class in the morning, so I'm going to let you go."

"Okay, what time should I pick you up, then?" He doesn't try to hide the excitement in his voice. I kind of love that.

"You don't give up, do you?"

"One o'clock it is!"

This time, when I answer him, I'm pretty sure he can hear my smile over the phone.

-Five-

Deo

"You called her?" Cohen's voice sways and slides through the dark as he navigates pissing off the side of my grandpa's deck. Grandpa is passed out on the couch, snoring so loud I can barely hear my friend's question.

"Yup. Wooed her with my many charms." I pop the dilapidated lawn chair on its back two legs and balance my feet on the deck railing, letting the sweet buzz of too much beer mix with the memory of Whit's dark eyes and hot, sexy kisses.

I hear the up-pull of Cohen's zipper. "What charms are those again?" He throws his body down in a sagging lawn chair recliner.

"Bad-ass charms, hot-as-hell charms, got-balls-of-steel charms. The usual charms that tempt the ladies. You may want to learn from my example." I let the chair thump onto all four legs and throw a red plastic cup at him.

It hits him on the side of the head, and he groans. "You're gonna be so damn hungover tomorrow, that poor girl's gonna be stuck holding your hair back while you puke." He burps and groans.

"You just can't handle your cups, my friend." He and I polished off a bottle of Sambuka in seventh grade and he puked on Kylee Chase's shoes the next day when we met up with her in the park. Since then, he always has to be a tough-nut about how much he drinks, even though he can't take it. "I have a genetically gifted liver."

"No damn joke. Your grandpa drank three times more than both of us, and that old bastard could have ridden a damn unicycle through an obstacle course." He burps again, and I wish he'd just go throw up and put himself out of his misery, but he's got pride about drinking.

"Like I said, I'm blessed with amazing genes. Which is why Whit was all over seeing me again." Okay, maybe that's a little bit of lie. Or a big ass lie. Maybe it was more like me forcing her to come out and hoping she actually shows up.

"So what's the deal with this girl?" Cohen throws one leg off the recliner, so I know the stars are spinning like mad for him.

I rub a hand over my scruff. I need to shave pre-date. "I really don't know. She's hot as hell, but she's kind of got a stick up her ass."

Cohen turns his head and looks at me through one painfully squinted eye. "Stick up her ass? That's so not your type. Are you losing your beach-bunny appetite? Going for responsible girls now? Are you sure you met this chick at a tattoo shop and not the bank or the DMV?"

"Fuck off," I chuckle. "She may have had a stick up her ass, but she was definitely running to a booty call. And she's all neat and proper, but sexy as hell. She has a tattoo behind her ear."

"Behind her ear?" Cohen drums his fingers over his stomach. "That's kind of rebel hot."

"She's all kinds of contradictions." I roll my shoulders out. "And I gotta get to sleep so I have the energy I need for this date, if you catch me."

"Cool. I'll just chill out here for a while." His voice calls to me before I'm in the house. "And happy birthday, old man!"

"Don't fall asleep out here. The mosquitoes will suck your rotten ass dry!" I close the sliding door, but not before I hear Cohen sneak to the side of the deck and heave. Gross, but I'm glad he did it.

I head to the kitchen and rifle through the fridge for my grandpa's anti-hangover remedy. The trick is, you have to drink it the same night you get shit-faced for it to work completely. I have no clue what's in it. It tastes like tomato juice that went rotten with a side of sour, but that and two aspirins and I'll be golden for my date, so it's down the hatch.

I collapse into my bed, and my dreams are populated by one very sexy dark-eyed, uptight girl who's all about letting her wild side peek out just for me.

When I finally wake up the next afternoon Cohen is gone, Grandpa is outside in his overgrown vegetable garden pulling weeds like a maniac, and I get ready to meet up with Whit. When I go out back to tell my grandpa I'll be gone for the day, he snickers.

"What's so funny, old man?" I ask, dodging a dirt-clogged weed he tosses my way on purpose.

"You look so pretty. Who are you all gussied up for? Not a floozy." He wipes wet dirt on the sides of his work jeans and tips back his old straw cowboy hat, grinning like a fool.

"Not a floozy," I agree. "A nice, respectable girl I'm gonna try my best to corrupt."

He shakes his head and goes back to his peppers, his shoulders shaking with his bouts of laughter. "Wear a rubber."

"Will do. Don't get sun poisoning. I don't want to deal with your old ass peeling and crying for a month again." I catch the pepper he throws at me and take a spicy bite.

"Get lost, pain in my ass." He pulls one of my birthday cigars out of his pocket and lights up, knowing the smell will send me running. Those cigars were definitely for pros, and a pro I am not when it comes to tobacco.

I hop in my Jeep, and sail down the highway, driving too fast and whistling totally off key to the random sappy love song on the radio. I'm a shit whistler, but I don't care. I don't care about anything but seeing Whit. And then I pull in on the beach that I texted her directions to last night and see her.

She's sitting on the hood of her LeBaron, her knees pulled up to her chest, her dark hair blowing back from her face in the salty ocean wind. She doesn't notice me at first, and I take a minute to watch her, lost in thought, looking small and huddled with the backdrop of the waves crashing loud around us. She must sense my eyes on her, because she looks up and smiles.

That smile hits me low in the gut. I jog over and put my hand out, helping her slide off the hood and onto the sand next to me. Her hair smells like the ripe grapefruits my grandpa coats in sugar and eats for breakfast.

She eyes me suspiciously. "You look pretty damn chipper considering how drunk you were last night."

Last night she was all dolled up, with dark, sexy makeup and glossy hair. Right now she's scrubbed clean, her hair slightly wavy and tossed by the wind, and she's wearing cutoff shorts and a practically see-through tank. Last night's look was hot, but today's is soft and touchable.

And I so want to touch her. All over. Without stopping.

"My grandpa has a secret recipe," I confess. "When we go out and get sleazy drunk, I'll bring you back to my place and give it to you before we…snuggle." I box her against the car and she leans back with a lazy, sweet smile.

"You have pretty high hopes for our supposed future dates." She narrows her big brown eyes at me, but she can't totally tuck away a smile. "Snuggling, huh?"

"I'm an awesome snuggler. You have no idea. You know that bear on the fabric softener commercials?"

"Snuggle the bear?" She giggles. I notice she has a whole sweep of freckles on her nose and cheeks.

"That's the one. I taught that fucker everything he knows, no joke." Her laugh loosens something good and happy in me. I stretch my arms wide. "You want a little sample?"

She has one hand over her mouth and laughs so hard, she's doubled over, but she doesn't accept my hug invitation. "I thought we were supposed to explore the beach."

"I'm a man of many talents." I point to the ocean and the swelling, crashing waves that always feel like home. "You ready for this? It's not a snuggle-a-thon, but it has its perks."

She nods, walks to me with those damn sexy swaying hips, and traces her fingers over my arm while I focus on not hyperventilating. I clear my throat and try to keep things light and loose. "The deal is, I show you all the super awesome secrets of this particular beach, and you let me ogle you in your bikini. But it's gotta be a super small bikini. If it isn't small enough, I'm totally cool with hunting down a nude beach."

She rolls her eyes and pulls her shirt over her head slowly. Two tiny red triangles and some string cover her smooth skin, and I feel like I'm twelve years old again, sneaking my grandpa's Playboys in the crawlspace under the porch. As I'm doing my best to cover the beginnings of a raging hard-on with a well-placed beach towel, she lets the tiny shorts slide off her hips and there is a very limited amount of black fabric and some more string. My head spins like I bashed it hard. Super hard. All normal body functions shut down, and I am fairly sure I'm probably drooling down my chest. And I don't give a flying fuck.

"Small enough?" she asks, but there's a hitch in her voice, and I notice her arms stiff at her sides, like she's resisting the urge the cover herself up with them.

"It'll do," I manage to get out. "So, did anyone ever tell you that you were made to wear a bikini? Because I'm going to go ahead and suggest you only wear them, like exclusively. The only thing I can imagine you looking better in is nothing, and I get that you'd be cold a lot of the time if you took that route."

She laughs and her arms relax a little. "Um, no one's ever told me anything about how I look in a bikini, because this is my very first one."

A flare of possessive goodness flicks through me. "Your first bikini? Right here, today?" With me. *For me?*

She nods. "I've had it for a few weeks, but I never actually wore it. Before." She has no idea where to look, so she's kind of letting her eyes dart on anything and everything except me.

"Right here, right now, we're popping your bikini cherry?" I clarify.

She nods, and that shy way she moves her head mixed with those sweet freckles set up against that sexy barely-there bikini knocks the wind right out of me. "What is it?" She wiggles her toes, painted a sparkly blue, in the sand.

"I'm just thinking that twenty-two is probably going to be the best year of my entire life."

-Six-

Whit

His words twist in the air around us. How do you even respond to a statement like that? Especially when he's looking at me *like* *that?* So I don't.

I change the subject. "What do you wanna do?"

"I've got a few ideas. You're not in Pennsylvania anymore, are you Dorothy?" His smile is ridiculously contagious.

"Yeah. It's been an adjustment."

"So, what brought you to our lovely hamlet? School? Family? Strapping young man who blows up your phone with inappropriate text messages while you're at work?"

My face is on fire. I should deny it, but I don't. I just let him stew in his vision for a minute. Let him think what he wants.

"Mostly school. And that young man? You know, I wouldn't say he's strapping, but he makes it worth my while," I say with a wink.

His jaw goes slack. He's surprised. And turned on.

"You're trouble. I can tell." He points at me and shakes his head slowly, his words trying to be stern around his grin. "I mean, the bikini was a dead giveaway, but that right there, what you just said? Hardcore proof."

I grin back at him. Flirting is easier than admitting the real reasons I bailed. Because there was no way I was going to let my parents pay for school after everything that happened. Because I was determined to change my life and take care of myself.

He takes a deep breath of salty, scrubbed-clean air and throws me another version of that lazy, sexy smile. "And let me get this straight. You've seriously never seen the ocean?"

I nod. I don't know why, but I feel embarrassed by this fact. Like I'm not as experienced. Or wordly or something. Probably because I'm not.

"Awesome. Let's do this up." A confident smile covers his face. He rests his rough hand on the small of my back to lead me toward the water.

"Okay," I say. But what I *want* to say is, *Can we leave because when you touch me all soft and sweet like that, I want you. Bad.*

We walk down the beach to the water. There are a half dozen guys on surfboards, sitting out in the vast expanse. Just sitting. I don't get it at first. Until I really relax and *look* at the water.

"So it's safe to say you've never surfed? Unless there's some kind of Pennsylvania lake and stream surfing we ocean dwellers don't know about," he says with a small laugh.

"That's a negative." My feet sink into the soggy sand. It's slimy and cold and wonderful.

"I'll teach you someday. If you want. But you need to be ready to surrender to me, body and soul. Surfing isn't just a sport, it's really an art form." His eyes are a warm, light brown, and they shine when he talks about the ocean and surfing.

The passion in his eyes transforms him in a way that's even more appealing, even more crazily attractive, and it honestly throws me off balance. I'm already slipping dangerously deep into lust and maybe more than like. So I attempt to joke it away. "Oh Jesus, dramatic much?" I swat him playfully in the ribs before I realize. "Shit! I forgot about the tat. Sorry!"

He cracks a smile around his wince and shakes his head. "Damn, you're lucky you're gorgeous."

We stand there for a while, like the surfers out in the water. Just watching the waves lap up onto the sand with a fricative whisper. The biggest body of water I've ever seen is Lake Erie. I remember going on summer vacations there when we were younger in the RV. I'd get up early, before everyone else and go and stand by the lake. It felt massive, and I was just a minuscule speck. I feel the same way right now, staring out into the Pacific. Totally and completely insignificant.

"Come on, there's something I want to show you." Deo is wriggly-puppy excited, and it's a weird contrast, his bald, uninhibited energy mixed with his laid-back, tough-guy sexiness. I stay back a few paces, watching the confident way he walks back up the beach. He's shirtless, though there is a wrap covering his new tattoo, and his board shorts are slung low around his waist. The sun beats down onto his back, deepening his tan by the minute, but it's like he isn't even aware of his clothes or lack of clothes or body.

I, on the other hand, feel like every single person must be staring at me, because I'm practically naked in public. I wasn't lying about my choice of swimwear; this is the first time I've worn this or any bikini. My best friend back home, Lindsey bought it for me as a going-away present. She said it was a first step, a necessity in my new life.

We walk for a while, Deo glancing over his shoulder every few paces to make sure I'm behind him. I've lost my footing several times, and, I swear, all I need to add on to my feeling of being watched by every person in a mile radius is to eat shit on these rocks in this bathing suit that offers about as much coverage as a Kleenex.

"I'm coming!" I reassure him. We're climbing over some pretty gnarly rocks and I didn't exactly wear the right shoes for this. "Where are we going anyway?"

"Here," Deo finally announces, his voice coiled tight around his excitement. "Check it out."

We're standing on some more rocks that aren't really just rocks at all. They're a home. Their cracks and crevices are filled with crabs and sponges and dozens of other types of unrecognizable sea life.

"This is incredible." And it is. Everything is vibrant and alive. It reminds me of Wakefield. Or at least how I want to remember Wakefield. A sudden crush of panic presses down over me. Maybe I'm creating a vision of him in my head that isn't even the right one. How can I not have the right vision of him? He's my brother.

He *was* my brother.

Suddenly it's hard to suck any air into my lungs, and I desperately need to focus on anything other than the horrifying thoughts ripping through my skull.

I crouch down on the rock next to the one Deo is standing on to get a closer look. The waves don't really reach us up on the rocks, I guess because the tide is too low, but cool water still pools around my ankles. A bright something moves slowly in the rippling water.

It's life-filled. Unlike Wakefield.

I press my eyes closed and shake that thought away.

"Can I touch this?" I point to a sea star. "I've only ever seen these on TV." Deo bends down next to me. His face is close. His hangover remedy must work wonders, because his eyes are clear and that weird, gorgeous light brown.

"You can touch it, but don't pull it up. You could tear its tube feet." Deo is definitely in his element here.

I bite my bottom lip and slowly poke the water with my index finger.

"Relax." His voice is low and reassuring. He wraps his large hand around mine and guides two of my fingers toward the sea star. His other hand presses lightly on the small of my back. It does the opposite of helping me relax. His touch is electricity.

And we're in the water. It's a buzzing, pulsing electric shock.

It's too much. It's different than with Ryan. Ryan is easy. Uncomplicated. Ryan is fun. That's the whole point. To be living big. To not be tied down. To not waste a single second of life. To not get too attached or too weighted down. *Deo*...Deo is someone who could mess up my whole plan.

I jerk my hand out of the water and slam it into the rock to steady myself.

"Fuck!" I yell.

"Oh shit! What'd you do, Whit?" he asks. He looks worried, and I feel like a grade A asshole.

"Nothing, I just cut my hand on the rock." I hold up my battered palm as evidence. There's a nasty gash right through the center of the tender flesh that's ugly and bleeding. My chin and throat burn with the tears I'm trying to hold back. There is no way in hell I'm going to cry in front of any guy. *Ever.*

"Holy shit, you banged that up good." Deo's eyes squint with sympathy for my pain, and that just brings the threat of tears even closer.

I clutch my hand to my chest to keep him from holding it. It's a stupid idea because now the front of me is covered in blood.

"I think we'd better go." I'm not a total wuss, but I've never been super great with seeing my own blood. Especially when I already feel exposed as heck out here in this stupid teeny-bikini. Damn Lindsey. Necessity my ass. What I really need is a tube of first aid ointment and some gauze.

"Come on, my mom has got some Calendula oil that will heal that in no time." Deo stands and gets his footing on the treacherous rocks.

"Some what?" I ask weakly.

He reaches for my hand. "Trust me, she's a pro."

I start to follow him, but I've only taken a few steps when he turns around and scoops me up like a small child. He cradles me in his arms, my nearly-bare skin pressed to his scorching chest.

"Second thought, I'd better carry you. I don't want you busting your ass again."

-Seven-

Deo

There's this romantic misconception that when you carry a girl in your arms, she's light as a feather and all that. It's crap. I've got inches and pounds on Whit, but when I scoop her up, it's work to carry her. Her long, lean limbs and sweet curves have a good kind of substantial feel to them, and she's holding her body funny, I think because she's attempting to not get blood all over me. What she's actually doing is making herself an awkward pretzel.

But I like this girl, so I like the work of getting her safely over the rocks. Cause let's face it; if sweeping girls off their feet, literally, was so damn easy, it would make it that much less awesome when a guy went all out and did it.

I manage to struggle the passenger door of the Jeep open with the hand that's under her knees.

"Just put me down," she protests, wriggling like crazy. "I didn't hurt my legs."

I do put her down. In the seat. And buckle her seatbelt. I take the opportunity to pretend the buckle apparatus is a hell of a lot more complicated than it is so I can smell her, all sweet grapefruit, salt-on-skin, and sexy, mind-quaking girl. "What kind of knight in shining armor would I be if I let you hoof it over the rocks? Seriously?"

"I'm definitely not a damsel in distress, Deo," she huffs. "It's one little scratch on my palm."

I pry said palm from her chest, pop my glovebox, and take out a handkerchief. Her eyes widen in what I'm sure is germ-afraid horror. I chuckle as I pull her hand closer and tie the soft cloth around it. "Clean, I promise. My grandpa has all these old fashioned ideas about guys and handkerchiefs. Don't even ask, okay? Bottom line is I always have one ready for these kinds of catastrophes."

She makes her hand into a soft fist and stares at it, and when she looks back up, her eyes are rimmed with tears. "Thanks," she croaks. She opens her mouth like she wants to say more, and I want to hear what she's going to say, but she stops, I'm sure to plug up the tears. I don't want her to feel uncomfortable around me, so I close her door and hop in the driver's side, pull out, and head to my mother's place.

"Do I have to meet your mom in a bikini?" she asks, worried.

I reach in the back, find a bag of laundry from my last trip to the laundromat, and pull out my favorite shirt. "Here you go."

She pulls it over her head and runs her hand over the worn cotton. "The Pixies?"

"I know. I have epic taste in music." I tug on the sleeve of the shirt, loving the way it looks on her. "I hate to admit this, but it looks a hell of a lot sexier on you than it does on me."

She smiles, and then it's quiet in the Jeep for a long stretch of minutes. I glance over and Whit is looking out the window, her bandaged hand still clutched to her chest, her dark hair whipping around her face from the rolled down windows. I like the way she fills the passenger side of the car with her sweet-and-sour self. Her mouth is turned down on the sides in a little frown and her eyes are unfocused, like she's miles away from me and this ride and this date. I wish I knew how to pull her back and get her to tell me what's on her mind, but I don't. So I settle for the fairly comfortable silence.

When we pull into the parking lot of my mom's place, I warn her, "She's a lunatic. But she's amazing. I think you two might get along really well."

Finally a smile. "You had to throw the lunatic thing in there, didn't you?" she asks, and I'm relieved to see a little eye roll. The patient is doing better already.

I come around to get her door, but she puts her hands up and says, "No carrying me. I'm fine. Totally fine."

I put my hands up and let her get out on her own. I take her uninjured hand and lead her to my mother's hippie dippy store, complete with tie-dye rainbow wall-hangings, all kinds of weird bells and chimes, crystals on every table, Janis begging someone to take a piece of her heart over the speakers, and a huge assortment of jars and bottles with herbs and oils. Mom looks up from her Kindle when we walk in, a smile on her face.

My mom's face is pretty much always smiley, and I love that about her.

"Deo! I'm so glad you stopped by. And you brought a lovely friend." My mom comes from behind the counter, barefoot, jangly silver anklets and bracelets and rings and earrings making her sound like an explosion of bells, her long hair swinging around her waist. She holds her hand out to Whit and says, "I'm Marigold. And you are…oh no! Bleeding! Get right over here. Deo, the Calendula, now!"

I poke through all her weird glass bottles and find the one she needs, the one that she used on all my scrapes and gashes growing up. And I was a super scraped up and gashed kid, so I hope my mom took out stock in Calendula. She has Whit sitting on a squishy chair and she's leaned over, washing Whit's cut with warm water and some kind of freaky soap she makes from who knows what. If my mom hadn't miraculously healed every single ailment I ever had, I'd be worried about her crazy potions infecting my girl.

"How did you do this?" Mom asks, her voice all clucking with mom-ish sympathy as she takes the bottle from my hand and applies.

"Deo took me to the beach. I was looking at a starfish, but the rocks were really jagged," Whit explains quietly.

Mom's smile is half-hidden by her hair as she fixes some gauze over Whit's hand. "A beach date, huh? Very romantic."

"Mom," I warn. "Whit's just a friend. Stop trying to marry me off." Whit looks up, her dark eyes wide with panic. "Relax, babe. She's like the village matchmaker. She does this all the time."

It's weird. I thought my explanation of my mom's particular brand of matchmaking crazy would make Whit happy, but she looks sort of disappointed.

"I guess I got overexcited. I've never been to the ocean before." Whit puts her hand back in her lap and eyes my mother shyly. "I'm Whit, by the way."

"Whit." My mom pulls her name out like she's enjoying the taste of it. "I love that. It suits you perfectly. So you were a land-bound girl before coming here? I can sense it. I was born and raised in the flat farmland of Michigan."

Whit's smile is warm and relaxed. "I'm from Pennsylvania, right by Amish country." She wrinkles her nose. "I know a lot about preserving jam and raising livestock. I'm really happy I got to trade goats for starfish."

"You're preaching to the choir, hon." Mom laughs and it brings out a reactionary bubbly laugh from Whit. I love that sound, the mingling laughter of these two awesome women in my life. "So, you have that brilliant college girl vibe about you. Am I right?"

"I don't know about brilliant. But I'm a freshman at Imperial Coast College, just getting my core done this semester and sitting in on some lectures in areas I might be interested in.

So no major yet. Everyone always wants to know my major," she explains, tucking her shiny, dark hair behind her ear.

I never even thought to ask her major, and now I feel like a jackhole.

"Oh, sweetie, I've been to enough college classes to have two BAs by now, but I never could settle on a major. I just have a ton of credits and a crapload of student debt." My mom shrugs and chuckles. "All that college led to one of the most exciting romances of my life, Deo, and an unexpectedly useful semester as a business major. So, you know, don't sweat the major thing too much. I get an amazing vibe from you, Whit. You'll find your path." My mom winks.

Before Whit can answer, the bell over the door jangles and a clutch of old biddies comes in, calling to my mother in high, excited voices. "Ah, my senior gals are here. Listen, why don't you kids come by on Saturday? I was going to make some risotto. Maybe Rocko can come by, too."

The idea of a double date with my mom and my tattoo guy is kind of creepy, but Whit says, "That sounds like a lot of fun." Since I'm down for more one-on-one time with Whit, I guess I'm also down for a double date with my mother. Not exactly my idea of romance, but I'll make it work.

Whit and I leave the store before the laughing, screaming, demanding grandmas hopped up on herbs can trample us. "Your mom is so cool," Whit gushes as we walk to the Jeep.

"I'm glad you like her. You remind me of her." I check out her ass in those little black bikini bottoms, hanging out of the bottom of my shirt. I like the view. A lot.

"Really?" She nips her bottom lip between her teeth and hops into the passenger seat. "Because she's basically who I want to be."

I slide in the driver's side and start the engine. "A hippie?" I never would have pegged Whit for a Grateful Dead groupie.

"No," she laughs as I pull onto the highway. "An independent woman. Someone who chooses her own path and makes her own decisions without regrets. Your mom didn't do everything perfectly, but she's happy with what she did and where she's at. She has her passion, her store, her life. Her own life, with no one else's expectations pressing on her. I think that's amazing."

I grip the steering wheel and grit my teeth. "Yeah, well, she's cool, but it's not all rainbow flags and psychedelic music with my mom."

Whit slides her feet out of her flip flops and puts them on the dashboard. "We all have issues, Deo."

"Not all of us go into month-long depression tailspins over the same worthless asshole every year or two." My words bite out harsher than I mean them to. Whit wrinkles her forehead and bites her lips, and I'm suddenly pushed to confess all kinds of things I've kept buried deep forever. "My dad has been yanking her chain since before I was born. When he's around, he's all she can focus on. When he's gone, she does her thing, but underneath it all, she's just waiting. Waiting for him to come back, for him to call, for him to throw her a bone before he goes off and ignores her again."

Whit drops her feet to the floorboards. "Rocko said he was kind of dating your mom?" Her voice is careful after my little outburst.

"Oh, she dates. You know, that whole 'casual fucking to tide her over until her true love comes back' bullshit." I see Whit's shoulders go tight, and feel like a scumbag on so many levels. "Sorry, Whit. I'm sure you don't want to hear all this. My mom's cool. It's just frustrating that she gets caught up in that crap over and over. You'd think she'd learn."

"I guess some relationships are just like that." Whit pulls her hair back like she's making a tiny ponytail, then releases it so it swings back around her chin. "I get you, though. If someone is going to suck you in and wring you out like that, is it worth it to be with them? I'd rather just keep things casual and keep a handle on who I am than fall so completely in love and lose myself."

"Agreed. Very sensible of you, College Girl. So, I never even asked your major or any of that. I guess that was pretty shitty of me." We're back at the parking lot next to her car. She looks over at me and throws this sweet-as-hell smile my way.

"That was pretty non-boring of you. I don't really feel like talking about school. And right now? I don't really feel like talking at all." Her voice is low and inviting.

"Really?" I nod her over. "You never cashed in on that snuggle I offered you before." I raise my eyebrows and she giggles, even though she's trying hard not to. "Come sit over here by me."

"You mean on your lap?" She narrows those sweet brown eyes my way.

"You've never sat on a lap until you've sat on mine. You know Santa Claus? I taught him everything he knows." I crook my finger at her.

She plugs up her ears and laughs. "Stop it! You are corrupting my childhood."

"Why? Have you been a bad girl this year?" I love that I can make her laugh. I love that she's considering coming over to me. And then, though she's acting like it's pure torture, she moves from her seat to mine, squeezes herself between my body and the steering wheel and presses her face close.

All the joking around comes to a sudden total stop. "This is a stupid idea," she says, her voice a whisper.

"I'm known for my charming stupidity." Then I stop talking. I run my hands up from her knees to her thighs and let my fingers press just under the edges of her bikini bottoms. She pulls a breath in through her teeth.

I catch that pouty bottom lip and suck it in, loving the salt and sweet taste of her mouth. I slide my hands around the curve of her ass, under my Pixies shirt, up her back, and pull her tighter, kissing her fast and hard so she won't have time to change her mind.

Not that she seems like she will. Whatever doubt she might have had flips off like a switch, and Whit spreads her legs wider so she's crushed against my instant hard-on. She moans into my mouth, tugs her hands at the bottom of my shirt and pulls it half over my head, leaving it hanging off one shoulder. I tear my mouth away from hers and kiss along the soft line of her neck, back behind her ear, right over that 'W,' the one that doesn't stand for her name.

And mid hot-as-all-hell makeout, I wonder if 'W' stands for a guy? Someone she left behind in Amish country? First love, first heartbreak? We talked a good game about not getting tied up in any one person and she knows I know about her booty calls with the random douchebag. But this is rattling my cage for some reason.

It all is, suddenly. I realize that every minute I spend with Whit makes me more possessive, and I suck hardcore at sharing.

My fingers tug at the strings of her bikini top and loosen it at the back. My hands come around and coast over her soft, hot skin, moving up under the loose fabric of her top and filling with the perfect weight of her tits. Every shred of testosterone in me is full-drive ahead. Her hands are in my hair, running over my shoulders, moving down to unbuckle my jeans. I skim along the inside of one thigh and slip my finger under the fabric of her bottoms. She's slick already, and my mind loses any control over where we're going or what we're doing.

The barking hoorahs of a bunch of idiot jarheads jogging on the beach cracks the quiet of my Jeep and makes Whit's head fly up. Her eyes lose their sexy glaze and snap, bright and totally full of regret.

"No. No, Deo. This…I haven't been honest with you about…I just can't…" She trails off, desperately trying to tie her top back on under my shirt. She scuttles back off my lap and onto the passenger seat, sticking her feet into her flipflops.

I'm still half in a sex daze, and reason is blurry. Why isn't she on my lap? Why aren't my hands on her? Why does life suck so much suddenly? "Is it about the other guy? The call you took last night? Because, trust me, Whit, I'm no fucking angel." I watch her pat her hair down and look around, frenzied, like she's afraid we'll get caught together.

"It's that. It *is* that, but other things. You're…you just aren't like him. That other guy. And I don't want…what we have is not the same as what I have with him, and I don't want to mix it up. Or fuck it up. God, I'm fucking this all up." She puts her head in her hands and her dark hair slides over her pale fingers. "I didn't expect this to happen, and I think it was a mistake. Okay. That's all."

"That's all?" I'm irritated as all hell. *That's all.* "So it's back to your dickhead fuckbuddy tonight?"

"That's none of your business, Deo." Her voice is icy.

"Maybe it wasn't. Then we had this day together, and you and me make a hell of a lot of sense, Whit. What we had today was real, and I'm not about to go in reverse for no reason."

"Everything is real." Her voice is the unexpected jagged puncture of glass in my foot at the beach. "Every damn thing we do is real because we're here living right now." She's close to tears.

I drop the attitude. "Okay. Back up, alright? I'm just confused, Whit. We were together, right? We were having a good time, right?" She nods and relaxes, her breath less labored and her hands less shaky. Good. "Then a bunch of meat-head soldier clones ruined the mood and now we're here. What happened between all that, cause something doesn't make sense, and I can't connect the dots."

She'd been calming down, but her eyes snap and her lips curl. "Don't say that! You keep your goddamn mouth shut, Deo!"

She grabs the door handle and slams her shoulder against the door, popping it open. She tumbles out and rushes to her car, snatching the little bundle of clothes she shed this morning. She yanks the shorts over her hips, rips my shirt off and throws it at me, then pulls her tank on.

I make it to her and grab her by the thin shoulders, trying to steady her, but she's a ball of rage, slapping at my arms and pushing against me. "Get the hell away from me!"

"Whit. Wait, what did I do? What did I say? Don't leave like this. C'mon, you're upset. Let me drop you off. This is crazy, Whit. Whit!"

But she isn't listening to me. She pushes me hard enough that I take a step back, then slides in the driver's seat, smashes the key in the ignition, and pulls her car in reverse. I can see her face through the windshield, streaked with tears, and I'm left feeling like I just got jumped and beat to hell.

I don't know how long I stand in the sandy parking lot, but I finally realize she's not coming back and I'm not accomplishing anything by being here. I bend down to pick up my t-shirt, and when I bring it up to my nose, her smell clings to the fabric.

I get in my Jeep and drive back to my grandpa's, the smell and taste of this girl on my body and in my mouth, and her number snug in my phone. I want to call her, find out what short-circuited, why we went from bliss to meltdown in three minutes flat.

But when I get to the privacy of my room, shades of my parents creep up. The tantrums. The fights that ended with fist-shaped holes in the sheet-rock and piles of gasoline-soaked clothes and pictures burning on the front lawn before the inevitable apologies and vases of roses and long, locked interludes in the bedroom.

I know what crazy emotions like that lead to, and I don't want it. I can't have it. Going through it once was enough for me. I consider calling Cara, my go-to friend-with-benefits, but I know no girl is gonna do it for me after I had Whit in my arms so recently.

I spend the next few hours on the back porch with my grandpa, trying to drown my pissed-off fury and regret in as much powerful liquor as we can find in his cabinets. Not the way I was hoping my first day of being twenty-two would end.

-Eight-

Whit

I blow off my evening class because that's what you do when you almost fuck some guy in his Jeep and then he offhandedly insults the one institution that, if you think about it for a single second, has the power to gut you. It's my day off, but I call Rocko to see if he needs me anyway. I've got to find something to do to keep from thinking about Deo and the feeling of his tongue grazing across my collarbone and that hungry look in his eyes that made me want to give him anything in the world just to make him feel as good as he was making me feel. And then he had to screw it all up.

But Rocko insists things are fine at the shop. No one's come in for ink all day. He tells me to go out and have fun. I don't really know what that means anymore. Fun hasn't been on the agenda in a while. Unless you count my twice-weekly hookups with Ryan. That gives me an idea. I text Ryan.

You up for round two? My place this time.

I know he'll say yes. He's never let me down. I get that sex isn't a good coping mechanism for grief; I'm not a total moron. That's not why I'm doing this thing with Ryan. I'm doing it because it feels good. The main reason I left Pennsylvania was that there was too much emotion all the time. Too much feeling. It's exhausting. There's none of that drama with Ryan. It's just pure fun. I can detach from everything else and just enjoy the ride, figuratively speaking, naturally. There's a line, though. Ryan never asks me out, we don't go to the movies or even to Taco Bell. Deo tried to cross that line, and I won't be stupid enough to let him that close again.

I peel back the wrapper on a sticky pastry and cram it into my mouth just as Ryan replies, saying he's on his way. Before I shower, I grab my phone one last time. And, with a shaking hand and a burning lead ball in my gut, I delete Deo's number.

"Come in!" I yell from my cozy spot on the sofa. After my shower, the effects of having been out in the sun all day do a number on me. I stifle another yawn as Ryan lets himself into my craptastic apartment. By the time I decided to take the free ride to Imperial Coast College, rather than my first choice school, the University of Delaware, all the dorms were full and my financial aid and the money I make at Rocko's shop don't exactly afford me a penthouse. Still, it's mine, and that was the whole point of the move, right?

"Looking fancy," Ryan says. He motions toward my choice of attire. Not the usual form fitting, uncomfortable skirt and heels. No thick layer of pin-up style makeup. Just me. Freshly showered in cotton shorts and a tank top. I laugh and wave him over, glad that things are back to normal for me. *This* is what I want; easy, no-strings-attached Ryan. *Not* complicated, drive-me-crazy Deo. My hand is bandaged, and I notice Ryan glance at it. He doesn't ask what happened. I don't know why I sort of thought he would, and I'm not sure if I'm okay with the fact that he doesn't ask or not. But that's not our thing, I remind myself. Just like I don't ask what he does the other five nights of the week, he doesn't delve into my life outside of our meetings. That's what makes this all work.

Right?

"I think I like this look even better." Ryan smiles appreciatively at the minuscule shorts.

"Just for you." I force a smile. Ryan knows exactly how to walk that fine line between complimenting me in a way that I appreciate and saying anything that takes my breath away and makes me feel all light-headed. Deo has no concept that there even is a line. And I'm usually good about tossing little blase compliments back and forth with him, but what I just said is a bold lie.

This clean, scrubbed, laid-back look isn't neat and nice Pennsylvania Whit and it isn't sexpot, pinup California Whit. It's me.

Just me.

And I never felt comfortable enough to show it to anyone until my date with Deo. Now I just feel overexposed, which is stupid. Ryan has seen me in the naughtiest little lacy numbers I had to go to sexy specialty lingerie shops to get. So why do I feel like covering up now?

I swallow hard and shake those thoughts out of my head, faking a sexy smile I don't really feel, and crooking my finger to get back into the mood. Because I need to do this, now, with Ryan, so I can get Deo firmly out of my system. "Now come over here."

He does as he's told and hustles across the room and within seconds, he's got us both stripped down and his hand between my legs. It feels so damn good I couldn't fight it even if I wanted to. Which I don't. Because the whole point of him being here is to make me forget about Deo. I switch my brain to autopilot and try not to let it wander. Ryan knows what I like, and I like that about him. Forgetting about Deo is something I'm going to have to work hard to do.

Except that the way that Ryan's touching me is just reminding me of Deo more. And how his hands felt different. Not so rushed, but still eager as hell. Sweet and slow and perfect, like he had an internal map to parts of me I didn't even know existed.

I push Ryan's hand away and decide to take charge, since thinking about Deo while Ryan's touching me is obliterating all my "forget Deo completely" goals and making me feel a sharp, ugly pain in my heart that I recognize and hate with a blind terror. I tug at the hem of Ryan's boxers with determined purpose, then wrap my hand around the familiar length of his shaft. Ryan is blessed. And he knows it. In fact, that's how we hooked up originally. I had literally just gotten into town. I'd just stepped off of a plane that had been delayed three times and made an extra stop. I hadn't slept in what felt like days, wanted to brush my teeth, and I needed to find a bathroom like, literally, yesterday.

I hauled ass to the closest one, barged in and found Ryan, mid-zip.

He didn't blush, or even feign embarrassment. Instead, he smiled and asked if I wanted a closer look.

I should have been appalled.

Pennsylvania Whit would have been and Just-In-California Whit was half an inch and one indignant tell-off away from driving a pointy kitten heel into his foot, but then I stopped and remembered the whole point of this trip; it was to open up, to live life and have wild, crazy experiences. And wild, crazy experiences didn't start with an awkward date at Longhorn and end with a kiss on the front step before working up to nice, sweet sex after you catalogued all the necessary facts and information about the other person.

Wild, crazy experiences happened in the bathrooms of tiny airports in California with guys who had gorgeous faces and even more gorgeous bodies you could just tell they knew exactly how to use. I was ready to dive headfirst into that crazy, uninhibited territory and have Ryan teach me some of what he knew so well.

Well, I was almost ready.

First I backed out of the restroom, apologizing profusely, my face hot with a Pennsylvania farm-girl blush. I found the women's bathroom and hoped the shade of red I'd turned wasn't permanent. And then I did that cliche thing where I looked at myself in the mirror, really looked, and told myself that if I wanted this new me, this daring me who didn't play by the rules, I had to take a chance. And, as far as wild first chances went, this gorgeous, supremely confident guy was a one in a million stroke of pure luck.

I found Ryan waiting for me outside of the tiny airport, and when he smiled at me, I didn't bolt the way I wanted to. I took a deep, big girl breath and flashed him the sexy, come-hither smile I'd practiced for ten minutes in the grimy airport bathroom mirror.

He introduced himself, took me to lunch, then back to his place. I was so nervous, I almost backed out a dozen times, but I decided to force myself do something uninhibited for once to kickstart my new life adventure across the damn country from my old existence. Plus that, Ryan was unlike any guy I'd ever known back home. He didn't fumble too much with manners and stilted, awkward silences; he was direct and positive about his own abilities and charms. He actually inspired me to unleash those things in myself.

And I sincerely grew to like him as a person. Because, despite our scandalous bathroom meeting, he really isn't a skeeze ball. He's a genuinely nice guy. He just knows what he wants. And it's what I want, too.

Except, as I'm holding him in my hand, all rock hard and curving up, eager for me, I don't feel the same sense of power I normally do. His eyes are closed and he's breathing heavy. I can't quit now, obviously. So I stroke him harder, faster, and maybe a tiny bit mechanically, until he clenches his fists at his sides and moans deeply.

"Jesus you're good at that," he says in between pants.

I just shrug. My parents would be so proud. I attempt to smile, but a sudden sense of dark, unsettling regret and possible disappointment weighs down on me.

"You're turn." He flips me onto the couch and crawls up the length of me, but his touch and weight are suddenly claustrophobic, and I don't want him here anymore. I wriggle around out from under him.

"That's okay," I say all casual, like I'm passing on an hors d'oeurve or something, even though my heart is hammering and I feel like I've been kicked in the stomach.

He hops up off the couch too and closes the space between us. He finds that spot on my collar bone he knows I can't resist.

He doesn't know when my birthday is, what my favorite food is, or the fact that, before today, I'd never seen the ocean, but he does know how to turn me on like he read my body's personal instruction manual. That used to be enough. That used to be better than enough. Now it feels robotic and soulless.

Not that this is supposed to have soul. That's not the point. This is supposed to be about our young, hot bodies rubbing against each other in the most carnal ways. This was never about feelings or emotions. Those are messy and just screw things up. Look how they're screwing up the perfectly good time I'm supposed to be having with Ryan.

"I got mine, and you're the one who called me all the way over here. You're not even going to let me make you feel good?" He nips at my neck, and it's the strangest mix of feeling good, technically, but also cloying and too much and too little all at the same time. "That hardly seems fair."

"It's not a big deal, there will be other nights. I didn't realize how beat I was." This time, I fake a yawn. I don't know why I'm trying to get rid of him. Letting him remind me of what we have and why it works is exactly what I need right now. I tell myself that, but I can't stand the sight of him, and I feel like a major asshole. I just blew off my fuckbuddy. Can I go any lower?

"Whatever you say, Whit." He pulls on his pants and checks his phone. He cracks a small smile at whatever is on the screen. I wonder if it's another random girl somewhere. If Deo had gotten a message from a girl while we were out, I would have had to resist the urge to shatter his phone. In this case, I'm actually hoping someone else is calling Ryan away and that he'll be distracted enough to just leave me to wallow. "If you're sure, I guess I'll take off then." He gives me a cool, detached look.

I relax. He's going. Good. Problem solved. Problem I invited over and then didn't want to deal with solved, but still. "Yep. I'm gonna head to bed. Have fun."

"Cool." His phone buzzes again, and he gives it his full attention.

He doesn't bother kissing me goodbye or anything like that. We don't do that. He pulls his baseball cap down low on his head and a few fine, brown curls peek out the sides.

"Hey, Ryan?" I ask, just as he's pulling the door open to leave. He glances over his shoulder, but doesn't turn all the way around to face me. "What's your favorite beach?"

"Huntington. They've got the hottest—why?" he asks. His brows pinch together, trying to figure out my motives. Why am I trying to learn anything about him now? He looks like he may run scared at the thought of me wanting to actually get to know him.

"Just wondering. I'd never seen the ocean before today." I don't know why I offer this bit of information. Deo seemed so amazed by that fact, maybe I'm hoping to intrigue Ryan, too.

"No kidding. Weird," is all that Ryan offers before walking out the door.

The bell above the door jangles as I push through it, and, with that noise, I'm emotionally right there back at Deo's mom's house, where she's holding my hand and dabbing her special oil on it. It's been a long time since I felt taken care of. It was awkward and somehow, warm-feeling. I could easily see where Deo got his laid back side, but there's another part to him that I haven't placed yet. I shake my head. I came here to forget about Deo. Whether Rocko wants me here or not.

"Hey, kiddo." Rocko peers over the counter. "I thought I told you not to bother coming in today. Like I said, there's a whole lot of nothing going on."

The place is dead. It doesn't look like Rocko's done a single piece of art today. There's no ink left out, no guns laying around. He hasn't even bothered to turn on the typically blaring 70s rock.

It's just quiet. I set my purse down on my desk. I'm staying.

"I know, but I didn't have much else to do. I can at least get the deposit together and run to the bank."

"What happened with Divo?" he asks.

I pull my hair back away from my face, like I'm going to put it in a ponytail, before remembering that I hacked all the length off the night before I moved here. I still haven't gotten used to this blunt bob. Gone are the long waves that I loved. This haircut says I'm fierce. Unapproachable. At least, that's how I wanted people to see me.

I laugh at Rocko's lame attempt at at joke. "Deo. His name is Deo."

Rocko nods and cracks a smile. I'm pretty sure he knew his name.

"Right. Well, why don't you kids go enjoy this sunshine? On second thought, why don't you kids go catch a bite or see a nice movie? I want your guy to stay away from the sun and the water.

I don't want that tat fading before it even has a chance to heal right, and he seems like the type that doesn't respect the rules."

You have no idea.

"Deo isn't *my* guy. We aren't even friends or anything, Rocko." I dig through my desk drawer. Mostly as a distraction. Also, because I'm sort of looking for that handkerchief that fell out of Deo's pocket while he was getting his tat, and that I might have hung on to and stashed in my desk. I pull the small square of fabric out and fight the urge to smell it. That's probably freaky grounds for a restraining order.

Rocko pulls his funky tortoiseshell eyeglasses down on his nose so that he's peering at me over the tops of them. "Listen kid, these glasses are purely a fashion statement. I'm not blind. I know what I saw the other night."

"What are you talking about?" I recoil, the handkerchief clear evidence of my guilty moping.

"The way you were looking at him, like you wanted him to be looking at you. And the way he was about to jump off that table mid-tat when he thought you were leaving before he was. Don't get me wrong, he also looked like he wanted to bend you over that couch out there—"

"Rocko!" Pennsylvania Whit is dying.

"Come on, kid. I know you aren't scrambling to get out of here at night with your phone going off like crazy to go home to your DVR. You're up to no good. And that's all good, because you're nineteen. I'd be worried if you weren't up to no good at your   age."

Rocko smiles smugly, obviously feeling like he's got me all pegged. And I guess, maybe he does.

He leans back in his chair and props his feet up on my desk. I knock his heavy black boots off.

"Manners," I say under my breath. I'm only half-joking.

"See, it's stuff like that, though, that confuses the hell out of me. Like that tat you drew for Divo—"

"Deo, and I didn't draw it *for* him."

"There's something more to you than the sexy makeup and heels."

"Rocko, I could so nail your ass for sexual harassment, you know that right?" This time, I'm totally joking. I love the free and fearless banter I have with Rocko. It's one of the most real things   I   have.

"So, tell me kid, what else is going on in that pretty little head of   yours?"

I haven't even started talking yet. But I turn to him, knowing that this time, I will. It's time, and really, I won't find a better listener, or anyone less judgmental than Rocko.

-Nine-

Deo

Cara is applying a coat of shiny purple nail polish to my toenails while I lie back on my stale-smelling sheets and count the cobwebs that have multiplied like crazy fuckers on the ceiling above my *Scarface* poster. It's been a little too dark to notice them lately, but Cara fixed the light problem with one snap of the sagging roller shade. She also tossed my iPod in my dresser drawer next to my bong and under my rolling papers to stop Robert Johnson's incessant, broken-hearted wail.

"You're harshing my mellow, Sunshine," I gripe, wiggling my toes and making her click her tongue when she paints the side of my foot.

Cara glares at me and swishes her strawberry blond hair over her shoulder so she can paint with more precision, but all that long hair is tickling my knee now. "You can't just hole up in here and listen to the world's most depressing music on repeat all day while you get high," she informs me cheerily.

"Robert Johnson happens to be a blues genius. And I'm not high," I protest, sitting up on my elbow.

She blinks her big, sky-blue eyes slowly. "Really? Why not? Too lazy to go out and hunt for more product?"

"You don't happen to have any you'd like to share, do you?" I make a kissy face at her and she tries to hide her smile by shaking her head.

She tugs out a little chip hanging on a cord from under her yellow sundress. "Deo, you know I'm sober now. Six months in a week."

I lay back on my pillow and sigh. "When did we all get so damn mature and boring?"

"Not *we*," she corrects. "*I* got mature and grew up. You're still a little boy who wants to get high and surf and do nothing with your life." There isn't a single ounce of malice in her words. Cara is like a surf-bunny Buddha. I irritate her sometimes, but she kind of respects that I do my thing.

Unless my thing is begging her to come over and then being a whiny little bitch who wants to be entertained.

"I don't do nothing." I raise my eyebrows at her. "Actually, there's something we could do right now. C'mon, Sunshine. Nothing lifts the mood like an orgasm."

She twists the cap back on the nail polish and looks at me closely. "I don't sleep with broken-hearted guys. It's too pathetic."

"I'm not broken-hearted," I insist. "I'm just in a slump. Which I'd have such an easier time getting out of if you'd take off that dress. I feel like I have to wear sunglasses when I look at it."

"Wow, you're so charming, how could I even consider saying no?" she asks dryly. "Look, we've been buds forever, Deo, and I treasure that. And when we were more than buds? That was also awesome. But times are changing. We're growing up. Well, some of us are." She puts her hands up to her face. I look at her with confusion. She picks up the bottle of nail polish and holds it like she's on a cheesy advertisement poster. I wrinkle my forehead. "Deo! You noticed the color of my dress, but not *this*?"

I sit up against the headboard and look at her hands. Among the silver sparkling rings is a particular one with a deep green gemstone on her all-important left ring finger. "Uh, is that supposed to be an engagement ring?"

She throws her hands in the air. "It *is* an engagement ring. I didn't want a blood diamond, so we opted for a fair trade stone." She looks down at it, her face droopy with disappointment, and I feel like a huge jerk-off.

"Hey, it's really nice," I say. She doesn't look up. "Sunshine?" She glances at me. "Seriously. It's beautiful. And I'm happy for you. I'm happy you're sober, I'm happy the pottery thing is taking off, and I'm happy for the lucky bastard who conned you into marrying him. Tell that punk I'll beat his face in if he doesn't treat you right."

She falls onto me, her warm, sun-dried sheet smell surrounding me as she hugs tight. "Thank you. So much. I wanted to tell you a hundred times, but I thought you might be upset." She pulls back and looks at me, those blue eyes shiny with tears.

I snort. "Upset? Me? I love you, kid. I want to see you happy. If this fair-trade-ring-buying douchehole makes you happy, you have my blessing. C'mon, you know all that."

She twists the ring on her finger. "I really am happy, Deo. And I wish…" She looks up and licks her lips. "I wish you could find someone for yourself. I know what we had was just fun. But I really think you're amazing. And I know the right person is out there for you. Somewhere. I know she's going to make you so happy. Maybe it's this girl, right now."

I chuckle and take her small freckled hands in mine. "You're sweet, babe. But this girl? She's not…this girl isn't the one for me. We're, like, from two different worlds, you know? She's got complications I'm not about to get involved in."

She raises her light eyebrows high.

"What?" I ask.

"Nothing." A knowing smile twitches on the side of her mouth.

"What?" I demand again.

"Nothing! It's just that you always take the easy way out, Deo. I mean, I know you never really thought you and I would get serious, but you've been calling me for, what, two years for booty calls? And you had to have had fifty girls you were interested in all that time. It was always the same damn thing. One, two, maybe three dates, then things were 'too complicated.'

I think it's code." She flicks her hair again like a damn know-it-all.

"Code for what?" I tuck my arms behind my head and look at my old friend and former fuck-buddy, the now-engaged Cara. Unreal.

"Code for 'maybe I like this girl.' Code for 'things are getting real, so maybe I'll pull back like an enormous pussy.'" She crosses her arms over her chest.

"Ooh, did you just pull out the 'p' word? Your feminist teachers would blow a gasket," I say.

"Desperate times call for desperate language," she sighs. "Look, I know you better than a lot of people. And I care about you. I really do. I've never seen you mourn a girl. Maybe it's a sign."

"A sign?" I watch her gather her little embroidered bag and slide into her sandals.

"A sign that times are changing, Deo. And maybe it's time for you to grow up and face those changes." She leans over and brushes my hair back, kissing me on the forehead. I inhale and drink in her clean, sweet smell. "I want happiness for you."

I grab her hand and kiss her knuckles. "As long as you're happy, I'm happy, Sunshine. See you around?"

"Of course." She pauses at the doorway. "Can I send you an invite to the wedding? I don't want it to be weird for you, but it breaks my heart to think of doing this without you there."

"I wouldn't miss it for anything," I say, and I drink in her bright smile before she darts out the door.

Cara is getting married. She's actually getting married.

It wasn't all that long ago she and I met at the skatepark, when she was just a scraped-kneed tomboy with moves every one of us guys secretly lusted after. And when she grew into those long legs and big blue eyes, I was right there to snatch her up and into my bed. It was always just fun and easiness with Cara, the sweet, sunny kid who never wanted anything more than friendship and sex. So why is her engagement shaking my world?

I pace out to the living-room and see my grandfather with a line of beer cans on the table next to him, watching a John Wayne marathon.

"What's up, old man?" I ask, falling onto the couch.

"That pretty redhead left in a hurry. You two on the outs?" my grandpa asks, watching the Duke draw his gun and try to talk the shaky-handed bad guy out of a duel that would definitely end with the big man's victory over his puny nemesis.

"Sunshine is getting married," I say blandly.

My grandpa nods his tanned, wrinkled head. "Well, that's what happens. You regret that it wasn't you that scooped her up?"

I crack a pistachio from the bowl he always keeps by his armchair and throw it in my mouth. "Nah. I mean, she's amazing, but it was always just friendship between us, you know? It's just fucking with my mind that she's engaged."

"That's the circle of life, kid. I was a piece-of-shit layabout before I met your grandmother. Goddamn, that woman was a sexy piece of ass," he says, while his eyes get this faraway look.

"Ugh, c'mon! I know you loved her, er, in every way. But seriously? She was my grandma, dude." I glance up at the pictures in their old wooden frames on top of his enormous TV. Gross as it might be for me to say it, my grandma was one hell of a knockout. And when she died, it gutted my grandfather for a few long, scary months. Which is a huge part of the reason I moved in and never left. "So, how did you know?" I ask.

"Know what?" His old, gnarled hands scoop up a bunch of pistachios, spread them on the worn arm of his recliner, and he starts cracking and eating.

"How did you know Gram was the one? How did you know you guys would be together for sixty years?" It shocked me right up to the end, how much my grandparents loved each other. You'd think my dad, growing up in a house with the two of them, would have had the whole happily-ever-after business down.

Grandpa laughs and cracks another pistachio. "She was a ball-breaker, and that's how I knew. I was a good lookin' kid. A lot like you. I had 'em fallin' at my feet, running after me and beggin' me to come keep them company in bed. Not your grandma." He chuckles and shakes his head. "Holy shit, that woman had me confused. One date I'd think it was forever. The next time we were together, I was pretty sure one of us was going to get arrested for homicide. But, in the end, she was worth all that work. No one before me ever bothered to chip through and see what was really in her heart. And her heart..." His eyes go glassy with tears, and I look right at the pistachio shells in the bowl like I've never seen anything so interesting in my life. "You know how much I loved that woman's tits and ass, Deo. But her heart? My God, I've never met someone who felt every damn thing with so much passion. I thank God every single day that I got to have a woman like that in my life. One in a hundred million, your grandmother."

There's nothing I can say to him. I'm all embarrassingly choked up, because it's the most amazing shit I've ever heard in my life, and I want it. What they had, I want that. I want it as much as I never, ever want what my parents have.

After a few minutes of watching John Wayne blow the bad guys away, My grandpa adds, "What the fuck are you still doing here? Your mom thinks you're going to that awful dinner she's cooking. Probably all rabbit food and shit."

"I'm not really in the mood," I say, settling back in my recliner.

"Fuck what you're in the mood for. When my mother invited me to dinner, I went to fucking dinner. I feel for you, cause your mother cooks some weird shit, but you get up and go. That woman suffers enough being hooked up with my piece-of-shit son." My grandpa chucks a few pistachio shells at me.

The guilt gets under my skin and spurs me to action. "Alright, alright. Stop with the violence, old man." I get up and stalk to my room. It's fruity as hell, but my mom likes when I dress up for this crap. I pull on a semi-clean, only partially wrinkled button-down and shorts that are stain and rip free. I head to the bathroom and take note that I should shave my scruff, but don't bother. My hair is messed up as hell from salt water and grease, but I don't worry about it much. I know hipsters who'd sell their man-purses to get the look from their expensive-ass hair products that I'm naturally able to rock.

I look good enough for Rocko and Mom, that's sure as shit.

I consider trying to see if I can score some weed before I get to my mother's, but after hanging with Cara, it makes me feel like a scumbag, so I say goodbye to my grandpa and just drive straight there. I hope my mom's got some good booze, cause the fruity wine she loves isn't gonna cut it tonight.

I stumble slowly up the short walk to her little cottage, which looks like it puked up an acre of herbs, a couple thousand little windchimes, and tons of hummingbird feeders. I duck under all the crap and walk in, following the trippy world music to the back patio, where I can see the flames from her firepit already licking high.

I sneak up on her and throw my arms around her waist. "Hey, Mom. Whatcha make me for dinner?"

She whirls around, and instead of the happy smile that's kind of my birthright as her only kid, I get a shocked sputter. "Deo! You're here." Her eyes dart back and forth.

"Gee, Mom. It's awesome to see you, too. You could at least pretend to be happy I dragged my ass over here." Maybe she actually wanted a sexy-time one-on-one thing with Rocko. I should have ignored my grandpa. Goddamn that old codger and his romantic stories and guilt plays.

And then I hear a laugh I know so well, it rips all the air out of my lungs.

"Whit is here?" It's not a real damn question. Of course she's here; I can hear her laugh. The real question is, *why* is she here?

"I didn't think you were coming, honey," my mom rasps in a low whisper. All of her silver bracelets clank up and down her arms as she throws them up. "Why do you never return my calls?"

"Sorry," I hiss. "I had no idea I needed to RSVP to dinner at my mom's house."

Before our little conversation can turn into a full-fledged double-sided tantrum, Rocko comes from the herb garden on the side of the house with a huge handful of tarragon.

"We got it, babe! You had a bumper crop this year. This risotto is going to kick...Deo! Deo. I had no idea you'd be here." He and my mother exchange a panicked look and Whit, unaware of the drama, comes running down the path.

"I have the mint! Do you mind if I take some home? It's my favorite...Deo!" She stops short and clutches the mint to her chest.

She looks so mind-blowingly beautiful, my heart definitely stops for a few dangerous seconds. It's not the pinup look from that night at the tattoo parlor. It's more like her laid-back beach vibe, but amped up. She has on this tiny dress, the same color blue as the ocean on a clear day. It's short and soft and makes her look like she's all long, tanned legs and smooth arms. Her dark hair shines and there's a thick red headband in it, which makes her look kind of young and incredibly sexy all at once.

"I, um, I was just here to drop off some...stuff. For mom. I wasn't staying," I stumble.

Mom looks like she wants to protest, but Rocko puts a hand on her arm.

"Yeah, so, nice seeing you guys. Bye." I give a nonchalant wave and turn on my heel, shocked by how my traitor wuss body is going fucking nuts over seeing her again. What the hell is wrong with me?

I'm all the way out to my Jeep when Whit's voice calls my name. "Deo! Wait!"

I stop, turn, and stick my hands deep in my pockets to keep from grabbing her and dragging her to my Jeep, shoving that sweet little blue dress off her body and showing her exactly how much I missed her confusing, stubborn, stupid, sexy ass.

"Sorry, Whit. I didn't mean to crash the party. I honestly thought it was just my mom and Rocko here. I didn't even want to come. My grandpa made me feel guilty." I'm rambling. I'm stealing time so I can look at her, be near her for a few more seconds before I go through another period of who-knows-how-long missing her like hell.

"It's okay. Really. I, uh, was going to call you. I mean, I wanted to, but I couldn't." She tugs that bottom lip in and nibbles.

I'm aware that she probably has no idea how much she's driving me nuts, but she seriously is. "You could have. I mean, I would have taken your call. Was it that bad, Whit? That we can't even talk to each other? I still don't know what the hell happened."

"No! I mean, it wasn't that bad. And I know you wouldn't have minded. But, uh, I kind of deleted your number." She grasps her hands in front of her body and twists them. "Don't be pissed. I…I had a lot of thinking to do, and I just thought I wouldn't be able to get anything figured out with you so…available to me." Her big brown eyes beg me to hear her out.

I nod. "Okay. So, you're doing okay now?" I take one hand out of my pocket.

She smiles, relief all over her face. "Yes! I'm great. It took a few days. Rocko helped so much. And your mom. I talked with her for, like, two hours one night. She must think I'm insane. But, anyway, I was actually kind of hoping you would drop by tonight. And if you didn't, I was going to beg your mom to give me your number." Her cheeks are a little pink on the edges.

I pull my hands out of my pockets, and the empty, howling hole that I'd been doing my best to ignore all these days without her suddenly feels like it's about to quiet. "I'm glad to hear that." I put one hand up against her face, rub my thumb along her cheekbone, and pull her closer, thinking that this night is about to get a whole lot better so damn fast. "So, you got things all figured out?" I smile at her.

She doesn't smile back. Her hand closes over my wrist and she moves my hand down away from her face gently. "I did. I thought about everything. And I really like you, Deo. As a friend. I think it would be so great if you and I could be...*friends*." She bites her lips after the last word.

I resist the urge to laugh at my stupid luck.

The girl I can't get out of my head just waltzed back into my life, looking like every fantasy I've never been creative enough to dream up, told me how much she's wanted to call me and how much she likes me...and dumps me right in the fucking friend zone.

Fantastic.

-Ten-

Whit

"That'd be my foot," I say. I flash a smile, but my eyes are all stabby. I push Deo's sparkly blue-painted toes off of my thigh, which is, you know, not my foot at all, but since we're at his mom's table, I decide against calling him out. It's the third time he's done it.

Once during the meal of Seitan tacos, once while his Mom and Rocko were debating how much hemp to put in the brownies for dessert, and just now, when his mom is busy telling me about how Deo used to work as a cabana boy. Which is, apparently, a real thing, and does, it would seem, include rich, sexed-up cougars. It's just one more exotic notch in California's belt, and it makes me realize all over again how far from Pennsylvania I really am. He blushes so hard when she tells me this, it's almost like she revealed he was a stripper, and I'm tempted to ask him if the uniform required a thong.

"Sorry 'bout that, doll." He winks and though it was obvious before, that smirk seals the deal and proves he isn't sorry at all.

"Not a problem, *friend*." I put an emphasis on the word "friend," since I know that's what this is all about. I threw him into the friend zone and he isn't man enough to take it.

It's not that I don't want Deo.

I do.

I want to be back there in that Jeep with his hands grazing over my skin like that's exactly what his hands were made to do. Because that's what it felt like. It was like he knew just what to do with them, and that mouth... But that's not reality. And the way Deo makes me feel is nothing more than magic. An illusion. Something that will disappear if I get to close to it or blow up in my face if I try to inspect it.

Reality is that you have to protect yourself from those things from the start. And Deo, Deo has this flighty bit about him. This, *I don't need a job or anything permanent at all* vibe, which tells me that being with him would cause an explosion doubly fast. It's better for me, right now, to stick with guys like Ryan, where everything is out there on the table and there's no chance for failure because there isn't anything to lose.

His cocky smirk falls at the word friend; I grin widely.

"So, friend--" he begins in a voice so low only I can hear, and so full of sarcasm, it automatically triggers an eyeroll from me.

"I ran into Cara at the farmers market the other day," Deo's mom says, not realizing we're in the middle of a semi-hostile friendly discussion. I don't know who Cara is, but Deo's posture becomes a little stiffer at the mention of her name.

"Ah, what a coincidence. I just saw Cara earlier today. She came over to hang out, like old times, if you know what I mean." Deo stares at me while he talks, gauging my reaction. I give him nothing outwardly, but inside I've hired a dozen cabana boys to give me a hot oil rub down while Deo cleans my Olympic sized pool and seethes with jealous rage.

A girl can have her exotic revenge dreams, can't she?

Deo's mom tosses her head back and laughs loudly, her dark hair falling back over her shoulders like millions of strands of silky threads. "Oh, cut the shit Deo. She showed me her ring." Her face softens and she narrows her light brown eyes in his direction. "It would make perfect sense if you were upset or thrown off by it, hon. She told me how unexpected the proposal was. Part of me always thought it would be the two of you. You and Cara had your fun when you were younger playing rumple the foreskin--"

"Mom! As usual, too far!" Deo yells.

I nearly spit my coconut milk across the table, which would be a damn shame because Deo's mom warmed it with mulling spices and I pretty much want to bathe in the stuff. This dinner is simultaneously one of the most enjoyable, sensory-rich events of my life and one of the most irritating, under-my-skin aggravating.

"Oh, please. If you were trying to keep your business private, I wouldn't have had to clean all those rubber wrappers off of your bedroom floor. Which, by the way--"

"Mom, enough. I'm gonna go outside and have a smoke," Deo says. He tosses his napkin onto the table and storms out.

"I thought you quit!" Deo's mom yells after him. But he doesn't stop. The back screen door slams loudly. And then, it's just me. And Rocko. And Marigold. And some pot brownies. And a whole lot of silence.

Marigold flicks a soft-browed, sweet-smiled look of sympathy my way, and her voice husks low and quiet. "Sorry about that, honey. I know he's trying to show off in front of you, and I just don't think it's right. He cares about you, and even though you aren't ready to be doing the lust and thrust with him, well, that doesn't mean he needs to be lying to you about what he's got going on."

Does this woman have no end to her collection of sexual euphemisms?

"Can't you just whip up some sweet love potion and feed it to these kids?" Rocko asks, definitely only half-kidding. After this dinner party, I'm willing to believe Marigold really *is* some kind of amazing, mood-altering witch. I assumed it was just a green thumb and a lot of people willing to believe holistic healing mumbo-jumbo, but maybe there is an element of scary magic to her. And I'd rather not be on the receiving end of any of her potions in any case. "Because I can tell this shit is going to get real old, real fast. And I've got to work with this one!" Rocko motions   to   me.

"I'll fix it," I rush to assure them. I push away from the table. "Thanks   for   dinner,   Marigold."

"No problem, sugar." Her long hair falls into her face and

Rocko is mesmerized. I haven't even picked up my plate to bring to the kitchen, but to them, I've evaporated.

I shiver as I push through the screen door. It's cooled off outside since I got to Marigold's tiny beach house. I rub my hands up and down my bare arms like I'm trying to start a fire.

"Hey," I say. Deo is sitting in a lime green Adirondack chair that desperately needs a fresh coat of paint.

"You cold?" he asks. Before I can answer, he's out of the chair and pulling his hoodie up over his head. "Here, put this on."

I don't object. I pull the thick cotton over my head and it's warm and smells like it's been dipped in the ocean and hung to dry in the salty air.

"Thanks. Hey, I thought you were coming to smoke?" I can't help but notice that there are no cigarettes around.

He drops back into the chair. "Mom's right, I quit. Along with all my other vices, it appears." He laces both hands behind his neck and exhales a long, sharp breath of frustration.

I dig my feet into the cold sand, wondering how far they can sink if I let them. Could I just keep going? It'd be easier to hide from things underground.

"Look, Deo, I don't know what's going on with you and Cara--"

He rolls his eyes and gives me a defeated three-quarter smile. "Nothing is going on with me and Cara, or didn't you catch that? We haven't been anything in a long-ass time. I said all that because I was trying to get to you, obviously."

Deo's sweatshirt instantly warmed my skin, but his words bring a fresh prickle of goosebumps to my arms. "Right. Um, why would you want to get to me? I thought things were cool?"

The partial smile disappears, and his mouth is all sexy-stern and his eyes focus in on me, the pupils so huge in the dim light, I almost can't see any of the golden color. "Things are great, Whit. Except I don't know how to be friends with someone so damn funny and gorgeous, someone who turns me on just by biting her damn lip, or making a face when she eats my mom's freaky hippie   food—"

"I   didn't—"

"Don't give me that, I saw it." His expression relaxes and he laughs, a sweet, sexy rasp that dissolves the goosebumps on my arms   and   makes   my   blood   simmer.

"I'm sorry I can't be what you want me to be." I'm surprised by how quiet my voice is; it barely carries over the repeated crash and suck of the waves. I sit down in the peeling yellow chair next to   him   and   pull   my   legs   up   to   my   chest.

Deo kicks at the sand. "That's the problem, Whit. You're every single thing I want. And for once, I can't have it, and it blows."

It's like he took the words right out of the deepest, most secretive part of my heart, the tiny room that's always locked up with the key swallowed for good measure. It's so tempting, so very tempting, to tell him that. But I know with absolute certainty that it would be a colossal mistake, so I try to offer him a truce we can both live with. "Look, I'm new at this whole friends thing, too. But if you want, we can sort of figure it out together? I promise, I'll be a much better friend than anything else to you."

"I doubt that," he says, eyeing my legs and grinning for the first time since I followed him outside. He runs his hand across the several day's worth of scruff on his cheeks and it sounds like sandpaper.

"You need to shave." He really doesn't. It looks sexy as hell on him.

His grin goes from reluctant to electric in a single beat. "If I shave, can we try again at sweeping the chimney?"

"Deo!" I swat at his arm and he ducks away, and laughs deep and mellow. " What does that even mean? And what is it with this family and their freaky sex talk?

"I'm kidding, Whit. Yeah, of course we can try the friends thing. But I warn you, it'll be killer trying to resist all of this." He motions to his own gorgeous body and flashes a wide, toothy grin heavy with pure confidence. I'm panicked to realize that, despite my resolve to not get involved with anyone, especially someone as flakey as Deo, I sorta think he's right.

****

Deo walks down the hot sand toward the water with a surfboard tucked under each arm. He stops and stabs the boards upright into the sand.

"This one is yours." He points to the larger of the beat-up boards.

"Why exactly is yours smaller? That hardly seems fair." I put one hand on the rough board and eye it up and down, silently praying my decent amount of natural athleticism will apply to this surfing venture, and I won't wind up totally humiliating myself in front of Deo.

He shakes his shaggy head and winks at me. "Shows how much you know. It'll be easier for you to learn on this one, trust me."

He runs his palm across the one designated as mine.

He leans so close I can smell the throat-drying mix of aromas from his skin; part clean sweat, part sunscreen, and part cool, sexy Deo. "I just stripped all the wax off and put a fresh coat on, so you should be good to go."

"Aside from the fact that I have no clue what to do." I pull my hair back into the smallest of nubs and secure it with a pony-tail holder.

"Well, yeah, there's that. But I'm an excellent teacher. First thing I'm gonna have you do is just watch the waves with me for a minute." He crouches down onto the sand and like a good student, I do the same.

"Why exactly are we doing this?" I ask, doing my best to ignore the bulge of his tanned leg muscles. "Shouldn't you be teaching me how to paddle-up or whatever?" It's hot, and I'd love to get into that cool water.

"Paddle-out, doll." He shakes his head and laughs. "Look, that wave right there?" He points out into the endless sea. "It may look small to you, but I bet it's double-your-head high. You need to get a feel for the current. You need to watch the sets break and see where you can swim if you get into trouble." He really knows his stuff. It's more than impressive. Every time I've been to the beach with Deo, he surprises me with his passion and it's quickly crossing the line from educational and interesting to irresistibly sexy.

I chew my lower lip hard and stomp those thoughts out. Friends. That's what we are. That's what makes sense. And I'm the one who recommended it, because I know how dangerously intoxicating he can be. But I can do this. We're just friends out surfing. Totally friendly. Not at all awkward or completely sexually charged.

"Stand up," he says, jerking me out of my embarrassingly guilty thoughts. He reaches his hand out and helps me up. I'm adjusting the ties on my stupid bikini that I'd sworn I'd never wear again when Deo pushes me. I stumble forward a few steps, kicking sand up behind me. "Thought so, goofy-footed." He looks triumphant. I glare, fuming over the fact that he almost made me expose one boob while I was trying to catch myself. "What the hell, Deo?"

As expected, his eye is right on that nearly naked tata, which I cover with a frantic snap of stretchy red fabric. His eyes are quietly appreciative, and it sends a warm, hot hum through me.

"Sorry, I had to figure out which foot you put forward. I couldn't warn you. In surfing, if you think about it, you'll fall."

"This is a ton of stuff. Are you sure this is safe?" Now that I'm as modestly covered as my teeny tiny bikini allows, my outrage shifts gears and turns into stomach-churning worry.

All the peeping-tom, mischievous, laid-back surfer elements of Deo's little show slide away, and his eyes become as calm and serious as his voice.

"Whit, I can't promise you much of anything, but I promise I'll never let you get hurt."

My heart leaps and thuds in my chest. That's an awfully big promise, especially from someone who currently holds more power than anyone else to do exactly that.

"Yeah, but you'll do anything," I say shakily, trying to lighten the mood.

He furrows his brow, then nods as if some piece to this whole million-piece puzzle we're putting together finally snapped into place. "Is that what's scaring you so damn bad?"

I suck in my bottom lip, just like I always do when I'm nervous, or totally brain dead and don't know what the hell to say. And he's staring at me, at my mouth, with a hungry, needy look, and I really think he's about to kiss me. And I may lean forward, just an inch, towards those lips that I know so damn well.

Even though that's not in the friend zone, at all.

He blinks several times and shakes his head, like someone said the magic word and he's no longer hypnotized. Or maybe I just stopped biting my lip.

"Let's get in the water and cool off," he says, his voice slightly strangled.

I just nod, since I don't trust my voice at the moment.

We wade into the salty water, and even its tingling crispness isn't doing enough to counteract the searing temperature from Deo's hand, burning a hole in me as it rests protectively on the small of my back.

I'm about waist deep when Deo looks at me and rubs a warm hand on my shoulder, as if he can sense my nerves. "Don't worry, we aren't going any farther. I think today, I'll just teach you how to paddle-*out*." He reaches up like he's going to touch my face, then seems to think better of it, and forms his lips into a tight line. "Okay, climb up on the board and lay your body on the center of it."

I try to maneuver my way on, but it's not as easy as he makes it sound.

"Don't lean back like that, you'll make the nose rise, that'll create too much resistance," Deo explains. He physically moves me onto the board, his strong hands gripping my hips as he slides me slowly around like the tasty shark morsel that I'm about to become.

I start to panic, all of my nervous fears suddenly jumping and crashing into each other under the black ocean waves. Every instinct in my body screams for me to get off this damn board and swim as fast as I can back to the safety of the shore.

Deo rubs his hands up along my thighs in a way that's more protective than sexual. "Whit, look at me." I turn my head in the direction of his voice. I register the sharp promise in his eyes. "I will not let you get hurt. Trust me. I promise you."

And, despite all shark-related, wipe-out-fearing logic, I do trust him. The look in his eyes calms my erratic heartbeat, and I feel sure I can do this, this crazy, amazing thing I've always wanted to do. Deo gives me courage to full-on attack every fear that's keeping me from trying. And keeping me from living fully. From doing what scares the crap out of me. I swallow hard, make my best attempt at a smile, and let myself just trust that he'll be there to watch my back in case I crash and burn. "Okay. Let's do this."

***

"So, what'd you think?" Deo asks as he carries the boards back up the beach. My arms are limp noodles, and my legs don't want to work properly. I keep stumbling and bumping into Deo as I attempt to walk again.

"It was great!" I search my mind for better words to describe the rush of being so immersed in the ocean, the thrill of mastering this skill that scared me for such a long time, the sweet realization that I could put my trust in Deo and let go for a little while. But all I manage is a wet, dopey grin.

"Come on, for real?" He stashes the boards in his Jeep and

opens the passenger side door for me, his body warm and so close I want to lick it.

Ugh, no! Bad friend, bad friend, Whit.

"Thanks, buddy," I say, even though I'm aware it's more than slightly obnoxious. I need to voice our boundaries before my addled mind and body forget and lead us somewhere we can't come back from. "I think next time will be better, you know, when I'm not so nervous. And maybe next time we get together, I can teach you something." My tongue feels weirdly thick, I assume from all the salt water and sheer, amazing exhaustion.

Deo starts the Jeep and grins. "Doll, I have no doubt you could teach me things. Where to?"

We end up back at my apartment, because, it's one of those perfect days with a friend that you're never quite ready to have come to an end.

"Do you want a beer?" I pace over to the fridge as he sprawls on my tiny loveseat.

Deo narrows his eyes at me. "Have you been holding out on me? I thought you weren't old enough to drink?"

I laugh and pull my wallet out of my bamboo beach bag.

"I have a fake ID." I proudly produce the Pennsylvania State ID that I paid a shit-ton of money for. The picture is just over a year old, and it's out of state now that I'm in California, but it hasn't failed me yet.

"No shit." Deo plucks the license from my hands. "Wow, your hair was so long. Doesn't even look like you."

That's because it's not me. It's just a girl I used to know. Someone who didn't understand how complicated and unfair life could   be.

"Anyway, beer?" I ask, holding the cold import up.

"What the hell." Deo comes up behind me, reaches around my body with the warm snake of one arm, grabs two and pops them both open. "Only if you're joining me, friend."

We both take a long pull from our bottles and, by the look on Deo's face, he's just as beat as I am. The unrelenting pounding of the waves and the sunshine have completely drained me. He takes me by the hand and pulls me back while he flops on the tiny loveseat. The way we're tangled so close, limbs twined, skin rubbing against skin could be friendly, technically. But I have to remind myself of the friendly nature over and over again as my body keeps sending my brain a whole different message.

"So, now that I'm just your boring, hot-as-hell, sexy surfing *friend*, I guess I should ask you the basics. Like how school is going." When I don't say anything immediately, he grabs my foot, which is laying on his thigh, and starts massaging it with sure, unbelievably amazing fingers. I pull my lower lip between my teeth to keep from moaning and his hands press quicker and harder. "Uh, if you want this to stay friendly, you'd better bore me   with   some   long-ass   school   story.   Now."

"You could stop rubbing my foot like th--aaah," I sigh.

He raises one eyebrow. "You really want me to stop?" His thumb slides along my arch, then rubs a heart-stopping line along the center of my foot.

"No. No, don't stop." I try to focus. "Okay. School. Right. I have this project right now for my anthropology class." He presses on the place right under my toes, and I swear I feel the stirrings of an orgasm. This is so not friend territory, and I'd be smart to stop it right this minute.

No one ever said I was smart.

"So what are you doing? Digging up bones of ancient Califonians? Robbing graves? Searching for the Holy Grail?" The mix of his joking voice and his tantalizing hands makes my head spin.

I look at him through half-closed eyes, and he's even more gorgeous slightly blurry. He needs to leave.

I never want him to leave.

"That's archeology," I explain. "I'm in anthropology. We're studying different cultures. So, my assignment was to watch people in a social situation and make note of any cultural details, like manners or gender roles."

"Ah. I get it. Not as interesting as fighting Nazis and almost getting your heart ripped out by crazy Hindus, but we can't all be Indiana Jones, right?" He drops my left foot and picks up the right one, treating it to the same mind-numbingly awesome treatment as its mate.

"Did you learn everything you know about history from Indiana Jones?" I ask, arching my back as he hits *the perfect spot* that I didn't even know existed on my body.

"All the important stuff." His hands move more quickly, but his voice slows to an almost slur. "So, bout this assignment?"

"I used your mom's dinner party," I confess, my voice bleary with the warring needs for him to stop immediately and never take his hands off of me. "And I got back the rough today. My professor wants to read it to the class next lecture."

Deo's brows press over his eyes and his smile is wry. "I could have told you that writing about me would get you an A." His cockiness melts away at my smirk. "What did you write about, exactly?"

I bat my lashes at him. "Oh, you know. The sad, desperate flirting attempts of young unemployed men."

He shakes his head, a smile curved on his lips. "You can't resist me. Admit it."

"I would say something smart, but this foot rub is amazing, Deo. I can't lie. I feel like I have no bones in my body. Where did you learn to do this?" I roll my neck back as he purposefully hits that certain spot that melts every tense spot in my body.

"It's in my sad, desperate flirting bag," he teases, then his voice goes low. "Seriously, I'm proud of you. Maybe I can see the paper sometime?"

"About that." I sit up on one elbow and catch his eye. "Deo, I want you to come to lecture with me."

"To sign autographs?" He wiggles my toe.

"No. I think...I think you might like it at college. If you wanted, you could come and see what I'm doing." I try not to sigh when he puts my feet aside.

"That would be cool, Whit. But, you know, I tried college. It just wasn't my thing. And don't you worry your gorgeous head about me. I'm a survivalist. I know right now I don't seem like I have decent prospects, but wait for the zombie apocalypse. I'll be leading civilization back from the brink and slaying those brain suckers left and right." He regards me from under his heavy eyelids and his easy smile is as sad as it is charming.

"Deo...it's fine if you don't want to go to college, but you may want to secure something. Just on the off-chance that I pursue biology and come up with a vaccine that will curb the zombie apocalypse before you get a chance to show off your skills. Which I have no doubt are amazing." I try to joke back, but today just proved all over again how amazing and passionate and smart Deo is. I hate to think about him wasting his life, his time. I don't think he realizes just how damn little we get.

"C'mon. Don't be sad. Many beautiful women have tried to reform me before. It's a lost cause. I'll just be your hilarious, uber-sexy sidekick. Good for a little surfing and a couple of beers, maybe with a semi-sexual foot rub thrown in once in awhile. I'm like the perfect no-strings-attached friend. Just like you wanted, right?" Though his tone stays light, there's a sharp edge underneath, and I decide to back off. He looks at me for a second, like he's debating saying something else, then changes gears. "Enough of this serious, depressing crap. You wanna see if we can rot our brains with a good zombie flick? Or maybe some shark attack show. Just kidding! I want you to surf with me again. I wish you could see your face right now. Priceless." He glances at the wall where most people would have a TV. I have seven small plants that are in various stages of death. "No TV?" Deo asks, turning in a small circle.

"I have one in my room. I don't watch a whole lot of TV, I just keep it on at night, for you know..." I sigh. He just finished laughing about my irrational shark fears.

But he drops the teasing and gets that sympathetic look that makes my throat scratchy. His voice is real and a little sad when he asks the next questions, and I have to resist the strong urge to curl into his arms and let him peel back all the fears that leave me shaky everyday. "What? Are you scared being here alone?"

Yes.

"No. It's just too quiet. I can't sleep like that. Total silence is just...weird."

Deo nods like he's not buying it.

"Do you wanna watch something...in my room?" For all my 'just friends' talk I sure seem to cross the line in a million different ways. Between the tiny bikini, the foot rub, and, now, the beer-fuzzy invitation to come to my room, my line in the sand is as indistinct as if it had been drawn too close to the waves at high tide.

"Sure. Mind if I grab another beer?" Deo swallows so hard I can see the tendons in his neck go tight.

I back away from him, needing a second alone to prepare

myself for Deo. In my room. With me. Alone. "Grab two, I'm gonna go change. And find something on TV."

I hurry into the bathroom and change into a pair of soft cotton shorts and a tank top. I don't even have the energy to shower, I'm that tired.

Back in my room, Deo is already leaning up against the headboard. His head is tipped back and his eyes are closed. I flip on the ceiling fan and start toward the bed, but Deo's eyes pop open.

"What are you trying to do, kill me, woman?"

"What are you talking about?"

"The fan, turn it off!" He's frantic. I haven't seen him like this before.

"Deo, it's a fan. Get a grip."

He crosses the room and flips the switch to off.

"Don't you know that ceiling fans cause Bell's Palsey?"

I want to laugh, but it is so apparent from the look on his face that he is dead serious.

"They do not. That's an old wive's tale. I've been sleeping under one forever," I say.

"Ask Marigold!" he challenges, knowing I more than believe in his mom's supernatural abilities when it comes to healing and health. He plops back onto the bed next to me.

The twitch in my lip can't be stopped and I burst into a full, rolling laugh.

"I'm sorry. That's absurd, Deo!"

He stares at me straight-faced, so I make an effort to pull my mouth back into a thoughtful, serious line.

"Fine. I can see this is a very sore subject with you, and as your friend, I'm going to drop it. And leave the fan off. On one condition." My voice shakes a tiny bit, but I get a handle on it.

"What's that?" Deo runs his hand through his hair and sighs. He looks tired.

I take a deep breath and just take the plunge, just ask him for what I want, even if I know this is making that damn fading line in the sand even sketchier. "Would you maybe stay here tonight? With me? Just as friends, of course."

I don't know if Deo is confused or horrified or what, but he doesn't answer at first.

He finally reaches over and cuts an invisible line down the quilt, dividing the bed into two sides, his and mine, and his voice grinds out, hard and rough.

"Sure. As long as you can stay over there, *friend*."

-Eleven-

Deo

Whit looks like an angel when she sleeps. She's all sweet, full lips, long, curly eyelashes, and a tumble of sleek, dark hair against the pillow.

She also kicks like a mule, snores like a bear, sweats like a hog, and steals the covers like a fat, menacing caterpillar about to cocoon herself before her metamorphosis. Which I keep hoping may actually happen and turn her into a relaxed, soft breathing, cool-skinned, cover-sharing butterfly. Instead she wakes up most mornings looking like a burrito with a small, sweaty, scowling girl's head, ready with crazy accusations.

"Deo, you were totally on my side of the bed all night. You were the one who made the divide," she snarls, while I sprint to the kitchen to get her a cup of coffee. I never pictured myself the kind of guy who'd be all whipped into getting a girl her morning joe, but I never encountered a person who was such a raging psychopath before her first cup of coffee either.

I shove the coffee, two sugars and a drop of cream, into her hands and she growls and laps up the dark liquid like the alpha wolf she is. When the caffeine has settled her frayed nerves a little, I venture to suggest she's not being entirely fair about our little arrangement. "Seriously, Whit? I'm considering growing out my toenails so I can get a better grip on the edge of the mattress. I have, like, six inches tops. You sleep like a bus wreck."

"So don't sleep here." She slurps another sip of coffee, and, when the caffeine takes a better hold over her ravaged brain, she gives me the sorry eyes over the rim. "Sorry. I'm such an awful human in the mornings. It's no excuse, but I am sorry. And thank you for the coffee. Did I mention you make the most amazing coffee?" She smiles hopefully.

I tweak her cute little nose. "Stop with the flattery. We both know you're just charming me so I keep doing your bidding."

She finishes the coffee and heads to the shower. She'll gather her stuff for school, drop a kiss on my forehead, and head out the door. I have my own key to her place. I examine it right now, running a finger over its bumpy teeth. She handed it to me like it was no big thing.

"Just in case I leave before you, you need to lock up. Get that look off your face, Deo. It isn't a promise ring. It's safety. You're afraid of ceiling fans, I'm afraid of psycho killers coming in and slitting my throat." Her words were all tough, but her palms were clammy when she slid the key my way.

And I stay here. Most nights. Sometimes I take some time to hang with Gramps, but he's like a damn pioneer. He's the kind of guy who'd prefer if he could pump his own water and keep his own cows and live by candlelight. Except then he wouldn't get the UFC fights on his 72" LED. It's his one modern obsession, that TV, and he treasures his time with it and his beer and pistachios.

I stay here with Whit, but we're definitely not together. Not in any way, shape, or form. The foot rub a few weeks before was the most intimate thing that's happened between us.

Other than the snuggling.

I told her I was a hardcore snuggler, but she didn't believe me. But I know it was the snuggling that clinched her decision to basically move me in. Whit is scared shitless to be alone in the dark. She's never given me a shred of a clue about why. That's off limits, and we just don't go there. When the lights are on, we're jesting, sarcastic, friendly assholes guzzling beer, playing poker, and hitting the beach and various cheap area restaurants to satisfy her desire for pizza or fish tacos or whatever other weird craving she might have. We stay that way right up until we walk into her bedroom. She changes in a little huddled mass with her back to me or in the bathroom, and we both sternly establish that there's a line we don't cross in the middle of her too-small full bed.

Then I flick the light off and settle on the bed. In the shadows of her room, she wordlessly turns to me, and I wrap my arms around her. Her back curves against my chest, her ass nestles painfully close to my dick, and her smooth, long legs twine around mine, her toes brushing up and down the length of my calf. I run my hands over her without saying a thing. I trace my fingers from the rounded curve of her shoulder, down the long line of her upper arm, around the pointed curve of her elbow. She always lies on her left side, and her right elbow has a puckered bump. In the light, I can see that's it's from a pretty gnarly scar, but I don't ask about it. What happens in the night doesn't get talked about during the day. That's the way it works with us.

Usually when I'm running my hands over every sweet curve and soft length of a girl's body, it's because I want to hear her gasping for breath, sighing my name, begging me for more, and moaning with body-shaking satisfaction.

With Whit, I want the opposite.

I want to be the one who takes all the stiff-limbed panic from her, who eases her out of the tense-muscled pre-sleep ball she curls herself into and lets her have a few minutes of sweet, relaxed sleep. Once she's asleep, there's nothing I can do to ease the rest of the night for her, and some of those nights are beyond brutal. She kicks and flails, grits her teeth, whimpers, sobs, opens her eyes and looks at me without seeing a single thing, sometimes wailing indecipherable things, sometimes just choking on her tears.

When her upset thrashing wakes me up, I curve her back into snuggle position and run my hands over her damp hair, put my mouth close to her ear and whisper sweet, quiet things, pull my arm tight around her waist to anchor her to the calm reality I try to provide.

Sometimes it works.

Other times it's like she's a DVD that has a deep scratch and we keep watching the same painful scene over and over on repeat. In the morning, we both wake up spent and grouchy, and all the menace of the night swirls between us, unacknowledged and heavy as a ton of cement on our shoulders.

I'm scared as hell to push anything further. I want to help her work through all her shit, but she won't let me touch it. And, as unsatisfying as it is to be so close to her but closed off, I'm glad for what I've got and won't run the risk of losing it entirely. Soon enough she'll meet some fuckwad who'll take my place, and they'll be more than just friends and snuggle buddies.

That thought makes me see red, so I try not to think it. I just take lots of long, self-satisfying showers, like I'm in eighth grade all over again, and I try to enjoy every second I get with her.

I'm on my way to meet Cohen at the beach after seeing her to class on a normal Tuesday when I hear the beep of her answering machine. She's old school, so she still keeps a landline, and I can't help but overhear the message.

"Ms. Conrad, this is Louise McKellan from Imperial Coast College. I'm afraid we weren't able to process the second check you sent. Unfortunately, you won't be able to get your grades at the end of the semester if this doesn't come through. It also puts your application for study abroad in jeopardy, as your financial accounts must be current in order for your application to be considered. Your student ID is on temporary suspension, so all facilities are off-limits until this is cleared. Please call me as soon as you're able, and we'll get this all straightened out."

Her strangely jolly voice is followed by an ear-splitting beep, and I resist the urge to smash the piece-of-shit answering machine into fifty fucking pieces. Seriously? Whit can't get her grades? She'll lose a place in this study-abroad thing she wants to do? Her ID is suspended? How the hell does dip-shit Louise think Whit is going to figure this all out?

I know exactly what's going to happen. She's going to come home after a full day of classes, studying, and work, and she's going to be exhausted after the hellishly sleepless night she had the other night. She's going to crack. Whit, who seemed tough as nails and so put together before I really got to know her, has revealed herself as a wounded fighter barely juggling all the shit she has up in the air.

This is not what she needs right now.

Even though she's usually Ms. Secret, Take Care of It All Herself, I'm taking one giant step over the quickly receding friend-line and getting all into this business. I can do this. Fixing sticky situations and charming people is what I was brought up to do.

I flip open my cell. "Cohen? You have a suit I can borrow?"

Cohen meets me at the beach with the suit, sans socks. "Socks kinda pull the whole thing together," I gripe.

"Go see your grandpa. He'll hook you up. So, what's worth getting suited up for?" He takes a lint roller off his passenger seat. Thank God for responsible as all hell Cohen. I love this guy.

"Whit." I don't say anything else as he rolls my sleeves and back lint-free.

Cohen nods, opens his mouth, closes it, and finally just comes out and says his piece. "Look, man. Whit is hot as hell. And smart. Too smart for you. And she's gonna grow up to be a real adult who buys groceries and has health insurance and all that. So if you can hook up with her, you have my blessing. But if you're just fun and games for her...don't do that, okay? I know you don't have the fucking job and degree and all that, but you've got your good qualities. Okay? Don't waste time with her if she doesn't know that." Cohen gives me a half smile, and I clap my hand on his back.

"Advice taken, man. And I swear to you, I will not wind up on your couch crying and playing video games for months if she does break my heart." I tug on my tie and slip my feet into my beat-up Vans before I pull out, leaving Cohen looking like he's predicting my imminent doom.

Maybe his predictions will be dead on. But she's worth the gamble. Whatever time I get with her, whatever it winds up meaning, she's worth it.

I pull into my Grandfather's driveway. He limps out of the garden and I glare his way. "When did you get so old? You need a walker?"

"I need a cane so I can smack you upside the hard-ass head with it!" he calls back. "What's your ugly mug doing back here? I thought you were shacked up with that pretty little thing with those miles of legs, staying out of my damn hair. Why don't you bring her over, by the way? Afraid she'll leave you for a real man when she sees me?"

He pokes his lined, tanned face into the truck, and my smile fades when I see how bleary his eyes look and how buckled over his back is. Is it just that I'm noticing this stuff now because I've been away for a few weeks? Or is he doing worse?

"You doing okay?" I ask.

"No. I need you to come home and tuck me in at night," he growls. "What do you need?"

"Dress socks. And shoes, if you have them." I smile at the look of outrage that spreads over his wrinkled face.

"What man doesn't have dress socks and shoes?" he asks pointedly. "You wanna grow up to be a hobo?"

"Yep. Just like my grandpa." He turns away, chuckling, and I follow him into the house where I head to my room while he gets the shoes and socks, muttering about my stupidity. I slide under my bed, careful to keep my white shirt out of the dust. I find a box in the back and wipe the top clean.

It's been a long time. A long time. I honestly never think about any of this shit, because it just amounts to a bum's pipe-dreams. I slide the lid open and the gold coins wink up at me, bright as some pirate's treasure.

I run my fingers over the bumps and grooves. I just checked the stats on them. I only need to pawn a few and, no matter what Whit owes, it will take care of it. Part of me wants to sell the whole damn lot, just for spite. And waste it. Maybe on a bright yellow Mustang. Something that would irritate my father because of how showy and everyday it is. Because these coins aren't for bullshit. They're part of a vow I made with my dad when I was too young to realize he talks so much bullshit, even he can't keep track of it all.

Every time he got the chance, had someone in a tight spot, found a rare coin for a ridiculously good price, he'd snatch it up and send it home to me. We had enough under my bed for everyone to live in a shitty mansion, but Mom and Grandpa wouldn't touch them. And I was under strict orders to keep my grubby paws off of them until I was ready to invest them. My dad wanted them to go to a set-up for treasure hunting. Real fucking treasure-hunting, months or years on end on a boat, cruising dangerous waters, racing other idiots for a piece of huge deposits, sunk to the bottom of the ocean and waiting.

Waiting for me and my scumbag dad to get our shit together and come scoop it up.

Of course, Mom and Grandpa don't believe that horseshit anymore. But they do expect me to do something amazing with the coins. Set myself up. They don't care if it's a dumb-ass dairy farm or a pottery studio; they just want me to do what I love.

And right now, what I love is Whit.

I almost choke on a dust bunny I sucked into my lung too quickly.

Love? Love Whit?

That was a little...what I meant was...I was trying to say...

I'm a fucking dumbass.

What I was trying to say is that I love her.

I love Whit, love the nights I spend getting my ass kicked in her bed, love the way she smells like grapefruits and girl and feels like sand-rubbed, sun-kissed skin, love talking to her, love the scratch of her key in the door. I love her enough to steal from the only dream I've ever had, even if it is an embarrassing, pathetic, little-kid, stupid dream. As long as I had these coins, I was invested in. Practically a trust fund baby. But I'm tired of living that what-if dream. I need to take care of the girl I love right now, and accept the fact that my dream is a day late and a motherfucking dollar short.

I grab the three I know will cover what I need, slip them in my pocket, thank my grandfather for the shoes and socks, and ignore his look. The look that says he knows exactly what I'm about to do, but can't believe I'd actually betray this promise to my vague dream that I've held onto my entire life.

I know the pawn shop to go to, and only get marginally ripped off. I follow the road to Whit's college and attract the attention of every lady there with my suit. And my business card, stolen from the pawnshop lobby. I'm Joseph Morgenstern, Attorney. Smiling, handsome attorney in charge of Whitley Conrad's financial accounts and so, so sorry to have caused so many problems for these lovely women, who already have enough on their plates everyday.

Thirty minutes, no ID check, very few questions, a good chunk of change, and several flirty smiles later, I leave the office and have paid Whit's semester and the down payment on her semester abroad. My phone has three messages when I take it off silent.

Whit. And the messages freak me the hell out.

I drive to her place with the gas pedal sunk to the floorboard, not giving a single fuck about red lights or cops. I run up the stairs and into her apartment, and she's sitting on the floor, her head in her hands, sobbing.

I kneel down next to her, take her shoulders in my hands. "Whit. Whit. Stop crying, baby. Stop." She lets me unfold her and take her clumsily in my arms.

"Deo, I'm screwed! I'm so screwed! My parents need that money, they need it! I can't ask. And I thought some financial aid was coming through, but it's been denied. I didn't know they could say they'd give it, then not do it, but they can. They can! And I'll have to leave. I'll have to leave California and go back home, and I'll be a loser! I'll be a huge disappointment. What am I going to do? I couldn't get anyone at the financial aid office to pick up the damn phone! Oh, Deo! What the fuck am I going to do?" Her sobs are harsh, and it hurts to listen to them.

I wipe her tears away with my thumbs. "Listen to me. Listen. I fixed it."

Her head snaps up. There are dark rings of mascara under her eyes. Her hair is stuck to her cheeks with tears and sweat. The tip of her nose is bright red, and her lips look swollen. She wrinkles her forehead when she looks at my suit and tie. "What did you do?"

"I worked some Deo magic." I try to keep my voice light, but her night terrors mixed with this new, extreme sadness are kind of freaking me out. "All settled. By the way, when were you going to tell me about your study abroad in Italy? Did I ever tell you I love spaghetti? And the David? And passionate women with awesome accents? You were just gonna leave me to rot in this shithole? Not cool."

"How did you fix it?" she asks carefully, and I'm still not sure she's going to be okay with my explanation, but I just have to stop being a puss and tell her.

"Don't be pissed, okay?" I know that's almost like asking for her to *be* pissed at me and throw a hissy fit. But I decide on telling the truth and trusting Whit to get it. For once. Even if it's so not our thing.

So I start with my sorry-ass childhood, looking up to my loser father like he was some kind of god, and that box under the bed that was so full of pipe-dream possibilities I never bothered to make good on, because as long as it was under my bed, there was still this potential for me to be amazing, but the minute I started to use it was the minute I had to admit that I might make huge fuck-up failure-based decisions. And how I'd never wanted to use any of it, not a single coin, ever. Half because, fuck my father, and half because I'd show everyone with my awesome whatever-the-hell-I-was-going-to-do-with-it-one-day. But all that took a back burner when I heard Mrs. Red Tape Asshole leave her chipper-ass message, and it felt good to finally be able to make something right in my long, loserish existence.

It's a long-ass, rambly-ass story, and Whit winds up getting me a beer and one for herself, kicking off her shoes, wiping her eyes, and settling down to just listen and sip her brew while I wah-wahed through my story.

When I come to the end and give her my fake business card, her face is unreadable, and I'm betting on the fact that I'll be kicked out of her apartment at any second for interfering in a huge way. Forget crossing lines. I've hacked through so many, it's unbelievable and irreparable. I've finally dragged us out of no man's land, and I might take a bullet in the head for it.

"You did this all for me?" Her voice is cracked.

"Of course. We're homies forever, right?" I attempt to joke.

Her eyes tear over me. "You got a disguise? You stole an identity? You flirted with those awful business ladies? You pawned your booty?"

"You're making it sound way tawdrier than it really was." I wink at her. "I'm good at being a liar. And a flirt. And a pawn star. Wow, that sounds wrong."

Then Whit does something I don't expect at all. She puts her beer down and climbs on my lap. "You're not a liar. You're amazing. You are so goddamn amazing, and I can't believe I'm lucky enough to have you in my life." The tears slide down her face silently. I sop them up with the cuff of my shirt. "I will pay back every cent, Deo. Every single cent, I swear to you. Thank you." Her lips come down on mine.

I squeeze her around the hips and try not to pass out from pure shock. Whit, sweet, soft, ready Whit is on top of me and kissing me with such hungry, nipping kisses, I can hardly focus. When I get my thoughts straight, I pull back.

"Wait. Wait a second. This is not why I did that." I pick her up by the hips and move her to the cushion next to me, no matter how much I wish I'd just shut my brain off and give in to what she started. "I did what I did because I lo—care about you. I care about you." I watch her eyes go perfectly round when she realizes what I really meant to say. I rush to cover my tracks. "And I'm collecting every penny back, with interest. That sad little stack of coins is all I got to my name. You? You'll be rich as Midas one day. Maybe I'll mop the gold-tiled floors in your thousand-story office building. Don't laugh. I'll gladly work in your shadow."

"Why can't you see how amazing you are?" she asks, and takes my hand. She tugs me closer and kisses me, her eyes closed. I know because mine are wide open. "I. Want. You. Now." She takes a deep breath. "Please."

I know it's one of those ideas that sounds good in the moment, but winds up being bad business.

But she's loosening my tie, unbuttoning the buttons that go down my shirtfront, and pushing my jacket off my shoulders. Her small, soft hand slides in the gap in the shirt and runs over my chest. Her lips brush over my neck, along my jaw. She sucks in on my earlobe and lets her tongue trace around my ear, breaking my arms out in chills. I yank her back onto my lap and rub my hands between her shoulder blades, knocking the ribbon straps of her sundress down off her shoulders.

I lower my mouth and kiss the skin where her straps were, the skin under her collarbones, the skin that pokes out of the top of her tiny, lacy bra, pink as a Valentine. I push the dress down to her hips and run my hands over the lace of her bra, down the smooth skin on either side of her spine, let my fingers tangle in the waistband of her thong.

She pops a button off my cuff yanking the shirt off, and her fingers fumble at the button of my pants and try to pull the zipper down, but I'm rock hard and pressed awkwardly against it.

"Deo," she gasps, and I lift her up, off the too-tiny loveseat. She wraps her long legs around my waist and I stagger with her in my arms into her dim bedroom. I set her down on the bed, and she yanks at my wrists, making me topple half on top of her. Her fingers comb up and down my ribs and her fingernails dig lightly into my back before her hands dart south and manage to get the zipper down. My pants hang half off my ass, and her brown eyes are wide, dark, and inviting me.

The happiness I feel over that look is second-guessed by a nagging voice in the back of my head. A voice that reminds me that what happens in this room tends to stay in this room. And, hard as it was to keep my nights spent holding her in my arms locked in this tiny space, I know for sure I'm not going to be able to keep earth-shaking sex in here, too.

She shimmies her dress down her legs and grabs at the elastic waistband of her thong. I put my hands over hers and shake my head, begging her to let me do these sexy-as-hell things I've thought about a million times in my endless morning showers.

I pull the little scrap of fabric over her smooth thighs, watch her mouth part as it bumps over her knees, down along her calves, and I untangle it from her ankles. I kneel in front of the bed where she sits, her chest rising and falling in time to her frantic breathing. I reach behind her back and unsnap the pink bra, letting it fall aside. And then I lean over her and kiss along those perfect, exactly-a-handful tits, pulling her nipple in my mouth and listening to the gasp that comes like clockwork from the twist of my tongue on her. I rub my face along the sweet, soft skin on the underside, and let my mouth suck and lick until she's whimpering. I pull back to look at her and totally love what I see.

Strange how completely different she looks naked than she did in a bikini.

Maybe because the bikini was for everyone. Just Whit, just all her soft, tanned skin is for me and me alone. I kneel back and kiss her knees, watching the goosebumps prickle up her thighs. I follow their bumpy trail, leaving wet kisses imprinted on her soft skin, until I make it right to the top.

"Open your legs." We never talk when we're together in this room, but I want to. I don't want this to be silent. I want to hear her voice during this.

She drops her head back and does what I tell her to. I lay my palms flat on her thighs and run my hands up to her hips, let my fingers grip her hard and kiss along the sweet, wet center of her. I assumed that Whit was experienced based on her booty calls before we starting shacking up, but she presses her thighs closed and slides back on the bed, away from my mouth.

"No," she says, shaking her head and trying to pull me up to her mouth.

"Yes," I counter, hooking her under the knees and pulling her back with one tug.

"No." This time it's fainter, because I'm kissing and licking whatever I can, and she likes it. And wiggles away from it at the same time.

"Why not?" I ask, kissing the tops of her thighs and dragging my mouth down to her knees.

She looks down the length of her perfect, sweet body at me and bites that sexy-as-hell pouty lip. "It's...too exposed."

I trace my thumbs along the wettest, slickest lines of her and watch her head roll back. "I'd like to." I keep my voice soft. "Every single part of you is beyond sexy to me. It will make you feel good. I promise you that." She squeezes her knees together, then loosens them. "I really want to. I've thought about doing it a thousand times." She moans a little and opens wider. "You can trust me, Whit. I promise."

Her knees fall wide to the sides, and I put my mouth on her, licking and sucking until her breath changes from steady and labored to panting and frantic. Her hands ball the sheets and pull up, her heels push against the bed frame, and her entire body shakes as her hips lift off the mattress.

"Deo!" Her head is thrown back and, suddenly, I want her so badly, I can't imagine a single damn thing that could stop me from being with her.

"Are you sure you want this. Whit, you want me?" I'm going crazy, but there's no way this is happening unless she wants it. Absolutely, no questions, wants it.

She rolls over on the bed, her sweet heart-shaped ass facing me, pulls open the drawer next to her bedside table, and grabs a condom. She rolls back over and sits up, pulling down on the waist of my boxer briefs with a rough yank and rolling the condom on my dick. I kick my pants and boxers the rest of the way off, and lock my mouth over hers, sweet, open, and busy gasping and pleading my name. Her tongue twines quick and sure in my mouth, and her hands go low with mine. I slide one finger, then two into her and her teeth catch my bottom lip. One of her hands pushes mine away, and she leads me to the slick, hot center of her.

I want to wait, drag it all out, prolong what I've already waited so long for, but I slide into her and she's hot and tight and her hips are pressing in a frenzied rhythm against me. I press my forehead into the space between her neck and her collarbone and focus on making it good for her, on holding back and not thinking about how sweet and warm and slick she is, so ready for me, I know she's probably imagined it as many times as I have.

I hold out until I feel the very beginning of her shudders, proud as hell of myself for not letting go before. Her fingers brush through my hair, then fist in it and pull as her shudders deepen. My name flies out of her mouth fast and urgent, and there's not a thing I can do to stop myself from coming, hard and satisfied against her, into Whit, in this bed we've slept in dozens of times but never done *this* in.

Her breath comes out hard and harsh, and I pull out slowly, remove the condom, and throw it away. She's curled on her side, not looking at me or anyone or anything. Her eyes are closed. I pull the covers down under her body, already heavy with sleep. I crawl next to her and pull the blankets up, our naked bodies pressed against each other's, and snuggle her in an entirely new way tonight. This time, she sleeps with loose limbs and easy, gentle breathing while I'm tense and worried.

"Whit," I whisper in her ear like a pussy, knowing she can't hear a single thing. "I love you. I hope to hell this didn't change anything." I run a rough hand over her shiny hair, dreading the dawn.

-Twelve-
Whit

"Did you know that if you have a cat, they'll eat you several days before a dog will? Like, cats will only wait a day or two before they start chomping on your brain matter, but your dog will wait like a week. Isn't that crazy?" I peer into my lukewarm cup of coffee and notice the congealed skin of cream on top. Should I drink it? How much do I need this caffeine exactly? I can't believe I'd actually consider drinking this.

Deo narrows his eyes at me. "And pretty insanely morbid, Whit. What the hell are you studying in that weird-ass class? Last week it was the people who breastfeed till their kids turn eight, and now face-eating pets. Also, why are you even worried? We don't have any animals."

I can't help it. I flinch when he says 'we.'

"Wait, are you even studying? Like, are there face-mauling cats in that chapter, or are you thinking about zombies again? Because, I told you, I have us covered if the apocalypse breaks out." He picks up a rubber band he finds on the floor across the room and shoots it at me.

I deflect it with my book, then slam it shut. "Just my morbid imagination hard at work. I guess that means I'm ready for a break. You want to go get something to eat?" I've been sitting cross-legged on my bed for hours staring at this damn book. I try

LENGTHS   131

to stretch, but everything just aches.

"No need." He tosses a dish towel over his shoulder, looking so very delicious. And domestic. "I made us some dinner."

"No kidding?" I toss the book aside and follow Deo to the kitchen, breathing the enticing aroma of home-cooked food deep into my malnourished lungs. It smells incredible; I must have really been into that anthropology book to miss the scents and sounds of Deo preparing this meal. "This looks amazing."

"Sit." He motions to the bar and I pull up one of the stools. Deo has cleaned off all of the clutter- the mail, keys, clothes and whatever else we toss up here on our way in and out of my apartment. In place of the junk are two mismatched place-mats and an even more mismatched pair of place settings. But somehow, it's perfect. "So, pan-roasted chicken with roasted tomatoes and white beans."

Deo scoops a heaping portion onto each of our plates and then takes the stool next to mine.

"Are you sure you made this?" I tease.

"Hey, Marigold is the one that can't cook. I learned from my Gramps. He used to be a Navy cook, you know. Every time he makes a damn pizza, there's enough to feed the whole freaking town." He gives me an eager smile and waits for me to try it.

I stab a forkful of chicken and pause before taking a bite and moaning over the flavor explosion in my mouth.

"Mmm. Mmm, seriously. Amazing." I point to my mouth and moan again. "But what's the occasion?" Deo has basically been living at my place for the last couple of weeks, going home just to check in on his grandfather, or grab some extra clothes. Neither one of us has cooked in all that time, and, instead, have been surviving on a diet of Honey Nut Cheerios and rice cakes. I'm starved for a decent meal.

"Your last final is tomorrow. Would I be a total dweeb if I confessed that I can't wait for you to finish up the semester, so we can surf and you can seduce me anytime of the day?" He lets his fingers tip-toe up my arm. I reach over and mimic the movement, but this time, I move up his thigh.

I hop off of the stool and press my lips to his throat. His skin is salty like the ocean air and once I start, it's always hard to pull away.

"Hey, hey, why are you being so nice? You know that freaks me out," Deo jokes, pulling back from me.

He's right. I enjoy every second of our nights together, but it's been a struggle to carry that same strong connection during the day. It's too much, still. And way too scary. I just can't allow myself to give in to the happiness or the fallout that Deo could bring. It's bad enough that I feel like I keep running right up to the edge of the water, but stopping before my feet dip into the waves. I can't force myself to jump in, no matter how amazing the water might be.

He pulls my hand to his chest and disrupts my spinning thoughts. "Feel my poor, shocked heart. It's beating out of my chest."

The feeling of his racing heart is familiar, since my ear is usually pressed against it at night. I listen to that steady thump as it goes from pounding with lust, to slowing with sleep and satisfaction. Then Deo rubs his hands over me in slow, relaxing circles and our limbs tangle together in the most perfect mess ever. And I steady my breathing and try to concentrate on that rhythmic beat alone.

I know Deo assumes I'm asleep, and, sometimes, the sound of his voice cuts through the simple sound of his heart beating.

Like when he tells me how much he loves me, or how he'd do anything to make me happy.

I'm a horrible person for not saying anything back, or even letting him know that I've heard him at all, but I just can't. No matter how treasured and wonderful and perfect it makes me feel, I just lie there next to him, petrified with this crazy mix of perfect happiness and absolute terror.

The terror I feel in his arms could maybe be measured if you took my fear of sharks, my horror at the shadowy loneliness of my apartment, and my nervousness about possible future pet cats eating my corpse when I die alone and squish them all together and multiply their ugliness by a trillion. And then you could stick me in a dark house with zombies bashing in at the windows as the terror cherry on top.

"Seriously,   what's   up?"   Deo   asks.

"What are your plans for the summer. I mean, other than

impressing me with your sexual prowess?" Which, for the silent record, is damn impressive. I'll never tell him that, since his ego is already big enough as it is. But, man, that boy knows how to use what he was blessed with. Deo shrugs and evades, his usual tactic when I bring up anything more substantive than our dinner plans. "I hadn't really given it a whole lot of thought."

I don't know what Deo has planned for the rest of his life. His future is all very vague, and honestly, I just can't handle that. I need plans. I need to be independent and be around happily independent people.

That's why I'm here, on my own. That's why I gave up the dream of living in the plush dorms at the University of Delaware, and, instead, settled for this crappy apartment, the most liberal college in the country, and a mediocre job (apart from Rocko) to help pay for it all.

Except that I'm not actually all that independent.

Because I had to accept Deo's help, which totally goes against everything I thought I believed in. And, despite how much I appreciate what he did, and despite the realization that I'd be so screwed without his help, it's also, strangely, one of the things that's holding me back with Deo.

I want to want him because I made the choice as an independent person. And I want him to want me for the exact same reason. Once we start basing the reason we're together on dependency (which all started with my freakish fear of being

LENGTHS   135

alone, so I take full blame), we run the risk of getting entwined in a way that isn't good for either one of us. I want a relationship that still lets me keep a piece of myself, and Deo and I run the risk of being all-consuming.

I know what happens when a love is all consuming, then gone.

A big piece of you winds up gone, too, and once you get back on semi-solid footing after a blow like that, it's scary as hell to imagine falling into that much pain and sadness again.

So I try pushing him to be more independent, and less wrapped up in what I'm doing. I want him to have his own plans, his own life. For his good and mine.

So I tell him the plan I've been trying to put in motion for him. "Because, my anthropology professor mentioned today that she's looking for an assistant. Just someone to do some organizing, and data entry and I thought, since you were once in the service industry," I wink at him, knowing he's shy about his cabana boy days, "you'd be perfect for the job."

"And?" Deo presses, because he can tell by my coy smirk   that   there's   more.

"So, I *maybe* gave her your number and she should be calling you tomorrow?" I say it like it's a question, like it maybe didn't happen.

Deo sighs and rubs a rough hand over his tan face and seriously sexy five o'clock shadow. "Whit, I don't need you to find me a job. I can take care of that on my own."

"I know that." I kick my foot out and rub it up and down his calf, because he can never resist smiling when I pull that trick out of my bag. "I know. And I know that you don't care about going to college, but I thought maybe just being around school might help change your mind. Maybe?"

Deo pulls my foot on his lap and starts another one of his bone-melting massages. "What am I going to do with you?"

"So you'll talk to her?" I have a hard time asking the question without moaning over the way he's handling my instep.

His fingers continue to work their magic while he sighs and rolls his eyes. "There's no limit to the lengths I'd go to to make you happy, doll."

I smile at him and he drops my foot and grabs my stool, sliding it across the floor to get me closer. He laces his fingers behind my neck and pulls me in. His lips glide over mine smoothly, his warm, sweet breath fills my mouth as his tongue traces over mine, flicking and teasing.

My phone vibrates on the edge of the bar. Deo pulls away with a slow, sexy groan.

"Sorry, I'll be quick!" I promise. I round the side of the bar to catch the phone before it jumps off the edge of the counter or goes to voicemail. I'm still waiting on a call to sort out all of this financial aid bullshit, and the sooner I get that taken care of, the better. Then, I can pay Deo back and not feel like I have this weight hanging over my head.

"Is it that tool, Ryan again? I thought you told him that he was done sampling the goods?" Deo tries to joke, but there's a fierce flicker of jealousy in his eyes.

I giggle and reach for the phone, but Deo grabs it from me in an athletic swoop and grab before I can answer.

Ryan has been calling off and on, even though I did tell him we couldn't keep up our arrangement anymore. More than likely, he's just bored, or hoping to catch me when Deo and I are on the outs. Deo has been dying to grab the phone when he calls and give him a little good-natured ribbing. Or, I suspect, to properly mark his territory.

"Rich and Paula?" Deo shows me the iPhone screen.

It's not Ryan.

It's my parents.

"Give me the phone." I practically leap over the bar to rip the phone from Deo's hands.

"Easy there, killer, I wasn't going to answer it." He shakes his head at my outburst.

I silence the phone and toss it into my purse.

"Seriously, Whit, I wasn't going to answer your phone. You don't have to hide it away." Deo takes a few steps toward me to close the space between us and pulls me in by my shoulders. He presses his lips to the top of my head like he's comforting me, but he has no idea why.

"Okay," is all I offer. Inside, I'm fighting the urge to recoil and tell him to leave. To stay away from me, because I ruin everything. Because I make brothers make decisions they shouldn't have to, I make parents choose, I ruin things, I destroy lives. *I* *leave.*

"But, are you going to tell me who Rich and Paula are, at least?" Deo's mouth is still pressed into my hair as he speaks. He knows I won't be able to do both- look at him, and open up.

I shake my head, curling myself tighter to him when I do.

"Whit..." he breathes into my hair. "It's not going to change things with us, you opening up a little. You know that right? You can open up a little. Let me know what's going on. I'm not just here to cook you delicious food and rub your feet. I'm also hear to listen to you gripe about annoying people you don't want to talk to on the phone. And to keep cats from eating your face, just on the off-chance that any of those furry bastards get any funny ideas."

The guilt of my inability to share this simple piece of information without him having to drag it from me while I kick and scream makes me feel like a coward and a fraud. I'm also well aware that we can't keep existing in our current state of cohabitation. Every single day Deo moves a little closer to my heart, and I try to block him with more defensive shields. One of us is going to press the other too far any day now.

"It's nothing. Rich and Paula are my parents. I'm just not in the mood to talk to them." My words are cold and dull, like I'm some kind of robot.

Deo stiffens for a second, his shoulders and arms suddenly tight. "Or about them. Or about anything that has to do with your life since you got here. All I know about the girl I share a bed with is that you don't sleep well at night, you hate to cook, you draw amazing tattoos, give even more amazing head...and that's not good enough for me, Whit. I want to know you." He runs his hands up my arms from elbow to shoulder and rubs my neck with quick, gentle pressure, the way he knows will make me goose-bumped and ready for him. "Not that I don't also want to get head, because, and I think I may have told you this a couple thousand times, but I'll say it again; you have a true gift. Seriously."

He slides his hands to my face and squeezes my cheeks until my face is so squished I can barely see his smile through my squeezed eyes. "But what else is there? I know four things about you, and I'm under your spell. Imagine if I knew seven or eight things! I'd be your slave forever."

I pull his hands down by the wrists, irritated by his goofiness and doubly irritated by my irritation at him. "There's nothing to tell, Deo, okay? I had a super boring life before I moved here. I work for Rocko because the hours are perfect, I go to school because I want to have a kick ass job one day. I live in this crappy apartment because I don't want my parents' money." *Just drop it, Deo. I can't go there.*

I can't tell him that I moved here to escape. That I'm here because *here* is so far from *there*, and *here* I don't have to relive what I lost every damn day like I had to *there*, over and over until just the thought of getting out of bed and seeing reminders of him everywhere sapped all of the strength from my body.

I couldn't look at the damn poster of Eleanor Roosevelt above my bedroom door that he drew a moustache on and laughed about like a hyena, or the bathroom mirror he cracked when he threw a marble during a tantrum when he was seven, or the tree in the backyard he swore was safe to climb, but wasn't, and left him with two broken ankles, or the Thunderbird he bought with four years worth of dog-walking and yard-raking money, rotting under the carport where we shared our first bottle of vodka, stolen from our parents' liquor cabinet by him while I distracted them in the kitchen.

I couldn't look at any of it because I'd remember, and it was too raw and painful to have to accept over and over, everyday, that he was gone. For good. No more. Eleanor Roosevelt and the bathroom mirror and the old tree and the Thunderbird and my parents' vodka would never be disturbed by Wakefield again, because he was dead and gone, and I can't even add 'and buried' to that list in any real sense, because there wasn't enough of my big, beautiful brother left to put in a box and send home.

And, as if I didn't find a million ways to torture myself missing him every damn day, the community we'd grown up in rallied to keep me in eternal misery whether they meant it or not. Every time someone back home saw me, they'd get this look on their face. First it was horror, like what had happened to me was somehow contagious, like you could catch having a dead brother. Then it was guilt, because my brother got blown to hell for their freedom and all that.   Then it was one of two things. If I was really, super lucky, the friend or neighbor or former shop teacher would suddenly get really interested in a sale on peaches or concentrate on walking their dog or see someone they knew and had to talk to right away. If I wasn't lucky, if the guilt was too heavy for them, they'd amble over with long, sad faces. Faces Wakefield would have laughed at. And trap me with stupid, bumbling words that made me sad and furious and tired and guilty all at once. Day after day.

Wakefield would have hated it. Hated the whole thing. My brother had the brains and the looks in my family, lucky bastard, and, to top it off, he was a riot. Seriously, I cannot remember a holiday or birthday when Wakefield didn't have me laughing so hard, I was snotting sparkling grape juice or cake icing out of my nose. Our parents used to complain that they couldn't take us to movies or plays or church because we were always doubled over, giggling like two fools no matter what was going on on the screen or stage or in the pulpit. I know most kids cried during *Bambi*, and I have no clue what Wakefield said that made a mama deer getting shot in cold blood hilarious, but that movie is still classified as a comedy in my brain.

How the hell did *he* die?

How did something so full of life suddenly wind up empty of life?

And how have I managed to keep going now that he's gone?

My hands shake, my stomach churns, and my head swims. I know exactly how I managed to keep going. By pushing it all out of my head.

I drag my Wakefield memories into the middle of my brain, dump them in a huge chest, and slam the lid shut. That's how it has to be. Period.

Deo pulls back from me and leans down so that our foreheads   are   touching.

"You're the only girl I've ever met that doesn't have any pictures out. You don't answer your phone when your parents call. You don't ever talk about home. It all points to one thing, Whit.   You're   hiding   something.   So   what   is   it?"

-Thirteen-
Deo

There's something epically depressing about cooking a girl a romantic celebration meal and ending up alone in the kitchen putting the leftovers in questionable Tupperware instead of rolling around in the sheets with said girl.

But that's what I'm doing, because Whit doesn't like people pawing around in her life and I'm like that cat that got all fucked up by curiosity.

By the way, I guarantee that stupid curious cat wound up yowling from the top of some junkyard fence, lonely, with a raging set of blue balls. If he wasn't dead. Or eating someone's face.

I shake my head to clear it of all cat-related thoughts and try to put together a plan. Whit said she needed 'space,' which seems like a colossally bad sign to me. Isn't 'I need space' the universal couples equivalent of 'I need you to pack your shit and get out of my life'?

I have no clue, since I've never really done this couple thing. I'm winging it and brilliant plan number one is just to keep busy and hope she cools off and comes back. But there are only so many dishes I can wash or piles of junk I can move around before I start to get antsy and wonder where Whit went. She grabbed her keys and her wallet off the table, but left her purse, which has her phone in it. So she's driving around, possibly pissed and upset, with no phone.

I definitely hate all of this.

I decide to do a drive-by of Rocko's. If her car is there, I'll know she's safe and come back. I can stay on the couch until she kicks me out or wants sweaty make-up sex. I'm seriously hoping for the latter. My brain is spinning jokes to keep things light and help aid in my anti-panic plot, but all comedy and calm goes flying out the damn window when I've circled the parking lot for the second time and realize Whit isn't here.

Maybe she's at the beach. But she's scared of sharks, so she's not swimming, and I told her how the cretin crazy-ass crackheads troll the shitty areas at night and to stay away. I wonder if she listened to me.

Maybe she's just cruising around, clearing her head. But her Lebaron gets dick gas mileage, and she doesn't usually have money to waste on that.

Maybe she called Ryan.

For a minute I lose my trademark calm and smash my hands on the steering wheel over and over, screaming like a deranged maniac. I don't give a goddamn who sees me or what they think. This is about Whit, my Whit, out somewhere, possibly not safe, and I'm feeling so out of control, I don't really know what to do.

I'm either going to break my steering wheel or my hand, so I kick the door open and closed and stalk into Rocko's store.

He's just finishing giving some cougar a tramp stamp when he sees my face and asks the woman, "Would you mind waiting a minute?"

She looks me up and down, and I can practically hear her purr across the shop. Painful flashbacks of my cabana days punch me upside the head. Rocko has me by the shoulders in a minute flat.

"Deo. You look like you saw a ghost. Everything okay?" He stares at me, and I can't get the words out for a minute. "Is Marigold alright? Your grandfather?"

I nod twice, and when I manage to find my voice, I have to tear it out of my throat. "Whit."

His eyes go wide. "Doreen," he calls over his shoulder. "I have a family emergency. If you could be a sweetheart and let me finish tomorrow, I'll do the color on your shoulder piece for free."

"You got it, baby." Doreen slides off the table and saunters out, but not before she gives Rocko a sticky kiss and shoves a scrap of paper in my jeans pocket. I'm sure it has her name and number on it, and I'm also sure I'm never, ever going to look at it.

Rocko is already flipping the lights off and turning the sign to closed. "You want to take my car?" he asks.

"Yeah. I came over in the Jeep, but it's sort of low on gas at the moment. I don't mind stopping to fill up if we need." Rocko says we'll just take his car, and I don't even bother to lock my doors. My Jeep will be fine in front of Rocko's well-lit shop. Plus that, I know this area backward and forward, and have more than a few car thieves in my band of merry friends. It'll stay put.

I jump into Rocko's cherry-red Camaro. "When did you last see her?" He pulls onto the highway and heads for the beach.

"An hour ago. I made dinner for her, and it was all going alright until she got a call from her parents she wouldn't take. I asked a question or two, and you know Whit." I shrug and lean my forehead on the passenger window of his car, watching the bright white of the lights shine intermittently into the interior.

"I do. Know Whit." Rocko's voice is calm and cool. "Deo, how much did she tell you about her parents?"

"Um, let's see. I learned their names today. And I know she's living in a shithole because she won't take their money." I lean my head back on the seat. "I don't think I'm being all weird about things, you know? It's normal to want to know things about someone else, right? Someone you care about?"

Rocko nods and runs a hand over his slicked-back hair. "It's normal. It is. But Whit is…look, I've never met anyone with as much need for control as Whit has. That girl is dealing with a ton of shit that would buckle you and me. But she just plows on. I don't know how she doesn't collapse."

I don't tell Rocko that I know exactly when she does collapse. It's when she falls into bed at night, shaking with exhaustion and shuddering in my arms all night long. "So, what is it? What's the big secret she can't tell me?" I look at him, his mouth pulled down in the dim light. "Her parents are satanists? She was kidnapped at birth? Drugs? Sex? Rock n' roll? Give me a hint at least."

"You know that isn't my story to tell. I want her to tell you. I think you kids make a hell of a lotta sense together. But whether she tells you or not isn't my decision." He's about to say more when his phone beeps. He switches on the speaker. "Marigold!"

"Hey babe." Her voice is a low, scratchy whisper. "I just wanted you to know that Whit is here and she's fine, but she may not make it to work tomorrow. She's had a really rough night."

Rocko looks my way, his eyes bugged out, and I shake my head, letting him know he should keep quiet about me being in the car. "Um, did she mention what happened, Mari?"

"Just that she's been dealing with a lot. Poor thing. She's overworked and overwhelmed. I thought Deo was staying at her place, but maybe he went back to check on his grandpa? Anyway, she's going to stay the night with me. I'm going to run her a lavender bath and give her a massage. She has the back of a fifty year old drill sergeant! I thought she and Deo were doing the dirty work at the crossroads if you know what I mean, but she's so tense! I think she needs to get lai—"

"Uh, someone just came in to the shop. A customer. Just walked in. So I should go, Mari." Rocko does not make eye-contact with me, and I'm grateful.

"I gotta go, too. I didn't want Whit to know I was calling. She's all about being independent and that whole liberated woman thing. But you, my love? Get ready to park your yacht in hair harbor later tonight!" My mom's whisper is all kinds of dirty and so wrong, I wish for ear and brain bleach to cleanse it all away.

"You bet! Will do! Gotta go, baby!" Rocko fumbles to end the call, and I consider that he might wind up driving us off the road in a fiery car crash.

After hearing that little convo with my mother, it doesn't seem like such a bad end to my night. Rocko u-turns and takes me back to the shop. Now that I know Whit is safe, I expect to feel relieved, but it's more like I'm deflated.

"Sorry about all that with your mom—" Rocko starts, but I wave my hand at him in a desperate plea for him to allow me to begin the immediate process of forgetting.

"It's cool. I know you two, er, are adults. And thanks for covering for me." I rub my eyes. "I have no fucking clue what to do now. What do you think?"

"I know you're not going to love hearing this." Rocko looks over at me and gives me this sad, sorry little smile. "I think you're gonna have to give her time. And, you know I can't tell you without Whit's permission, but let me just say, what she's going through is real. It's the kind of thing people spend their entire lives trying to get over." He pulls up next to my Jeep and cuts the engine. "And I meant what I said about you two. I'm rooting for you guys to figure this all out."

I clap my hand on his shoulder, appreciative that he gave me advice, even if I have no plans on taking it. I like Rocko. Even if he and my mother are near constant breakers of the TMI code. "Thanks, man. I appreciate the ride."

I get in the Jeep and think about taking a long, fast cruise along the twining ocean roads, but I don't feel like bothering to fill the tank, and I'm exhausted anyway. I'm old-man tired, and I consider going to my grandpa's house to revel in my codger-dom, but the only place that I feel like going to is Whit's apartment.

I know I made a mistake as soon as I open the door and walk in. Without Whit, this is just an overcrowded, cluttered, dirty little depressing space. I pace back and forth, tempted to drive to my mother's house, when I notice her laptop open on the coffee table.

I don't go through other peoples' shit.

I don't do it because it's disrespectful, and also because I don't care to dig for information on people who just don't matter all that much.

But Whit matters. She matters more than anyone else ever has. And I care. So much.

So much that I break my own moral code and click the machine on. It was in sleep-mode, so I don't have to be a dirtbag and try to figure out her password. I can just be a dirtbag and spy on her shit.

There's an icon for a web browser at the bottom of her page, and when I click on it, some super boring anthropology article pops up. Blah blah wedding practices around the world. I open a tab and type in 'Facebook.' I have a page I haven't logged into or checked in a few years, but girls tend to like this stuff better.

My intention is to log-in as myself and search for Whit. But I'm not sure if I can even remember my password after all this time. And her user name is already in. And the little password box is filled with circles, like the computer automatically saved her information. I click the log-in button like I'm having an out-of-body experience, and a picture of her with the long, wavy hair that she has in her ID photo pops up. She's not really looking at the camera and not really smiling. It's a picture that makes me sad for reasons I can't put my finger on.

I quickly find that Whit and I have one thing in common. Neither one of us checks our Facebook account often.

I click her 'information,' but I already know her gender and birthday and the fact that she loves Eleanor Roosevelt quotes and zombies and is scared of sharks.

She has no photo albums set up.

Her last update was months before, something about naked Ewoks. So she's a Star Wars geek? And aren't Ewoks always naked? I'll have to find a non-incriminating way to bring it up.

The rest of her page is mind-numbingly boring. A tiny part of me feels letdown that I threw my morals to the wind for this disappointing lack of anything substantial.

Then I click on her wall.

And people I've never met fill in the blanks Whit never told me about.

RIP Wakefield. <3 You were the brother I never had.

Thoughts prayers and love to your family whit.

I know no words can ever make the hurt go away, but time heals all wounds. It's the truth.

God bless your brother and all the brave men and women who gave their life for this country. Forever in our hearts.

I can't believe he's really gone. I was just gonna call and ask him to a drag race. I hate the days when I forget and have to remember again.

Whit, if you need me, I'm here. I know we grew apart this summer, but you're never alone.

Luv to you and yours whit. Wakefield was one of a kind. Never be another one like him.

There's a picture someone tagged her in. Her arm is around a guy with her same brown eyes and wicked smile. He's in an army uniform and he's hugging her close. Whit's face is glowing in a way it never, ever has in all the time I've been with her. The caption underneath says, *You two were always so tight. I know what he meant to you, Whit. Wakefield will always be in your heart.*

The 'W' behind her ear isn't for her name.

I push the lid on the laptop closed and jump up, pacing from wall to wall.

The day at the beach, in my jeep, when I insulted the army guys jogging past.

I punch the door-frame, scraping my knuckles and leaving the imprint of my fist in the dozens of layers of paint.

The lack of pictures. The lack of phone calls. Running away from her home. Avoiding any talk about her past, her family.

I pace to her room and fall into the bed that smells exactly like her and feels cold as the Arctic and empty as the Sahara without her. I spread across the entire bed. I roll myself into the covers. All of the covers. No one sweats, snores, or kicks me. And I'm miserable. Too many thoughts and worries crowd and jumble for space in my head.

Sometime in the early dawn, I hear the door creak open. Keys drop on the counter. Feet tiptoe to the room. I watch between my eyelashes as she shimmies out of her jeans, unhooks her bra and pulls it through the armhole of her tank top and starts for the bed, the smell of my mother's lavender on her body and hair.

"I was worried."

Whit jumps and slaps her hand over her heart. "Deo," she hisses in a whisper, even though we're both wide awake. "You scared the shit out of me."

I hold my hand out to her and she takes it. I pull her onto the bed, and she moves toward me on her knees. "I'm sorry about last night," she says, her voice low and dark. "I was in a shitty mood, I didn't want to talk about things. I had no idea I left without my phone. I would have called."

"My mom called Rocko. I went to him because I was panicked out of my damn mind." She runs a hand over my jaw, but I don't nuzzle against her skin like I normally would.

"I'm sorry. Very, very sorry." Her voice goes sexy, and I know how totally upset I am by my ability to resist this amazing, irresistible girl. "Can I make it up to you?"

"I don't just want to fuck and pretend everything's alright," I grind out.

She had been lying half on top of me, her arms limp around my neck, her mouth hovering above my face, but she stiffens and sits up. "I said I'm sorry."

"I heard you," I snap, my patience fried, my conscience on fire, my brain addled from zero sleep. "It's what you *didn't* say that pisses me off."

She swallows hard, and I watch the way her neck moves, the way her fists ball at her sides. "Did you and Rocko talk tonight? Did he...did he tell you about my family?"

"Nope." I let my mouth pop around the word. "He respects your privacy. Which I guess is easy to do when you trust him with important facts about your life. I wouldn't know about that, would I?"

She sits cross-legged and twists her hand in her lap, her eyes on the bedspread. "If Rocko didn't talk to you…"

"I opened your laptop. I snooped like a pathetic dirtbag," I admit, ashamed of myself.

Her perfect little mouth drops open. "You went through my files?"

"I just logged onto your Facebook page." I watch her face and see her eyes go wide. "How could you keep that from me? How could we be together all this time, and you never felt like you wanted to tell me?"

Her cheeks go bright red, bloomed with rage. "I kept it from you because it was none of your goddamn business, and you have no right snooping through my shit, Deo!" Her voice gets louder and shriller with every word.

"Sorry," I growl. "Sorry I had no choice but to snoop around like some deviant on your computer to learn a single damn fact about you. I tried talking to you, I tried asking you questions, I tried giving you time and space and getting close to you. Not a single thing worked, and I was worried about you. Do you realize you spend most nights crying or screaming in your sleep? You're petrified of the dark and being alone, you don't eat enough, you run yourself ragged. And I had no fucking clue why! How the hell do you expect me to hold you in my arms, comfort you, cook for you, and not even know who you are or what's making you so upset?"

"Don't do any of that if you don't want to." Her voice is mechanical, and she's staring at her hands. "No one's forcing you to be here and do all that."

I move across the bed, because the pull of her is more than I can resist. She feels so small and fragile in my arms, like she'll explode into thousands of pieces if I don't hold onto her. "I want to. But I want you to tell me why you hurt so bad." I run my hand over her hair, damp from the bath I know my mother made her take. "Tell me."

"You already know," she whispers.

"Not from you. I don't know your story, so I don't know anything. Tell me." I pull back to look at her and she jumps at me, her hands and mouth everywhere at once.

I'm not made of stone. She's gorgeous, so sexy, so ready, and I want her. My entire body is jumping and stomping with a crazed need to take her, now, while we're both wild and relieved and sorry and horny as hell.

But I know what it's like with us, how we fall back on sex and that's all it is. So I hold her at arm's length.

"I want you," she breathes, reaching for me again. "Let me touch you."

"No, Whit." I rub my hands on her shoulders. "Not tonight."

She looks at me for a minute and her warm brown eyes go hard. "I want to fuck you. Are you saying you're not interested?"

Everything in my pants scream mutiny, but I swallow hard and shake my head. "Not interested in sex. Talking, yeah. Sex, no way."

She chews on her bottom lip before she looks at me, a cool, dare in her eyes. "Get out then."

I raise an eyebrow at her. "You'd rather have me leave than agree to tell me what's going on with you?"

Her voice shakes hard around her next words, despite their bravado. "I told you pretty clearly what I want. If you can't give it to me, I'll call someone who can."

It's a sucker punch. A low-down kick to my balls. It's spit in my face.

I get up off the bed and nod. "Alright. If that's what you want, I guess I got the message." If it was still going to be dark, I'd hit the couch. No matter how much this girl is breaking my damn heart, I wouldn't leave her alone in the dark. But dawn is breaking. She can sleep in the room. It'll be lit up in no time.

"You don't have to leave, you know." She pulls her knees up to her chest and looks up at me, her face so gorgeous and sweet, it rips at my heart.

"You wanna tell me? You wanna talk?" I ask. She scowls in response. "Alright." I pause in the doorway and turn to look at her, flopped over in the fetal position on the bed. "Call me if you need anything. I'm pissed as hell at you, but I…I love you, Whit. I mean that."

I take the long, slow walk down the hallway, grab my wallet and keys, stuff my feet in my shoes, and, maybe, a little part of me waits for Whit to come flying down the hall after me, telling me she's ready to open up and tell me everything and that she loves me too, so much, and has been afraid to say it and that she wants to use my body in deviant ways after we spill our guts.

But it doesn't happen. When I'm in the parking lot, I swear I hear wild, screaming sobs, but it's got to be my overtired brain and my wild imagination. Whit's apartment is three stories up and the windows are always closed tight and locked. Plus that, Whit never loses it like that, not even when she's at her lowest, I realize as I get in the Jeep and pull out of the apartment parking lot. Whit is cool and totally in control unless she's sleeping.

That's one thing I know about her, no question.

-Fourteen-
Whit

"You heading out, Whit?" Rocko calls from the back of the shop.

"Yeah, in a minute! I want to run the broom over this floor one more time." Or eleventy-billion more times, because really, I've got nowhere to be but my quiet-ass, depressing apartment. And nothing to do except lie in my bed. Which should have a place carved out neatly for Deo next to me, but, instead, is empty.

There's something strange about coming home to an empty apartment after having someone there with me round the clock. I never really thought about it before, because I never really had anyone there with me before. It was just me, on my own, when I first moved out here, and that was kind of the big independent plan. And now, it's just me again, and it's taking some getting used to. Even though it's been a couple of weeks since Deo stormed out on me, being so alone again still hasn't gotten any less weird. I still come home from the shop at night and expect him to be sitting there on the couch, waiting for me to tell him about all the inane details of my workday. And maybe even rub my aching feet.

But he's not there anymore. Because he screwed up. He

couldn't just leave it alone. He had to keep pushing, and pushing. I gave him a clear warning, and he made his decision.

Rocko shakes his head and shoos me away. "Get out of here, kid. I'm sure you've got something else to do."

I shrug and my sweater falls off my shoulder. "Not really." I yank it back up, feeling a chill. I don't know if it's because Rocko has the air cranked as usual, or if it's that I'm just exhausted and susceptible to chills. I don't dwell on the fact that I've been chilly alone in my bed at night to the point where I haven't even wanted to leave the fan on. This does *not* have to do with Deo. I had a life before him, and I sure as hell have one now that he's gone. One that doesn't need to revolve around how much I miss him.

"How about getting something to eat? No one's come in for ink since this morning. Let's close up early. I'm headed over to Marigold's now, why don't you come with me? You look like you could use a decent meal." Rocko eyes my gorgeous jade dress, which fit all my curves a few weeks ago, but now seems to bag in all the wrong places.

I don't know how much of Marigold's food would be considered a "decent meal," but I'll take it. By the time I get home at night, I'm so beat from working all day that I haven't been eating much. I ended up taking the assistant job I'd told Deo about with my anthropology professor, so I work there till four, then I come into Rocko's shop till closing. When I get home, I'm completely wiped out. And, okay, maybe a little, tiny bit   depressed.

"Sounds perfect," I tell Rocko, and he looks both surprised and relieved by my acceptance of his invitation. I have to try to be more upbeat. I don't want to worry Rocko, who's always a little nervous about me no matter how well everything in my life is   going.

Marigold is serving tofu scramble. I guess there are worse things in life. At least the company is good. Marigold and Rocko sit next to each other at the small, bamboo table and clutch hands while they talk. Of course, being here makes me think of Deo. It makes me wonder, and maybe even secretly hope a little bit, that he'll come over unannounced like he did that time before.   That he's in desperate need of chopped up tofu and veggies...and   maybe   even   me.

But that's far-fetched. Because I know for a fact that Deo is a hardcore carnivore and is probably chowing down on some Flintstone-sized chicken leg with his grandpa. And there's also the fact that he hasn't so much as texted me since he walked out. I knew he was mad. I maybe even knew I deserved it. But to not come back? All he's doing is proving all of the reasons I should've   kept   my   distance   in   the   first   place.

I wish he could just understand all of the reasons I can't open up...without   me   having   to   actually   open   up.

"So, you and that son of mine still playing hide-and-go-seek?" Marigold asks, tossing her long, dark hair behind her shoulder. I pause for a moment to consider what she's said, and realize that, for once, she isn't making some sexual innuendo.

Still, I tense up at the mention of Deo. All night I've wanted to fish for information about what he's been up to, but have been biting my tongue over and over to keep from mentioning him.

I swallow hard and get my voice under control before I make my cool, calm, full-of-shit declaration. "I'm not avoiding him, I've just been busy."

Marigold nods her head and widens her eyes, the exact soft brown Deo's are, though hers look at me with an extra dose of sympathy. Deo's always had an extra dose of starved, sexy hunger. Her face pretty much says that she doesn't believe me.

"Well, he's been avoiding you," she says with a laugh. She claps her hands together and she's all sorts of clanging bangles and charms and flying hair.

"Nice," I mutter. Even though it's obvious, and she hasn't said anything wrong, I find myself tapping my foot manically, because I'm annoyed as hell. Like, was Deo over here talking about how he can't stand to be around me? Maybe he and his brand new girlfriend laughed about the time he wasted with the dour girl from Pennsylvania. Maybe he's been out surfing and drinking and dragging random girls who have drawers filled with tiny bikinis into his Jeep. My imagination gets wilder and angrier with every second that ticks by.

"Easy, Marigold. The kid is really broken up over this."

Rocko's voice is low and calm as he smoothes the sleeve of her paisley print dress.

"I'm just playing with her." Marigold winks at me and gives me a soft smile, and I know she didn't say it to hurt my feelings in any way.

"I'm not, for the record. Broken up about it. Deo and I had fun. It didn't work out. It's not a big deal." I push the gelatinous blobs of tofu from one end of my plate to the other, trying to spread it around so it looks like I actually ate some of it.

Marigold glances at Rocko and gives him a quick look before she leans close to me. "Did Deo ever tell you about his father?" she asks.

I nod, remembering the few details he gave me, always tinged with disgust and barely buried, seething anger.

"Then you know he's a worthless son of a bitch. Sure I loved him, but the best thing he ever did for us was walk out on Deo and me," Marigold says matter-of-factly. "He wanted more than this little town. He wanted to see the world and build a big name for himself. Me? I just wanted to stay here in this beautiful little place and put down roots. I wanted my son to fall in love with his home as much as I did, so that he never wanted to leave, either. But Deo has fought both parts. He's been stuck in the middle of both of our passions. Deo ignores that pull that makes him want to want to do big things that might take him away from here, I'm sure, in part, because he wants to prove that he is not his father in any way, shape, or form. But, on the other hand, he refuses to put down any sort of roots or even lay a small foundation, because that would mean he's stuck here. Like his silly old mama."

I stuff a bite of soggy vegetables into my mouth because I don't know what to say. They don't require any chewing, but I chew and chew and chew some more, because I'm clueless about what to do next.

"Sweetheart, point is, Deo has been fine doing nothing with his life. Don't get me wrong, I think he's the greatest goddamn kid in the world, but he doesn't really have a lot of passion for anything but waves. Well, he *didn't* have any other passions. Until he met you. Until he fell in love with you. Because he does love you, Whit. You know that, right, sugar?"

My chin and throat burn with the tears I refuse to let her see.

"Yes." My voice claps out, brittle and wooden.

"And, how bout you? Do you love him?" She holds her hands up and shakes her head before I can even open my mouth to answer. "That's not my business. Ignore that. Just know, it's okay if you don't. But if you do, just let him in Whit. Tell him about Wakefield. Tell him all the bad and the good and the things you miss, and the things you're angry about. Tell him about the guilt and why you avoid your parents. Just tell him. Trust him." Marigold tucks a piece of hair behind my ear and smiles a pleading smile, then looks down at my plate and laughs. "And for god's sake, stop pushing that food around. You're not fooling anyone. Next time, I'll order you a pizza."

She cuts the seriousness with a huge grin, and I can't keep myself from running around the side of the table and into her arms. I bury my face deep in her lion's mane of hair and relax as I breathe in the sweet lavender smell that reminds me of when I first met Deo.

The ride home is rough. I stop by every place I can think that Deo might be. The hole-in-the-wall pizza place he loves on 3rd. His favorite beach nook, tucked back behind the lifeguard stand on the pier. I even drive around the block his friend Cohen lives on a few times like a total creeper, hoping I'll catch a glimpse of his Jeep.

But I come up empty. He isn't anywhere.

He could be out on a date. He could be drunk at the beach. He could be in a different state for all I know. Because that's what happens when you shut people out. Eventually, they move on,   right?

I start to feel sick to my stomach. And not just from the tofu swimming   around   in   it.

I pull into my regular parking place outside my apartment, and it's like a light shining down from the heavens, because Deo's Jeep is parked right next to me. I try to yank the keys from the ignition before I even put the LeBaron in park. I can't jump out of the car fast enough. I run up each of the concrete stairs and my excitement mounts with the incline, because each step up is one closer to Deo. Closer to falling into him and telling him all of the things that I've been keeping hidden. All of the secrets I wasn't ready to confess that kept us apart these weeks. Because we just needed this space, and he respected my boundaries enough to give it to me, and, now, things will be okay.

I pause outside the door and stop to catch my breath and smooth my hair before I go bursting into the apartment all sweaty and insane-looking. I decide a quick dab of lipgloss wouldn't be too ridiculous, just in case we maybe kiss...who am I kidding? I'm ready to drag him into bed with me. It's in that second of quiet, with a little jar of raspberry lipgloss in my hand, that I hear them.

The three of them.

Deo.

And   Mom   and   Dad.

I sink to the floor outside my door, my heart pounding, my hands shaking, my palms sweaty from a mix of nervousness and upset and fury. I put the lid on my lipgloss with shaking fingers, so angry I was just thinking about being with Deo. Because I trusted him. Because I thought he understood me, understood what I needed in a way no one else in my entire life understood.

And now I feel like a colossal idiot on so many levels.

Because he didn't respect my boundaries at all. When I didn't give in, he went around them. No, he broke through them. Crushed them and stomped on them and did whatever he wanted   to.

I pick myself up, fist my hand around the doorknob, and fling the door open angrily.

Deo is leaning with his back against the bar, his hands stuffed deep into his pockets. His hair is the same disheveled mess it always is, the same mess I love to run my hands through while he kisses my throat. The same hair I ball my fists into when the lights are off and we're tangled up in bed together. But other than that, nothing looks the same. His typically unshaven, scruffy face is smooth, his normal board shorts are replaced with actual pants and the light blue polo shirt he's wearing screams *respectable*. I have to do a double take when I first see him. Was this new look strictly to impress my parents? To make him seem extra credible, so that he could be trusted with their daughter, who dropped out of their lives and is a total nutter?

Deo straightens when he sees me, locks eyes with mine, and slowly nods my way to acknowledge me. And the look of fury on my face. His eyes widen, I can see his Adam's apple bob when he swallows, and his mouth flattens. But he doesn't say a word.

"Whit?" Mom's voice chokes out from the other side of the room. She and Dad are sitting, shoulders touching, on my crappy little loveseat. They both look older since the last time I saw them, even though it's only been a few months. They look tired. Am I responsible for that?

Mom runs the charm on the end of her gold chain back and forth, back and forth. The zipper-like noise is the only sound in the room for a few long, painful moments. She and my dad look at each other, like they're trying to come up with something to day. She tucks a piece of her wavy hair back into her low ponytail, opens her mouth to say something to me, then snaps it shut.

I don't know what to say. I feel like I'm suffocating in the oppressive, uneasy silence of this room. I'm not ready for this. The pressure is so extreme, I can feel my heart hammer off the charts, and it's hard to regulate my breathing. I can't believe they're here, in my dingy little apartment, looking at the evidence of the craptastic life their only living child is barely managing to piece together. I can't believe he brought them here, to this, to see the way I barely live. They don't need this. I don't need this. This should never have happened.. *He* did this.

"Whit, we missed you so much," Dad says haltingly. He runs his hands along the knees of his pleated pants. He's wearing a sweater vest. In the middle of summer in California, because, of   course   he   is.

He and my mother have a gray pallor to their skin. They look thinner, less certain, older, more broken than I remember. Remembering how they were before, so energetic and full of laughter and hokey fun, compared to seeing them in their present shadowy shell-form is like looking at a sad, living metaphor for life when Wakefield was alive versus life now that he's gone.

The hurt is splinters shoved under my nails. It's a boot in my gut, a jab in my kidney, grains of sand kicked into my eyes, snapped bones, twisted intestines, every physical pain imaginable, multiplied by a thousand and slammed into me all at once. I feel like the will to live I so carefully collected and compiled here in

this sunny, exotic new place is spilling out of me like ocean water
in   a   sieve.

My eyes snap back to Deo's.

"What the fuck, Deo?" is what tumbles out of my
mouth before I can stop the word-vomit.   The room fills with
the   ugly   echo   of   my   voice.

"Whit, listen—" Deo starts, his voice as purposefully calm as
if he's talking to a rabid animal. I cross the room in a few furious
steps and yank on his arm, making sure to dig my nails in.

"Give us a minute, please," I snarl at my shaking, rabbit
parents. I drag him out the front door and into the dingy,
fluorescent-light   lit   hall.

"Whit, those are your parents, and they didn't even know
where you were living. You can't do this," he says, slowly, calmly,
arrogantly, as soon as the door closes. Yeah, sure, because he
knows what this is doing to them. To me. To my attempts to
move on. To their inescapable grief and disappointment. Because
he   knows   all   the   things,   apparently.

I've never wanted to slap someone across the face the way I
want to slap Deo. I clench and unclench my hand, and I have to
take a choke-hold on my emotions to keep from going into a
wild, spinning tantrum of pure temper and hate right in his face.

"You brought them here?" I finally manage to spit out.
"How could you do this to me? I thought you cared about me,
but all you care about is getting answers to satisfy your own
damn curiosity. It's not a fucking movie, Deo. You can't stage

the big reunion scene and, poof, it's all better! Why didn't you leave it alone? You just couldn't let it go! You couldn't let me have something that was mine, something that was just for me to know and deal with my own way." The words start and stutter, and I almost lose my hold on them a dozen times during my rage-filled speech. Who the hell does he think he is? What the hell has he done to my life?

His eyes shine with something that looks an awful lot like frustration. Seeing that look in his eyes lights fire to my already boiling blood. His voice is quiet, pleading with me to listen.

"Whit, you're so wrong. All that was yours was the pain. You didn't do this. You aren't responsible for what happened." He reaches out and grazes his finger lightly over the 'W' that is inked behind my ear. And I realize that he knows it all now.

The exhaustion I feel is so marrow-deep, I have to lean against the door to keep my buckling knees from letting my body slide into a heap on the floor. "So, they told you? They told you everything?" My voice is a whip of accusation.

Deo's jaw clenches. He moves his mouth back and forth and drops his head, shame slashed across his face. Then he looks up, his gold-hued eyes transmitting me an apology, and nods. "I would've rather found out from you."

I press my fingers to my lips until I can feel the imprint of my teeth, because I have to let a whole lot of words pass by before I'm sure I can open my mouth and trust myself not to full-out scream my throat raw. "I would've rather you never found out."

But he knows. Deo knows about that night that my parents sat Wakefield and I down and told us that Dad's retirement had gone to shit with the economy. He knows that they told us how they could only afford to send one of us to an out of state school, and the other would be stuck in Amish country going to community college. He knows about the tantrum I threw. How I *insisted* that I be the one to get the cash because I was the oldest, even if it was only by less than a year.   Deo now knows how long I dreamed about the University of Delaware. He knows how close Wake and I were, and how he'd never want to see me upset. So, it took him less than a week to make a decision. He was joining the military, and they would pay for school, even though he never had any interest at all in the service. He did it so that I could take Mom and Dad's money and go to Delaware and never look back. He'd take one for the team, like he always did. Because he just wanted to see me happy. He didn't even think twice about it. It would just be a commitment for a few years, then he'd have the cash for school and all would be right with the world. And best of all, I'd get my way. Again.

But now, Deo also knows the end of the story, knows that it didn't work out that way. That Wake was promptly shipped off overseas after basic training and blown to bits by an IED. That my brother sacrificed his life for nothing. Because, in the end, neither one of us was going to some stupid, private college. And now, neither one of us will lead a long, happy life.

LENGTHS   171

Now, Deo knows why it's unfair for me to be happy. Now he understands why I need my life compartmentalized. Now he knows about the guilt I carry over forcing Wake into a choice he never even wanted, a vicious, stupid choice that ended up costing him his life. Now he knows the reason why I moved out here-- because they gave me a scholarship I wouldn't have elsewhere, and it's far away from rural Pennsylvania, where everyone knows that I'm responsible for the death of their golden boy.

His voice is so sincere and patient, it makes me shake from the core of my being. I can hardly hear the words he's saying, because I'm so sick with coiling, lashing anger.

He closes the gap between us, but I twist just out of his reach before he comes in contact with my arm. "Losing someone you love, doesn't mean that you have to lose yourself, Whit. You can still live your life. You still deserve to be happy. You can't carry all of that guilt around forever. Your parents won't let you. And I sure as hell won't let you, either."

Everything is spinning. Flipping. Exploding, wide open. Because every bit of me is exposed. Every selfish, horrible thing I am is on display. Having my parents here only makes everything real again. It's too hard to keep away now. The pain is rearing hot and ugly again. He brought it all back to me, when I was trying so hard to keep it contained.

I can't do this.

He's still talking, and his voice is soothing, but his words make me quake with anger because he doesn't know. He has no damn idea. "Your parents want you to be able to move on, Whit. They miss him, but you're taking the only child they have left away by shutting them out like this. They want you to be happy. I want you to let me help make you happy again. I know you want that, too. Deep down."

Deo moves toward me again, but I flinch away. I don't want him touching me, don't want him anywhere near me while this cyclone of pain and pure rage is tearing through me. I turn the full force of my hateful, guilty, terrifying anger on the one person who couldn't stay the hell away when I needed my space, couldn't respect my privacy, and couldn't leave well enough alone so I could get on with my miserable life at my own slow-as-hell pace.

"The only thing that I *want* from you, Deo, is for you to get your keys, get in your Jeep, drive the fuck away and never look   back."

-Fifteen-

Deo

I knew it was moronic as hell to plot this whole stupid-ass plan.

I bang my hands against the steering wheel and growl with total frustration, then drive past the road that would take me to my grandpa's, past Rocko's, past the little shack by the sea where my mom is still mixing her oils and sending me thousands of texts demanding to know what's going on between me and Whit.

Nothing, Mom. Nothing because I went out on a limb and screwed it all to hell.

When I finally get to the tiny cove, it's too dark and the water's too choppy for this to be a good idea at all. And I decide to jump into the pit of my own stupidity with both feet. "Cohen? Pull the strongest shit you can find out of your liquor cabinet and meet me at the cove."

I can barely hear him over the incessant crash of the waves, and that's a good thing, because I'm half sure he's trying to ask a ton of questions I have no intention of answering, and I've already hung up on him.

I rip my blue douchebag polo shirt off and strip out of my jeans and boxers, not worried about anyone seeing my ass on this deserted stretch of beach. I have shorts in the back of the

Jeep to pull on, but I feel cold wearing just them. It can't possibly be because of the temperature outside. It's balmy with warm breezes, so why am I pulling on my hoodie?

Because what I had with Whit has been blown to hell, and I feel like a sailboat with no anchor, tossed and battered by the waves.

Cohen's headlights nearly blind me, but my aggravation abates a little when I see he's holding out a six pack. "That's the strongest alcohol you could find in your liquor cabinet?"

He raises his eyebrows. "Uh, no. I found half a bottle of Everclear from last New Year's Eve. Then I remembered last New Year's Eve, and I decided that I didn't need to see you dance naked and vomit for three hours straight. So, beer it is."

I jump up, wrap my arm around Cohen's shoulders, and shake him back and forth, then pop a brew for each of us and drag him to the still-warm sand.

"Cohen, you've always been here for me—"

"Dude, stop. Now. I can't stand sappy Deo, and you didn't even start drinking yet." He takes a long pull of his beer, then gives me a guilty look from the corner of his eye. Because Cohen can never manage to be all tough around me. Not since we were kids.

He cried right at my side when I ripped my arm open, elbow to shoulder, back when I was first learning to skateboard. I needed thirty-two stitches, and he grit his teeth with every single prick of the needle. He toilet-papered Rosie Mazo's house when she broke my heart and dumped me right before our eighth grade dinner dance. He got out of bed at 2 AM to surf with me on the morning after my eighteenth birthday, when it dawned on me that my loser father seriously wasn't going to make it. He's been by my side through it all.

"I just wanna say thanks, man. Other than my mom and my grandpa, you're the only person on this motherfucking planet who believes in me. That's rare as hell, and I appreciate it." I take a long sip of beer and hold my hands up, surrender-style. "That's all I'm saying."

"This is about Whit." It should be a question, but it isn't, because Cohen knows the answer.

"No," I lie.

"You called up her parents." Another non-question, and this time, I can hear my friend's frustration in the tight delivery of his words.

"Maybe." My voice is nothing short of a grumble, because I'm sick of this shit. I'm sick of putting it out there and getting smacked upside the head.

"So, what about 'that idea sucks' didn't make sense to you when we talked about that whole shenanigan-in-the-making?" Cohen finishes his bottle in a few gulps and crams it back in the cardboard holder, taking out a second before I'm half done. That's not typical Cohen, but maybe I'm rattling his cage more than usual tonight.

I twist the bottle in my hand. "You know, it was a big fight when we left. And then there were weeks of nothing. And I missed her like crazy. So I thought I'd come back with a bang, make shit right, get her attention." I yank at the pulls on my hood and let out a long burst of breath. "But that worked like shit."

Cohen's laugh is quiet around the lip of the bottle. "You're such a dick, man."

"What?" I snap a look his way so fast it almost gives me whiplash, because I did not anticipate that reaction. "A dick? Why a dick? I put my heart out there for her, Cohen. I found the thing she needed, the thing she was afraid of, and I helped her face it. Explain how that makes *me* a dick?"

Cohen shakes his head and laughs again. "Alright. It makes you a dick, you fucking dick, because you were so busy solving all of Whit's problems, like you're the great and powerful Oz, it never occurred to you that she needs to do it her own way? In her own time? Her brother got blown up in some goddamn sand trap because she threw a hissy fit about going to college. How do think that made her feel, man? No wonder she has night terrors. She's at a low place, and I think your whole bogus-as-hell plan shoved that in her face."

"So you think I should have done nothing?" I challenge, my temper really close to flaring.

"Nah." Cohen looks me straight in the eye. "I think you should've spent some time working on your own bag of crazy.

You're twenty-two, you've got no real direction, no job, no place of your own. You've got a pile of treasure you're hoarding under your bed like a little kid. If you want to make some big statement and win Whit back, take a look at your own catastrophe of a life, eh? Maybe, if you clean your shit up, it will inspire her. Because you're looking like more and more of a lost cause every damn day, and it scares the shit out of me."

My temper sizzles out.

Mainly because I just got schooled by Cohen, again, for the nine millionth time in our life together.

I let myself be pissed at him, though. Let myself think he's an asshole and wrong and stupid as shit and doesn't know his ass from his elbow. I drink through my first beer and half my second thinking that. By the time I've started my third, I know in my guts he's right. I know he's saying it because he cares about my inebriated, shallow, stupid ass.

I tilt my head back and look at the stars, so many they look almost murky in the midnight sky. "If you were me, what would you do?" I ask him.

"If I were Deo Beckett, what would I do?" He studies the bottle in his hand. "Well, I wouldn't be a fucking bum, first of all. I'd crawl under my bed and pull out all those gold coins I'd been hoarding like Gollum—"

"Is this another *Lord of the Rings* reference?" I groan.

"If you'd read Tolkien, like I did, maybe you wouldn't be the unmotivated loser you are today," Cohen observes.

"Dude, you run your parents' furniture store," I point out.

"Hey, it's gainful employment, and I'm in school for my business degree," he argues. "Do you want my advice or not?"

"Sorry. You were talking about me being some freaky, ring-obsessed goblin." I toast him with my beer and take another long sip to fortify me through this story.

"Gollum is not a goblin, by the way. Moving on, you are hoarding those coins because you think your dad's coming back." He pauses here, and I interject a laugh so sharp and angry, it startles me.

"Fuck that, man. I know that asshole is staying deep in the jungle where he disappeared. I'm not delusional, alright?" When Cohen meets my objection with silence, I feel the need to defend my stance, which is moronic, but I feel like Cohen's just picking at an old wound to get a rise out of me. "It's been years. He isn't coming back. I'm not like my mother, hoping he'll waltz the hell in and expect her to drop her damn life for him. I get who he is."

"Yeah, you get him," Cohen agrees. "You get him because you *are* him."

"Fuck you!" I point at my friend, all the fury from before built to a sudden head. "Fuck you and your bullshit, Cohen! That's some cold shit, right there." He looks at me steady, no guilt in his eyes this time. "That's a kick in the balls, you know that? Me? Like him? I'm nothing like him." He doesn't

LENGTHS   179

say a word, just watches me tantrum like an infant. "Okay, smartass, how exactly have I gone from being some goblin to my loser-ass father? Enlighten me."

"Your dad doesn't stick around for the hard shit. He's always looking for the easier way." Cohen shrugs like that explains me.

"Look, my dad's a champion dickwad, no doubt, but he works hard as hell. That guy has gone places and done things no normal human would go anywhere near." My father's medical records alone could fill a week's worth of *World's Scariest Injuries* marathons. The man has been everywhere from the top of icebergs to the rivers in caves thousands of feet underground. Adrenaline is more important than oxygen to him.

"I'm not talking about sticking around for work. I'm talking about people." Cohen taps his beer bottle against his palm.

"I was there for Whit. That's the reason I'm here," I snarl, losing patience with my friend.

"No. You were looking for an easy way through all the shit, and that's why you're here." He picks up his last beer and pops the cap. "You asked me what I'd do if I were you? I'd sell those coins, set up a surf shop, get my life in order, and show up at Whit's door with my shit in control, ready to be her rock the minute she needs me. Because I think she was waiting for someone substantial enough to lean on. And that just wasn't you, man. I think she wanted it to be you, but it wasn't." When he finishes talking, he takes a long sip and wipes his mouth with his hoodie sleeve.

We both sit and drink and watch the waves crash on the shore, over and over. Finally I ask, "And what if I just can't get my shit together? What if I crash and burn?"

"You wanna hit these while they're good?" Cohen jumps up and points to the waves with his glass bottle.

"Answer my question, asshole." I jump to my feet and glare at him. "What if I crash and burn?"

He takes his board down and pulls off his hoodie. "Then I spend the next fifty years bringing you beers and listening to you cry about the girl who got away. Enough talking. I feel like I'm at my kid sister's slumber party. Let's get out there before we lose this."

I follow him out, and for a few hours, it's just Cohen and me and the waves crashing full force on the sand under the star-strewn sky. By the time we're soaked, bone-weary, and stone-sober, the sun has been up for at least an hour.

"I'm going to be a zombie at work." Cohen shakes his hair out and loads his board up.

I raise an eyebrow. "How with-it do you have to be to sell a couple of recliners and end tables?"

"What the hell would you know about selling furniture? Or buying it for that matter? When you sleep in a bed that doesn't have a bunk, get back to me." I laugh and he slaps me on the shoulder. "Seriously. When your little surf shack is the hottest place on the coast and you have all the mad dough, Rodriguez Home Furnishings will give you a deal on getting your new pad all set up."

"Sounds good, man. Just tell them I'm not dealing with that shady-ass son of theirs."

He jabs me in the ribs and gets in his truck, rolling down the window to catch the cool morning air. He leans out and yells as he's leaving, "Get her back, man. Next time we hang out, more surfing, less whining."

"Fuck you!" I yell back, but he knows that it means 'thank you.'

It would be cool if I just got my shit together all at once. Like, in the course of one great movie-montage song, I drove home, got up the balls to trade in those coins, found some sweet property, and started doing my thing in a real way.

But years of slacking have made slacking my norm, so I basically sit around eating pistachios with my grandfather and think about what Cohen says while I wait for Whit to possibly call, which never happens.

A few days go by, slow and draggy. I get bored. I check my phone a thousand times an hour. My grandpa drags me around with him, doing odd jobs around the neighborhood, fixing our fence, cleaning the yard and the gutters, working on his truck. I think about calling Whit, but there's a new excuse every single day. And the days roll into weeks. And then the weeks turn into one entire month and more days add up. I'm getting desperate. I'm imagining every possible extreme-ass, bad-ass scenario about her in my head, and if I didn't get updates from Cohen, who I've bribed to drop by the tattoo shop now and then, I'd go completely crazy. I know she's safe and generally okay. And I'm positive she'll call. Any second. My phone will ring any second, any day, and it will be her.

But it's never her.

My mom calls. A lot. And there are lots of vague, cheery voicemails, which I listen to just to make sure she's okay. But I don't call her back. I have no interest in getting into it with her about Whit and how I should take advantage of what's right in front of me and all that.

So, I'm not all that surprised when she shows up at grandpa's house, a big box of something that actually smells edible in her hands after three weeks of phone calls I've studiously ignored.

"Marigold." Grandpa gets up and takes her in his arms. "You look gorgeous as always, baby. Did you bake us something?" Even my grandpa, who's half in love with my mother, can't do a good job of faking enthusiasm.

"Nope. And that look of relief on your faces says it all guys! These are creampuffs from Colletti's." She opens the box, and Grandpa runs like a kid to the dessert table to get plates set out so we can eat like normal people. Mom bustles to the kitchen and puts on the teapot so we can have tea.

Yes, it may be slightly ridiculous to be scarfing down creampuffs and sipping tea with my mom and grandpa like we're a couple of duchesses. But Colletti's is owned by baker/magicians, and if I have to play Pretty Pretty Princess to get to eat their wares, I will.

"Sorry I haven't returned your calls—Ow! What the hell, old timer!" I just nosedived into my dessert because my grandfather wailed me in the back of the head.

He shakes his plate at me. "You call your mother back. I swear to God, I don't know how this saint of a woman wound up surrounded by the shittiest men on the earth."

Mom blushes. "Oh, Johnny! If you'd been single when I was seeing your son, I'm telling you right now, he would have had a run for his money." My mom brings Grandpa a mug of tea and kisses his cheek. He takes an extra second to squeeze her around the waist. Suddenly she gets even redder and starts messing with her hair and twirling her bangles, classic guilty Mom maneuvers.

I take a big bite of creampuff, sip my tea, and send a suspicious glare her way. Or, I send as suspicious a glare as is humanly possibly while chewing a fluffy mouthful of pastry. "It was really sweet of you to come over like this," I say leadingly.

"Yeah, well...no one returns my calls..." She clears her throat, fidgets with her earrings, and, after about two minutes, the pressure is too much for her. "I have to tell you both something!"

Grandpa and I look at each other and put down our treats. The last time Mom told us "something," she'd used the money she inherited when my great-aunt died to buy her little hippie-dippy store. Mom had been struggling with this long bout of 'what it all means' crap as a legal secretary, but it was good money and health benefits. Grandpa and I were both pretty sure the beach-shack-essential-oils thing would tank and burn, but she made a huge success of it. Because my mom has work ethic like a mule.

"Tell us, Marigold." Grandpa's voice is soft and kinda old-man-sad. He has that Spidey-sense geezers sometimes acquire, where he knows when some bad shit is going down. And his voice sounds pretty prepared-for-doom.

Mom slides the big silver ring my dad sent her from the Ivory Coast off her left ring finger, where she's always worn it like a holding place wedding band, and she shows us a small, bright ring of purple flowers tattooed on her skin. "They're tiny irises. My favorite flower." Mom stops talking while we all wait.

"Nice ink. Was that the big news?" I'm totally confused because my mother has a huge lotus flower thing down her spine among a bunch of other smaller designs, so she's not exactly new to ink. What's with all the guilt and creampuffs?

"Don't be a complete idiot all your life, Deo," my grandpa snaps. He gets up and gives my mother a tight hug. "Who's the lucky guy?" he asks gruffly.

"Rocko," she says softly.

"Rocko what?" I ask, my mind clicking the pieces together way too slowly. My grandpa slaps the back of my head again, and my mother twists her silver-ringed hands around each other.

"Rocko proposed, Deo." She sucks in a deep breath, exhales, and announces, "And I said 'yes.'"

"Congratulations, love." Grandpa pats her back, his voice thick. "I wish it could have been my son who was smart enough to scoop you up. But, I want you to know, you'll always—" His voice catches and Mom and I both look away to let him get a hold of himself. "You'll always be my family. Always, sweetie."

"Oh, Johnny." Mom wraps her arms around Grandpa and laughs through the tears that are splashing on Grandpa's shirt.

The silver ring is still on the table. I pick it up and look through the hole, seeing my grandfather and mother through its circled border.

And it's like I'm seeing my mother for the first time.

I remember her being so sad, so helpless she wouldn't get out of bed for days on end when I was a kid. I'd have to make my own sandwiches and eat at the scratched kitchen table by myself. Milk went bad, cereal got stale, I spent all day on my skateboard or surfboard, Cohen by my side. Mrs. Rodriguez's hospitality was the only reason I had decent dinners any night I wanted to stop by their house. That would last for weeks, then, one day, she'd pop up like a daisy and soldier through months without him. Until he showed up again and set it all to shit. The cycle went on for years. Cost her jobs and boyfriends who were decent. She missed a lot, just sleeping and moaning in bed over him. And I guess I just never cleared that image of her out of my head.

Because, maybe I don't trust it's entirely gone.

I kick my chair back and stalk to the deck, letting the door slam behind me. I hear my grandfather and mother talking, his voice irritated and loud, hers soft and low. Finally she follows me onto the deck.

"I thought the creampuffs would soften the blow." She puts a hand to my face, her skin warm and scented with lemon oils, her rings cool and smooth on my cheek.

I grab her in for an awkward bear hug. "I guess this is where I say 'congratulations'?" I murmur into her hair

"Only if you mean it." Her voice waivers and I feel like a champion asshole for making her sad on her happy day. "I know this must seem sudden. But Rocko and I have been friends for years, and he mentioned this months ago. I've had a while to think it all through. And I'm sure about this. I want to be with him."

I pull away from her and look into her eyes, the same color as mine, but all wide and happy and sure the world is going to be good and amazing and full of positive Karma. I love that she's so full of hope now, but it also worries the hell out of me.

"I do mean it. Only…are you sure this isn't just a way to get Dad out of your system?" Her mouth goes slack, and I sigh. "C'mon. Be fair. I was with you through all that shit, and I hated it. I hated seeing you that way. But what suddenly changed that made you not need him like you used to? How do I know this isn't just gonna crash and burn?"

Mom presses her lips together and brushes her hands through my hair. "Oh, Deo, my gorgeous, warped boy. What the hell did I do to you?"

"You taught me to be careful, that's what." I jerk back from her touch. "Mom, I almost got serious with Whit. Then things broke off, and, you know what? Sometimes I think it's for the best. I don't want to be in a relationship like you and Dad were in. That was pure misery for years. I watched you, and I learned how to let go. Now I'm scared for you, because clinging to somebody was the trouble, Mom. Don't you remember all that?"

"Oh, honey." Mom wipes the tears from her eyes with her fingers. "You have it all backward. It's not clinging to someone that ruins everything. It's never grabbing on in the first place. Your father and I failed because we let go too easily. It was more him than me, but both of us let go of the love we had and put other things first. It broke us apart. But your father kept letting go. Of this town. Of his father. Of me. Of…of you." These words come on the cusp of a sob. "Something in him kept coming back and wanting this all, but he didn't have what it took to hold on."

"It's not like that with Rocko?" I ask, putting an arm around her slight shoulders.

Her laugh is wet with all those tears and…happy. So happy, it tugs at my heart. "Rocko is all roots, baby. He's twined around me and isn't ever letting go. I've never been able to hold on to anyone the way I can hold on to him, and he's holding right back. I'm happy, Deo. I'm so happy, and I want you to be happy for me, but I understand if you can't be."

I make a fist over the fat silver ring Dad gave her and kiss her soft, crazy hair. "Of course I'm happy. So happy. Congratulations. When's the big day and what do you need your slacker son to do to help?"

***

I'm back outside Whit's apartment for the first time in almost two months. We've had a few close calls coming in and out of the tattoo shop, but I haven't actually seen her in so long, my throat aches when I think about the Whit-sized hole gouged in my heart.

This may be stupid, but my mom and grandpa and Cohen have all gotten on board with my snail's pace life change, and I need to close this chapter with Whit properly. And make sure my mom's and Rocko's big day is as happy as possible.

I take the steps to her apartment two at a time, and when I get to her door, it takes a few minutes before I manage to knock.

She opens the door slowly, so I know she checked the peephole. I expect to be invited in, but she keeps her body turned slightly, blocking the entrance.

"Hey stranger." I smile at her, but her face is somewhere between stony and just plain sad. She looks younger, softer than the last time I saw her. Her dark hair is longer, down to her neck now, and it's wavy again. Her big brown eyes are ringed in shadows. Is she sleeping well? Is she eating right? Suddenly the idea of 'closing this chapter' blows up in my face, and I'm left with all the hopeful scraps of possibility Whit always makes me grasp at with the desperation of a drowning man.

"Hello, Deo. Do you need something?" She's using this professional receptionist-type voice like we're former co-workers and never held each other all night after having marathon sex in this very apartment.

"I do. Can I come in and talk to you?" I could conduct all this business right here, and actually had plans to keep it short and to-the-point. But now that I see her, catch the sweet smell of citrus on her skin, remember so fiercely that it aches what it felt like to kiss her, I want to stretch this out.

She tucks a wavy piece of hair behind her ear and shifts her dark eyes uncertainly.

"Please?" I keep my voice neutral, safe, calm. "For my mom and Rocko. They're why I'm really here anyway."

She wavers for a second, then nods. "Okay. Come on in."

The apartment still looks the same, maybe just a little more cluttered. I wonder if she kept that anthropology job she tried to get for me. It still makes me feel like an asshole to remember how I blew her off when she went through all that trouble for me. "Place looks good."

"It's still the same shithole." Her sigh is long and suffering, and she crosses her thin arms over her chest. "You wanted to tell me something?"

"I did. I do." I sit at the dining room table, the one where I served her what was supposed to be the first romantic meal of this long, amazing summer. "Come sit?"

She slides into a chair across from me stiffly and her stare is so point-blank, I feel jittery.

"Your tan faded. You haven't been on the waves much?" I ask. She frowns and doesn't give me a single inch. "All right. I get it. So, you know the wedding is in a week?"

She nods and suddenly takes an extreme interest in the place-mat on the table.

"My mom is dying for you to come. I mean, she's saying all that crap about how she respects your right to do what you need to, but it's killing her. She wants you there, and I want this day to be amazing, and I know the reason you're not coming is because I'll be there." I reach over to grab her hands, but she pulls them back. I curl them back towards me. "That day, with your parents? I was wrong. I thought I could force you to change your whole damn life when I wasn't even willing to change one single thing about mine. I want to apologize for doing what I did. It was completely out of line, and no matter how good my stupid intentions were, I should have respected your decisions."

She looks up at me, her big eyes wide and surprised. "I...uh....I accept your apology?"

"Is it a question?" I try to make my laugh easy, but it comes out shaky.

"No. I do." She pauses, licks her lips, and adds, "And, even though I was pissed, it got the ball rolling, and I've been talking to my parents. I'm not saying what you did was right, but I should know better than to waste opportunities. Wakefield would have been disappointed in me. You remind me...of my brother in a lot of ways. So, you did help." This time her sigh is one of pure exhaustion. "But I don't think going to the wedding is a good idea."

I nod, but my blood is coursing hot and fast with adrenaline. I had zero expectations when I came to see her, but now I feel like things may be better than I thought. That I might have more of a chance than I originally expected. And then I consider that I'm pushing this all too hard, too fast. I need to back off quick.

"Okay. I respect that." I get up to go, and Whit stands too, but before I can leave, my mother's words clang around in my skull. Her warning about how she and my dad let go too easily. How they didn't hold when things got tough.

I walk the few feet over to her and take her by the shoulders. She looks too shocked to even wriggle out of my hold. "But I'm going to have to argue the point. I *am* right this time. Again." She opens her mouth to argue, but I rush on. "Marigold and Rocko are important to both of us. And you're important to me. This may be too quick. It may be too stupid. You may be back with Mr. Booty-call Douchenozzle Fuckhead." The tiniest of smiles inches on her mouth. "But I have a week. And I'm going to use it to convince you to go to this wedding. Because Wakefield would want you to go."

The glimmer of a smile fades and she shakes her head. "You're seriously using my dead soldier brother to guilt me into doing what you want?"

My face cracks into the first genuine smile I've worn pretty much since she left. "Yeah. I am. You know why? It's what Wakefield would want." She narrows her sweet brown eyes at me. "It is. He'd want his sister to get out of her shit-hole apartment and come to some dipshit hippie wedding where they read poetic, sappy vows and serve tofu. Because he'd know that his sister would be surrounded by people she loves. People who love her. C'mon. Say you'll come."

This time the glimmer of a smile turns full-blown. "I'll think about it." She shakes her head. "Think. About. It. This isn't a yes or a no."

"Great. Not a yes or a no. Got it." I walk to the door, but pause before I walk out. "Just, when you get your dress, tell me the color so I can match my tie, alright?"

She holds onto the door for a minute, we lean close, and the kiss and more that I want to give her crackles in the air between us. "Good-bye, Deo."

She tries to make her voice cool and cruel, but I catch the hint of passion and happiness that slides under her words. Slowly, slowly I'm getting my life on track. And I'm about to woo Whit this week like she's never been wooed before.

Because Mom and Cohen and Wakefield are all irritatingly, totally right. Life is too short to waste on bullshit. And I've spent way too much time letting go when all I want to do is hold on with all my strength.

-Sixteen-

Whit

I fan myself with the thick piece of recycled card stock, hoping maybe the answers will float right off of the paper if I do it long enough.

"And you swear you have no idea what this is for?" I spin in the swivel chair and ask Rocko. He looks at me over the tortoiseshell frames.

"Darlin, I swear to Gaia, if I knew, I'd tell you, just so you'd shut the hell up. No idea what it is or who it's from." He looks back down at the VOID-stamp tattoo he is doing to cover up the name 'Dwayne' on his current client's hip.

"So, do you think I should go? I mean, do you think it's safe?" When I got to work this afternoon, there was an envelope on my desk with my name on it. All that was inside was a brown card with an address printed on it and a time, 10:00pm. Who in their right mind would think that's even close to enough information to be considered a proper invite?

Rocko shrugs. "I don't know, Whit. Do you want me to go with you? Check it out first? Just tell me what you want me to do and I'll do it."

"But it's probably from Deo, right? This isn't his handwriting, but it's all recycled paper and all vague like he always is... Maybe it's Marigold? The wedding's tomorrow. Is she planning some secret bachelorette party she doesn't think I'll go to if she tells me   about   it?"

I flick at the corner of the card and ponder this some more.

Rocko doesn't look up from the classy piece of artwork he's doing, even though it's so simple he could do it with the tattoo gun between his teeth. I've been talking about this card for the last   six   hours.   He's   clearly   annoyed.

"Do you want me to check with her?" he finally asks.

"No, that's okay," I tell him. "But, do you mind if I leave a little   early?   Scope   it   out?"

"Oh, sweetie, I would've let you leave hours ago," Rocko says before clearing his throat. "I mean, course not. I can handle things   around   here.   Call   if   you   need."

I pull up to 1100 Clove Street, and check the address card once more. Because this place is not bachelorette party-worthy at all. It's a two-story furniture store. Why the hell would Marigold want   me   to   meet   her   here?

I shouldn't even be here. This is just plain stupid. Like, there should be an audience full of people rolling their eyes at me right now, saying, *"You stupid bitch, you deserve what you have coming. You know   you   shouldn't   be   there   alone.   At   night."*

But, despite all the obvious dangers, I put my car in park, grab my iPhone, and walk slowly to the door. If someone has decided to lure me to a furniture store to kill me, this is a pretty nice one to go down in, I guess. The mattress in the window is on special for six-grand, so, there're worse ways to go, I guess.

I push on the door and it's unlocked, naturally, because killers don't want you to have to screw around with a locked door before they slice and dice.

"Hello? Marigold?" I call into the darkness.

"I was afraid you wouldn't show up," Deo says. He steps out from behind a massive fountain carved from a tree trunk. "I'm glad you did, though."

"Deo?" I say it like it's a question, even though it's obviously not. I'm just confused. I don't understand this. Why I'm here. With him. "What's going on?"

"Look, I wanted to hang out, I wanted to see you. But, I don't have a place of my own. Yet. I'm working on it." He pushes his messy hair out of his face nervously. "And it's not like I could just invite myself over to your place. So, I came up with this masterful plan instead."

"Where are we, Deo? I mean, a furniture store?" I turn in a slow circle and take in the cavernous space. As far as furniture stores go, it's nice, with lots of unique, quirky pieces, and handmade, clean-lined items.

He shrugs and throws me an irresistible grin that I use every scrap of will-power I have in me to resist. "Well, yeah. It's got everything we need here. And it's Cohen's family's place, so it's cool and everything. I didn't break in, if that's what you're wondering. Mr. Rodriguez gave me the keys, so it's all legit."

"I just...I don't really see what we have to talk about." I rock back on my heels and forward on my toes and avoid all eye-contact.

Deo's sigh is so long and sad, it sounds like he's deflating. Just when I think he's all out of breath and confidence, he springs back, a gleam of pure determination in his light brown eyes. "Please, Whit. Just give me a shot. Just tonight. Please."

And I can't say no. Because he's standing there, wearing that same carefree smile he always has and, even though I'm not close enough to him, I know how his skin feels sand-scrubbed except on his calloused hands and how he always smells faintly like the beach and summer and something very cleanly, essential guyish and Deo, and I just can't walk away from all the raging temptation   that   he   throws   my   way.

"Okay." I nod cautiously, reminding myself to keep my head around   him.

Deo pumps his fist like he's just won a giant stuffed teddy bear   for   his   girl   at   a   carnival   booth.

"Okay, so, come over here first." Deo has a little bounce in his step that I haven't seen him with before. He leads me through the maze of sectionals and end tables until we get to the massive selection of dining room tables. Deo has pulled a shiny, dark one slightly away from the sea of other tables and blocked three of the four sides off with decorative folding room dividers.

"Where'd you get all of this?" I ask. The table is covered in a burlap table cloth and dozens of small, burgundy colored candles.

"Honestly? It's extra from Marigold's wedding booty. You are coming tomorrow, right?" He pulls out one of the heavy wood chairs for me. I pick up one of the votives and smell it.

"These smell amazing," I say, inhaling deeply again.

"Chai and almond," Deo identifies. I glance at him out of the corner of my eye and he shrugs. "Marigold is as talented at making good-smelling candles as she is shitty at cooking edible food. These are supposed to be party favors or something. But you didn't answer me. Are you coming tomorrow?"

"I think I have to or I may lose my job," I joke. "But seriously, Rocko and your mom have been great to me since I've been here. I couldn't miss it." Or you, I think. I'd been wondering if he'd be bringing a date. Marigold had told me it was okay if I did, but I can't imagine anything more tacky than that.

"Good." He's staring at me in the same glazed-over, swoony way he used to before he fell asleep at night. When everything was good and safe and happy and we'd talk until neither one of us could hold our eyes open anymore.

"So, what's on the menu?" I ask. "Or are we just talking?" I blink several times to break his stare.

"Okay, so, I don't want you to get mad. Again. But I sort of asked your mom what you might like." Before I can react to what he confessed, Deo jumps up from his chair and takes two large dishes from the curio cabinet next to our table. I can't help but tense up at the mention of my parents. Even though things have been okay between the three of us since Deo brought them to town without asking me, it's still strange to think of him talking to them. Especially since he and I haven't really been talking.

I nod to let him know it's okay with me. At least I think it is. Pretty   much.

"I made pot roast and spaetzle," he announces proudly. He sets the two dishes onto the center of our table.

I'm having a hard time keeping my eyes in their sockets and my jaw off the table. "Wait, you made spaetzle?"

Deo laughs that deep, gritty laugh that draws me in and makes me want to gobble *him* up.

"Well, technically we still have to taste it. So you can be the judge of what I actually made, because it might just taste like dough balls and onion. But yeah, I tried." He uncovers the dish and shows off his creation. It looks so similar to the stuff my grandma used to make for me, I almost choke up.

"Wow, you really went all out," I say, and I have to rein my voice in to keep it from wobbling. Deo takes my bamboo plate and fills it with the spaetzle and enough meat and vegetables to feed a party of twenty. "I see you inherited your portion   control   from   your   grandfather."

"Too much?" He stops scooping and hands me the plate. I stab a forkful of a little bit of everything, and Deo watches me as I take the first bite. I don't know what I was expecting, but this is incredible.

"Deo, you nailed it," I say around the explosion of flavors

that trigger a thousand perfect, happy memories. "It's perfect, thank you."

It tastes like home. Like my childhood. Like every Sunday dinner at Gram and Gramps's house, when Wakefield and I played out by the lake until Gram had to drag us in kicking and screaming. We thought taking the time to eat would kill us. But, by the time we'd get cleaned up and sat down at her table, we couldn't imagine being anywhere else. This meal was all of those good things. And Deo had done it. For me.

I reach across the table and brush the top of his hand and he cracks the tiniest of smiles. But he pulls his hand back before I can really hold it. Because maybe he's trying to protect himself from me stomping all over him, or maybe he doesn't want me to touch   him.

"How's work?" Deo asks. Easy. Non-committal questions are apparently   the   name   of   the   game   tonight.

"Eh, both jobs are going well." I try to balance the experience of eating this heart-poundingly delicious food that brings back so many swirling memories of catching tadpoles and fireflies with Wakefield, with the most mundane, meaningless conversation Deo   and   I   have   ever   had.

"Both?" His forehead wrinkles with confusion, and I realize that my life has bounded ahead without Deo. For some weird reason, that makes me sad. It makes me even sadder to wonder what's been going on with him. Somehow, the stuff that's currently so boring was kind of magical and special when it was just ours, during our time completely alone together in my dark room, on my soft bed.

"Yeah, my job working for Rocko, obviously, and I took that job with my anthropology professor. The one I talked to you about?" I say with a tiny bit more acid than I meant to use. It's not meant as a dig, but it comes out as one.

"Oh," Deo says, and there's a whole world of regret and embarrassment in that one tiny word. He wipes his mouth with one of the brown, recycled paper towels.

I rush to smooth the tension that's extinguishing all the happy between us. "How about you? What's keeping you busy these days?" I don't want him to feel bad. We've already played that game, and it's exhausting and stupid.

He still seems to be stuck on the job barb, but he shakes himself out of his daze and gives me a version of that carefree smile. "Same old stuff, different days." But there's something hidden in his words.

"Hmm... Your mom said you've been busy with some project?" I venture into the topic of his possible project, even though Marigold had sworn me to secrecy.

His gold-brown eyes narrow at me, and he points at my dish, reminding me to eat my gigantic mountain of food. I pick up the fork and take another delicious bite, even though I'm already getting too full. When he's satisfied he answers. "Oh, she did, did she? Well, she's sort of a lunatic, if you hadn't noticed." Deo's laugh is completely self-satisfied.

"She is," I admit. "But I can tell by that shit-eating grin that you're hiding something. What's up?"

His hand reaches out, and I hold my breath, praying he's going to touch me, and internally scolding myself for being so damn eager. But he just runs one finger along the strap of my dress and meets my eyes. His are dancing with mischief, like he knows exactly what he's doing to me. "New dress?" Deo asks coyly.

I tug at the navy polka-dot fabric of the Rockabilly-style dress and hope the burn I feel on my face isn't noticeable. "Yep. Why are you avoiding the question?"

"Whit, I worship every damn thing about you, you know that. But you really don't have a leg to stand on when it comes to accusing other people of keeping secrets--" I can tell by the look on his face that he tried to stop the words from tumbling out, but still, they fall. I suck in a sharp breath and bite down on my bottom lip.

"Touche." I fight to make my voice come out light and unaffected, trying to play it off as if it doesn't sting like he's just thrown me into a buzzing hive of angry bees, but it does. And I deserve every bit of venom the words inject.

All the humor in his face dries up, and he takes my hand and squeezes it hard, moving quickly, before I can attempt to back away. "Sorry, doll. I didn't mean that."

His eyes are sincere and apologetic. I really want to know what the hell Deo is hiding, what project has kept him so busy, why his mom refuses to tell me. But I know better than anyone that I can't make him talk about it, that I can't make him trust me or open up.

"It's fine." I shake my head and force myself to put the brakes on my hypocritical interrogation tactics. I also realize, with a tiny twinge of humiliation, how someone can be digging deep and asking questions because they care so damn much it's scary. But I bury that thought fast, and move on to more pressing topics. Like Deo's possible dating life, which I hope is nonexistent, even if I have no right or reason to hope that.

"So, your mom's wedding. Tomorrow. Are you...bringing anyone?"

He raises his eyebrows and chuckles. "Whit, be serious. If I had a date for Marigold's wedding tomorrow, would I be here with you tonight?"

"Why are we here, Deo? After everything, it just seems..." I put my hands up, at a complete loss for words as the sweet-smelling candles flicker and glow between us.

Pushing his plate to the side, he leans forward and lays it all out, honest Deo style. "I miss you, Whit. And I'm sorry."

There are a million things I should say. Want to say. One is, *Thank you for everything you've done for me.* Another is, *I miss you and am sorry, too.* And, of course, there's that one that screams the loudest and makes my heart thump and my palms sweat, because I'm afraid it will jump out of my mouth: *I'm an idiot and I need you, so take me home and throw me on our bed and have your way with me right now.*

Instead I say, "This was really great, thank you." I push away from the table. Deo glances down at his watch and swallows hard.

He gets up and walks so close to me, I can smell the clean scent of him over the warm scent of the melting candles. "You're welcome. Hey, Whit. I know it's late and you need to get a move on, but I've just got one other thing planned."

My heart is still punching in my chest from his last words and my crazy internal reactions to them, but I'm so curious, I can't resist asking. "What is it?"

"Follow me." His voice is low and hard around the edges with a hint of pure stubbornness.

He leans over and blows out each of the candles, and then clutches my hand. He grazes his thumb over the place on my palm that now has a scar from when I busted my ass on the rocks that day at the tide pools. It's a simple gesture, but it feels intimate as hell. I doubt he even realizes he's doing it.

We make our way past the bunk beds, and water beds, and with each bed we pass, the knots in my stomach weave tighter and tighter.

"Deo, we can't do this." We've stopped in front of a massive sleigh bed. The only one in the store dressed up with soft, striped bedding and about a zillion and a half squishy pillows. "Just because this place has a king-sized bed, doesn't mean we have to use it."

"Well, first of all, it's a California King. There's a difference, trust me. And second, *we* aren't going to use it. *You* are," Deo says. My eyes clearly spell out, 'huh?' so Deo continues. "See that chair right there. Well, La-Z-Boy and I are about to become good friends tonight." He points to an overstuffed recliner a few feet away from the bed. "You curl on up in that bad boy, and I'll sleep in this chair."

"You're not sleeping in a chair. Deo, this is crazy. We're not sleeping in a store," I protest, for all the obvious reasons two normal, rational people don't just sleep in a random furniture store.

But Deo's never been normal or rational, and he's not backing down. "Would you rather us go back to your place?" Deo says, half-joking. His upper lip twitches and I want to nip at it.

I cross my arms and shake my head adamantly. "No, that's not gonna happen, either."

Deo takes three steps toward me. I know it's three, because with each step closer, I have to take another breath.

"Whit, doll, you look tired. Two jobs? Sleeping alone in that apartment? I mean, I hope you're sleeping alone. Not that it's my business, but if you aren't, just be quiet and humor me, okay? I know you haven't been getting sleep. There are a dozen down pillows up there with your name on them, nice and firm, exactly how you like them. You will have a fucking instant orgasm if I tell you the thread count of these sheets. And this is real Egyptian cotton. This bed is custom made, just for you, so you can get an amazing night's sleep. So, stop arguing and just climb up into the bed, and I'll be over here. I promise to keep my hands to myself." He holds them up to showcase his innocence.

"This is crazy," I repeat, but my hold on logic and sense is wavering in the face of all those heavenly pillows and Deo's soothing, lulling, sweet-as-all-hell voice.

"Maybe. But you always knew 'crazy' is how I roll." He shrugs. "Come on. It's going to be a long day tomorrow for both of us. Let's get some rest."

Deo pats me on the ass and I can't help but jump and squeal like a stupid girl.

"And don't you dare feel sorry for me in my chair. This baby reclines, vibrates, massages, you name it. My grandfather would sell his soul for this chair. Actually, I might feel slightly sorry for *you*. Cause that bed is amazing, but you're not getting a massage from it. If you want one from me, on the other hand, arrangements can be made." He plops into the thick fabric of the chair and pulls the lever that sends his feet up into the air.

This is a totally ridiculous plan and I know each second I don't hold my ground is a second closer to complete insanity, but it doesn't look like I'm going to get out of it. So, rather than argue, I kick off my cherry-red wedges, climb up onto the absurdly high bed, and slip under the silky, thick comforter.

The bed is heaven. The heavy fabric of the bedding weighs down on my weary body, and I feel like I'm tucked neatly into a cocoon. My head sinks deep into the soft pillows. I only wish I would've worn something other than this gorgeous, stupid, form-fitting dress. I consider wriggling out of it, but decide not to. No telling if Deo really did get permission to be here. It'd be bad enough if someone found us here in the morning when we weren't allowed to be; it'd be mortifying if I was in my skivvies. Not to mention, me stripping down is either a not-so-subtle invite for Deo to come a little closer, or a form of torture for him.

The massive store is dark and quiet apart from the fountain over by the entrance. It's a strange place, full of strange things, and yet, because Deo's here, I feel safer than I do in my own apartment.

As much as I fought this, I know that sleep will come quickly for once. I can't believe how everything aches in the best way now that I've settled into the bed.

"Whit?" Deo whispers through the darkness. I don't move. He doesn't want to talk. He wants the silence from me. He used to talk to me all the time when he thought that I was sleeping, and tonight I can go back to those perfect, tortured evenings from before. "I still love you. Obviously."

I sort of love you too, Deo.

Only, I'm not brave enough to say it.

-Seventeen-

Deo

"Deo! Deo, wake up now! Deo!" Whit's voice is calling from somewhere far away, and I want to answer her. Seriously, I do. I just need, like, five more minutes of sleep.

But then she starts shaking my shoulder back and forth, back and forth, and I can't ignore the sea-sickening motion. I open one eye and her gorgeous little face is glaring at me.

"Morning, doll. You wake up like a scary-ass starving bear in the springtime. Anyone ever tell you that?" I reach out to take her in my arms, and she rolls away, clutching her open dress to her chest.

"I need to pee, and you need to zip me up right now. And once I pee, you can explain what you were doing in bed with me and why I wasn't wearing anything but my underwear when I woke up." She turns her smooth, tanned back to me and I sit up, rub the sleep out of my eyes, and pull the long zipper up, sealing both sides of the navy dress and wrestling down my disappointment over covering all that perfect skin. Her shoulder blades go all tense and straight, and she crawls across the enormous bed with as much dignity as she can.

I make things as awkward for her as possible by watching, a big grin on my face, as she flounces uncertainly in the opposite direction of the bathroom.

"Come give me a morning kiss, and I'll tell you where it is!" I call out.

She turns her head and her eyes are hot, narrow slits. "I will find a vase and piss in that. Then you can explain what happened to your friend's parents."

"You used to *like* kissing me," I remind her, but she only bounces up and down on her toes and looks at me with a mix of anguish and fury. God, she's damn beautiful when she's full of piss and vinegar. Literally. "Take a left at the coffee tables and go straight past the fabric samples. Second door on the left."

She's stomping back in a few minutes, and the image of this beautiful, romantic morning vanishes and is replaced by reality. And I'm not even remotely disappointed. I missed my angry bear.

"Deo, I thought we had boundaries set last night. You in the recliner, me on the bed?" She crosses her arms and shakes her head. "I...Don't you get that I can't agree...Why don't you understand...Ugh," she groans low in her throat. "Forget it," she mutters.

I want her to come back to the bed with me. It's actually my bed. Or it will be soon. I put a deposit down on it a few weeks ago, and will pay it off every month until I get into my place. She doesn't know that. She also doesn't know I had a secret scheme to make my sheets Whit-scented. Pathetic? Maybe. There's that saying about desperate men. Totally applies to me in this particular scenario.

I flip the covers off and get out of the big, warm bed, and I definitely notice that Whit checks me out big time. She always did like to watch me walk around in my boxers in the morning.

I make my way to her, and put my hands on her tense little shoulders. "There is a perfectly reasonable explanation for how you and I wound up in that big, incredibly comfortable bed, spooning *like friends* all night long." Her shoulders relax under my fingers as I massage all her pent-up tension away.

"Mmmm. Okay. What's the reason?" She rolls her neck back on her shoulders and sighs again. I already have a raging hard-on, and all her sexy moaning isn't helping at all.

"The reason is; you asked me." She tries to yank away, but I pull her back and rub my thumbs along her spine. She wants to tell me to fuck off, I know it, but this girl has tension burrowed deep in her muscles, and she's not about to end this epic backrub.

"I did *not* ask you, you damn liar," she grits out, then her scraping, angry words tumble into another loose, sweet moan.

"Uh, yeah. You did. You said, 'Too damn tight. Too tight. Get this snake off of me, no more eating that cheese,'" I repeat.

For a minute Whit holds perfectly still, and then I have this uncanny feeling that even my magic hands aren't going to be able to convince her not to stomp away. She's a little shaky, and I try to get myself ready for the blow, because I'm fairly sure she's about to bitch me the hell out like nobody's business.

Then I hear her tiny, strangled laugh, and my lips tug up in response. "Deo! You...assface!" she gasps between choking laughs. "You know damn well I was dreaming!" She spins around and looks at me, her eyes wide, her head shaking slowly back and forth. "The dress was tight."

"I know. You told me. I thought you were just speaking metaphorically," I muse, and she grabs me by the shoulders and shakes me back and forth as best she can with those scrawny arms.

"Just when I'm prepared to be so mad at you, you pull out that magic charm." She holds her hands out in defeat, then looks from under her eyelashes, kind of sheepishly. "And thanks. For getting me out of that dress. It *was* super tight."

"Yeah. I know. You compared it to a boa constrictor." I take her hands in mine. "So, now that my super-human charm has wowed you out of your grizzly mood, you wanna grab some breakfast or some caffeine? Swing by and pick me up a tie? Get washed up for this shindig?"

She looks down at her small, nail-bitten hands, her fingers threaded through mine. "You don't own a tie?"

"You're seriously going to focus on the tie bit of my list rather than the coffee bit?" I study her dark, serious eyes for a minute, wanting to see her face relaxed and sweetly smiling again. "I have a tie, Ms. Conrad. I have many, many ties. But I don't have one the exact color of your dress. Which is, what, again?

She tilts her head to the side. "Deo. You and I don't have to match. It would imply that we're..."

"Both attending a wedding? Both honored guests? Both really into...purple? Why do I have this strong feeling you're going to be wearing purple?" I grimace. "Well, every guy needs a nice pastel tie."

Her eyebrows raise so high, they're practically in her dark hair. "My dress is *not* pastel purple." She wrinkles her little tanned nose, like an adorably offended rabbit. "I'm not five. Or seventy-five. Or going to an Easter parade."

"Salmon?" I faux-guess.

She gags.

"Puce?" I try.

"They do not make puce-colored dresses," she insists, then presses her eyebrows together. "Do they?"

I shrug. "See how bad I am with colors? Take pity on me and help me with this tie debacle." My smile starts her smile going, and soon we're both grinning like fools, exiting the store, which will be cleaned top to bottom by a maid service I sprang for as an extra 'thank you' to the Rodriguez family, and she's following me in the LeBaron. I wanted her in my Jeep, but so many things have been going my way, I decide not to push my luck. We whip into a local coffee shop, and her extra large caffeine fix works like a powerful drug, melting the last rough edges of her evil morning self and leaving her sweet and smiley.

Sweet and smiley enough to spin the tie display racks at our next stop, coffee in one hand, five ties in various shades of yellow draped over her arm.

"Yellow?" I flick each tie, running my finger on the underside of her forearm just for the pleasure of watching all those little goosebumps ripple on her skin. I look at her beach tan, her dark hair, longer and wavier than when I first met her, and her big brown eyes. "I bet you're a knockout in yellow."

She takes two ties and drapes one over my left shoulder and another over my right, takes two steps back and squints. She grabs the one on my left and smirks at me. "I'm a knockout in any color."

"No argument about that." I lean in close to her, and she makes herself extra busy fixing all the ties she took off the rack, still one-handed because she has an iron grip on her coffee cup. "I also happen to know that you're a knockout when you aren't wearing any color at all."

Her cheeks flash a deep pink. "Go buy your tie."

I do as I'm told, but I notice the big smile she's trying damn hard to hide from me.

After tie shopping, she and I decide to go our separate ways to get ready for the wedding reception, and I feel this wave of panic. It's been baby steps to get back into Whit's good graces after my stupid idea to emotionally atom bomb her with an unexpected parental visit. Last night was a special kind of purgatory.

The minute I climbed into bed with her and helped wrangle her out of that crazy dress, I was hoping for some clear reason to not get back into that recliner. When she rolled towards me and curled her body into mine, I felt right for the first time in more weeks than I could count. I barely slept because I was so damn excited to have her in my bed, but it was weighed down by this irrational fear that maybe it was only going to last one night. Maybe that's all I was going to get, and I should be happy about it.

Which made me crazy, because I had no intentions of being happy until she was one hundred percent mine again. So watching her LeBaron pull away bitch-slapped my heart, because I felt like maybe that was the end of me and Whit, and I'd used up all the crappy magic fairy dust I had in my romance arsenal.

And then I also realized what a raging dipshit I was becoming on so many levels, and drove to my grandfather's house. He was already in a suit, because that old man used to rock one on a regular basis, so he's comfortable to just lounge watching UFC fights and cracking pistachios while he's dressed to the nines.

"You got a suit to wear?" he asks, but his guy gets pummeled in the face before I answer, and I don't have a chance to remind him that he forced me to get one a few weeks back. Silly old man.

I had a bank-loan interview, and when my grandfather found out I was borrowing Cohen's, he gave me this long-ass speech where he pounded his fist on the table until pistachio shells vibrated all over the floor and lamented the end of Western civilization while calling me and my generation slackers who dressed like the slobs we were at heart.

That old kook kind of gets his jollies off running his blood-pressure through the roof, but I actually saw merit in this rant and decided to get suited. So, I'm ready for my mom's wedding, looking pretty motherfucking dapper in my new gray suit and yellow tie. Fuck dress shoes though. I don't need to be all pinch-toed. I did buy brand new Vans for the occasion.

Gramps grunts when I come out. "If you cut your damn hair and put on a pair of real shoes, you'd look halfway decent."

"Settle down, old-timer. This town happens to be big enough for two sexy men and their styles. Don't hate on my awesome look because you're so damn jealous." I lean back in my recliner and accept his gruff offering of pistachios until it's time for us to get to my mom's house.

"Deo." Grandpa puts a hand on my arm suddenly, mid UFC blood-bath. "I got something for you."

I have no clue what he's got up his sleeve, but I follow him back into his room, spartan after my gram's death with only a few homey touches; a black and white picture of my gram when she was a teenager in a bikini set out in an oval gold frame, a painting of an octopus I made when I was a kid hanging on the wall, and a little hand-carved statue of a bunch of running horses my father sent from somewhere practically unknown and awesome on the dresser. I stand in his room and look at his bed, still made up for two people, and it kills me all over again that Gram isn't here to cluck over his tie being crooked and drink her little glass of grappa with him every night while they listen to the oldies station and hold hands.

I get a lump in my throat, the same way I always do in this little room that still smells like sweet musk and powder, Gram's signature scent. Much as I loved her, it hurts too much to miss her right now, and I don't want to be the jackoff guy crying at the wedding, so I hope my grandpa can hurry the hell up and I can leave this ghost-clogged room.

He turns around with a red velvet box in his hands. "This was the ring I proposed to your grandmother with."

He doesn't give me the details, doesn't tell me for the thousandth time how he took her to the state fair and got her hopped up on cotton candy and root beer before he took her on the ferris wheel. When their car was at the top of the wheel, he handed her the box of Cracker Jacks he rigged, awesome romance style. There was a little paper packet in with all that caramel-covered popcorn, and when she tore it open, he got down on one knee and made the whole car tip and swing back and forth asking if she'd put the ring on her finger and agree to marry him. He's not telling this story, which I kinda love rehearing over and over, because he's as close to tears as I am. We've become two emotional assholes, living in this old house without any women around to keep us tough.

"Well, take it." His voice is scratchy and annoyed, and his eyes are bright.

"You want me to give it to Mom?" I ask, looking away when he uses the sleeve of his suit to wipe his eyes.

"No. That would have been what I wanted your father to do. Too bad he's a fucking moron. This is for you to give to her." He tugs on my yellow tie and snorts knowingly.

"Her who?" I still haven't taken the box from his outstretched hand, so he shakes it at me.

"Her, the little minx with the Bambi eyes and those sexy legs you were bringing around a few weeks ago, before you messed it all to hell." He shakes the box. "Take it, damn it!"

I take the box with clumsy fingers, fumbling it from hand to hand while my grandpa rolls his eyes. "Whit and I are nowhere near there, Gramps." I have a very, very strong feeling that if I so much as hint that I've got something like this to Whit, she'll turn tail and disappear unbelievably fast, leaving what little bit of a relationship we have a permanent cold case file.

"Then you're a goddamn blind idiot," he mutters, stomping out of the room. "Don't make me regret giving that to you!"

Ah. Words of encouragement. I open the lid and the hinges creak. The ring is white gold, and the stone is clear, dark, beautiful blue. Is it a sapphire? I don't know dick about jewelry, but it looks old, shiny, and expensive.

And it looks like Whit. I can imagine her rocking this vintage ring.

Then I remember it's not just a pretty decoration for her finger. This ring means something. It's a huge commitment.

And Whit's about as anti-commitment as a girl can get.

I slide the ring box into my pocket. The only other option is to stash it under my bed, but I'm not getting covered in cobwebs before Mom's big day. And I feel like it may be a good thing to keep close for now. Not right now, but near-future now. Maybe. Or maybe my grandpa's emotional craziness is scrambling my brain.

Which is about to get an extra dose of addling, because the minute Grandpa and I arrive in my mom's little backyard-turned-wedding-jungle, we're put to work setting up chairs, hanging pollen-filled bouquets from branches, stringing lights, and helping out with the thousand things my mom kept to the last second. Cohen and his parents wave at me from their place of indentured servitude near the catering tables. Mom put everyone to work.

Soon the place fills up with flowy-haired, goateed hippies in their best brightly patterned paisleys and new Birkenstocks, and I work hard not to gag on the waves of patchouli that are drifting through the air. Rocko shows up, looking scared as hell and nice as a greaser all geared up for his big day, and then Whit rushes out of the house.

She sucks my breath away. She's wearing a deep yellow dress that's tight on top with a flouncy skirt, kind of old fashioned, and totally perfect for her. Her soft, dark hair falls in waves almost to her shoulders, and her lips are so temptingly red, the only thought bumper-carring in my hiccuping brain is that I want to drag her to some dark, quiet corner and kiss all that lipstick off her lips. Before I can take my fantasy firmly out of PG-13 territory, her warm eyes find me in the crowd, and she rushes over.

"Deo." She says my name like she's been waiting for me. Like I'm the only one who can solve what's wrong in her life. She looks me up and down, takes a breath so deep, it's like she's about to go on a dive for pearls, then releases it in a long whoosh. "Wow. You look...you really look god. I mean good! You look good. Not like a god." Her flustered mortification is beyond awesome. Then she seems to remember something. "Oh, Deo! You have to get in there. Your mom is almost ready."

As if on cue, the raggedy bunch of musicians starts playing something that sounds like a Grateful Dead cover of the "Wedding March." Those ruby-red lips are begging to be kissed, but she's already nervous enough, so I leave her unkissed.

For now.

It's not easy, though.

I go inside and find my mother sipping a mimosa from a crystal champagne glass like she's royalty. Seeing her so damn happy makes me feel good. "Hey, fancy pants. You ready to roll?"

She's wearing an electric orange dress with purple flowers in her hair. On anyone else, it would look like a Renaissance Faire nightmare. On my mother, it's like she's some kind of exotic flower come to life.

"I'm a little nervous," she giggles tipsily, and her gold eyes are mirrors of mine, but half-filled with tears.

I hold out an elbow and she tucks her arm through it. "You look so damn beautiful," I tell her. She giggles again, like a teenager, and blushes a little. "Rocko is one lucky guy. I'm really happy for you two."

"Oh, Deo." She kisses my cheek and rubs the lipstick mark off with her thumb. "Well, should we get started?"

"Let's do this."

The walk down the aisle feels like I'm underwater, and I float through with no focus, only seeing pieces of all different things. Rocko's tortoiseshell glasses, Cohen's plaid tie, Grandpa's gold wedding band, the crazy mystic who's officiating's rainbow scarf...nothing is solid and whole.

Nothing except Whit.

She's sitting up front, yellow and dark, spine stiff and straight, one seat next to her empty, and, when I deliver my mom to the makeshift alter and kiss her smooth cheek, I beeline for that damn chair.

The service is all hokey self-written vows that are sappily sweet but make me squirm a little to hear, like I'm listening in on Mom and Rocko's pillow talk. Whit stares straight ahead, her big brown eyes unblinking and wide. I thread my fingers through hers, and she looks my way, a ragged smile on her face, and tries to relax.

When the vows are done and the kiss is kissed, complete with Rocko bending my mother back and all the hippies cheering and the band getting out multiple tambourines, we all throw birdseed, the bride and groom strip out of their fancy duds and into comfortable clothes, and everyone eats from a huge buffet of all kinds of weird but tasty food. My mom knew better than to even attempt to cater anything herself.

I look over at my mother and Rocko, smiling, kissing, hand-in-hand, and a tension I didn't even know I was carrying in my chest melts down. I feel warm. I feel happy. This is all good stuff. But I want better.

I want Whit.

I shadow her closely. I know she slept pretty well, but she still looks dazed and edgy, and it worries me.

"Oh no!" Three huge, oily olives stuffed with goat cheese tip off her plate while we're standing next to the buffet table. I catch two in mid-air. One lands on her skirt, leaving a nasty oil explosion on the silky yellow fabric. "Oh no." Her voice drops to a breathy whisper and her eyes pool with tears.

I take her plate from her hand, put an arm around her waist, and lead her inside, through knots of dancing, slightly high and mostly drunk revelers. I pull her into my mother's bedroom, all batik wall hangings and the sharp and sweet tang of essential oils. Now that we're away from all the guests, she starts to cry.

First it's little tears wobbling out of her eyes. Then it's big, breathy sniffles and moans. Then it's hiccuping, air-stopping sobs that sit heavy on her lungs and make every breath a gasp. "My dress! My dress!" she wheezes, and, even though I know this breakdown can't be about a dress, I put my hands on her shoulders and turn her, grab the zipper and tug down with a long, slow pull. Her spine curves because she's buckling over, falling onto Mom's bed. I help her lie down and pull the dress off her legs. She curls into a tiny ball, and I cover her with mom's blanket.

I want to get in bed next to her and wrap my arms around her, but she needs space. She needs to cry this out. And I need to show her I learned my lesson and step the hell back, no matter that it's like a dagger plunged into my heart over and over.

"Whit, I'm going to get the spot out of this dress, okay? My mom is a huge klutz, so she has all kinds of crap to get stains out of clothes. Don't worry about anything." I say the words calmly, like she's not hyperventilating on my mother's bed, and I go to the laundry room and sprinkle my mom's magic laundry stuff on the big blotch and put the dress to the side to sit. I head to the kitchen and put a few soaked rags in the freezer and rifle around the medicine box mom keeps on the tiled counter, collecting what I'll need to help her when she's finally ready.

I hop up on the dryer and listen through the wall to Whit, on the other side, her cries getting louder and less hinged, rolling into muffled screams, sliding back to wet, gasping sobs, and cycling through the whole process again. I ball my hands into tight fists and grit my teeth. I want to burst in there and make it right. I want to fix it. I want to smooth it out so she doesn't feel all this pain shredding through her.

But she needs to feel it. And I need to step back and let her.

It feels like hours before the wails turn into whimpers and the whimpers turn into uneven, half-choked breaths. I finally let myself walk back through the door, armed with all the kooky herbal crap my mom swears by.

"Hey, killer," I say. Her face is blotchy, her eyes and lips swollen, body drained and exhausted. I turn her onto her back gently and smooth her hair from her face. Then I put an arm under her shoulders and hold a cup to her mouth. "Bottoms up."

"What is it?" Her voice is so scratchy, I barely recognize it.

"Love potion." It's a joke, but she looks so worried, I tell her, "Marigold's heartbreak remedy. Take it."

She drinks slowly, and the lines on her forehead disappear. It's déjà vu time, the smell of this room, the sun slanting through the window just like it is, the echoes of a long, wrenching sob-fest, a beautiful woman, a ton of pain, a weird herbal drink; all shades of my mom and her breakdowns. There's still a part of me that wants to get up and run away from this, but there's also a huge part of me that realizes that me being the one who did this for my mother after my father left her hollowed out sucked. Me doing this for the girl I love? Well, that's what it's all about.

I push her back on the bed and press the cold cloths on her face. "You good, doll?"

"Sorry," she croaks. "So, this is pretty damn humiliating. I mean, it's a dress."

"Whit, babe, this is so not about a dress," I object, moving to cradle her head in my lap so I can rub her temples, her forehead, down her nose and under her eyes. She goes liquid-boned under me.

Her mouth is a tight line for a minute, then it relaxes. "Wakefield…" She stops and I have to force myself to keep rubbing her head, slowly, quietly, to keep her talking. "Wakefield had this girlfriend right before he joined the army. She was okay, you know? A little generic for my brother. And after he signed up for service, he was kind of excited. I think it was getting the uniform, you know? It made him feel bad-ass. Like a GI Joe. And he was so damn handsome in his uniform." A real laugh breaks through all her bitter words. "I joked that he could get any chick he wanted. But he wanted her. He went to her house in uniform with flowers and she told him it was all over. She just couldn't commit to someone because it would *hurt too much if something happened to him*." I checked her mouth, because I would not have been at all surprised if she had grown fangs that dripped venom. "And I hated her for being such a coward. Then, when we got the news about...when we found out he was dead, I went to her house, and when she opened the door, I went ballistic on her. Her parents had to call mine to come take me home, because I couldn't stop screaming at her and shoving her...all kinds of crazy."

"She sounds like a piece of shit." I brush her hair back from her forehead and press another cool rag on her face.

Her mouth twists. "I'm no better."

I run my fingers along her tension lines. "Are you kidding? You're awesome. I've never seen anyone bulldoze through all their crazy-ass pain like you can."

She rolls over and sits up, knocking the covers off her body. I try very hard not to ruin this moment of deeper emotional connection by ogling her hot pink bra and thong, but sleeping by her all night and spending the day at her side is kicking my horn-dog tendencies into heavy overdrive.

"I bulldoze because I'm too damn afraid to get my hands dirty and take a pickax to what I'm feeling." She bites her lip and looks up at me, her voice louder, stronger. "I loved sleeping by you last night. I've missed you. So much."

It's everything all at once. My heart and brain have rolled out the kegs, the fireworks, the waterbed with black silk sheets, the side-by-side Jedi/ninja parade, because this girl has finally said the words I've been waiting to hear. Well, some of them. There are others, but now I have fact-based hope that the rest of the words will be coming. Soonish, hopefully.

My honest instinct is to lay her down on the bed, take off the last tiny pieces of lace she's wearing, and rub my hands and mouth all over her body until she's hot and wet under me.

Why did I carry her to my mom's room so she could have her breakdown? This is a serious mood-blighter.

I find a gauzy white dress of my mom's and hand it to Whit before I wind up throwing her back on my mom's bed and start doing things I can't stop.

"I've missed you too. Wanna go say our goodbyes?" I'm trying to not sound over-eager, but it's not working all that well.

Whit stands up, her body such a few inches from mine, my hands are itching to make the feel of her skin more than just a really awesome memory. She closes the space between us, and her nearly-naked body presses against mine. Being in a suit, I'm wearing more clothes than I usually would be, and now I'm super fucking upset about it.

I rub my lips on hers, just a quick rub, just to taste her for one single second. She grabs onto my bottom lip with her teeth, then let's go and licks the place she nipped. Her mouth presses harder against mine, and I open against her, my hands on her smooth, soft back. I run my hands in that sweet spot between the bottom of her bra and the top of her thong, up and down, and I pull her closer with each move of my hands. She pushes my jacket off my shoulders in one rushed press, then drops a hand between our bodies and runs her palm down my chest, under my belt buckle, and over my dick.

Suddenly, I don't give a damn where we are or what memories there are in this room for me. My mouth drags over her face, down her jaw and neck. I kiss her shoulders, and the round swell of her boobs, jiggling in the lacy cups of her tiny bra. I pop them out and suck on her nipples, run my hands over their full weight, rub my face over her smooth skin. She walks back until she's leaned against the door, her fingers working on me hard and fast. I move a hand under the sweet swell of her ass and hike her up so she can wrap her legs around my waist, her back braced on the door.

My free hand is wild, moving fast over soft skin, eager to touch her everywhere and trying to slow down and savor what I've been missing like a madman for weeks. I lock my mouth over hers and move my fingers up her thigh, pushing the scrap of fabric that makes up her thong to the side so my fingers have free access. She's soaked already and pressing herself hard against my hand.

I slip a finger into her and she tilts her head towards me, bites my earlobe and tugs at my hair, moaning deep, hungry moans. I work my fingers harder and faster, sliding against her with less skill than I'd like. I want to focus on her, but it's all a crush of sweet, hot, wet need, and my brain is blurry as hell. My belt comes undone under her quick fingers, and she flicks open the button and slides down the zipper, her hand working under the waistband of my boxers so she can grab my dick and cup it softly, then work with quick, frenzied strokes that are making me see little bursts of silver at the edges of my eyes.

Her body bucks hard, going stiff and pulsing against my hand. "Now. Now, please, now," she pleads, her fingers pulling against me more quickly. I wrap my arm around her and move the few inches over to my mom's nightstand. I realize that my soul is about to flambe in so many levels of hell. Who the hell steals a condom so he can fuck his girlfriend in his mom's room on her wedding day?

I do. Damn straight.

I move her back against the door, just in case anyone feels like bursting in on us, and rip the wrapper open. Whit grabs the condom and fits it on me in one slightly awkward, eager roll, and I lift her hips higher, then settle her on my dick in one quick, long thrust. She bites her lip and rolls her head back on the door, arching her back, and pressing harder against me, her tits bouncing a few inches away from my mouth.

"More," she gasps.

I pump in and out of her, slowly, trying to draw this out, because she's twice as hot and tight and wet as I remember, and I've needed this for so long, needed her for so long. My mouth dips low and catches first one nipple, then the other, enjoying her moans and the way she yanks my hair. She jerks my head back with a rough pull and looks at me, her lips parted and shiny, her eyes wide and nearly black with total need. She drops her hands down, cupping my face and her eyes close and her mouth makes a small 'o' as she strains harder against me.

"Faster, Deo. I want you now. I want you…more…fast." She tears through the buttons on my shirt, my tie loose but still on, her fingernails raking down my chest and ribs as her body rocks against mine, with quicker, slicker pulses and total, focused concentration.

I hold her under her ass with one hand and use my other to pull her face closer. She kisses me, but absentmindedly, and I realize she's completely locked in her own world, pressing against me to get to the place she needs to be.

At this point I'm ready to be her whatever, do whatever she needs to get to her release. I rub my hand slowly over her face, down her neck as she tilts her head back. My fingers drag along her collar bone, pinch softly at the soft, sensitive peaks of her nipples, before letting them rub against the rough pad of my palm. Her breath hitches and she presses so hard against the door, her hair is flattened and pushed up wildly. Her hands clutch at my shoulders, fisting around them and then digging into the skin through the thin fabric of my shirt.

She grinds against me, and I press into her, holding steady as her mouth comes open, her breath pants in quick gasps, and she finally yanks at my hair, crushes her forehead to my neck and muffles a scream into my collar. The relief I feel at the hot, wet downpour of her orgasm is knee-weakening. I come hard, and hold her sweaty, limp body against mine for a few minutes.

When she looks up, her eyes are glazed and her smile is lazy. "Thank you so much. I needed that so badly." She rubs her nose on my shirt and takes a long, deep breath. "And I feel like a complete whore. We need to go mingle, Deo. This is your mother's wedding."

She unwinds her legs from my waist and stands on the floor, unsteady in the heels she never kicked off. I collapse my weight against the door and take off the condom, straighten myself up and button myself back together. I'm happy. This is good. Right?

But there's something a little too fierce, a little too wild about the light in Whit's eyes as she asks to borrow my mother's brush and slips on the dress I grabbed for her. She's kind of chattery, kind of happy, kind of unmoored, and I feel a prickle of fear, because this feels like I just got spit out of a tornado and sucked into the early surge of a wicked tsunami.

Her eyes shine like she's delusional with fever. "Let's dance, Deo! Let's drink! Let's be wild!"

I take her hand and follow her out the door, wondering why, just when I feel like I got everything I ever asked for, I can't shake the press of dread that looms over me.

-Eighteen-
Whit

Deo shields my eyes from the sun streaming in through the curtainless window. Because that's just Deo. Thoughtful. Gorgeous. Protective. All the things I've ever wanted someone to be, but wouldn't let them.

I blink the sleep from my eyes and roll over to face him.

"Morning," I grumble. Deo runs his hand through his thick hair and his smile is wide and sexy. "What?"

He puts the tip of his index finger between my eyebrows and slides it down to the tip of my nose, then brushes his thumb over my lips, his eyes lazy and a deep, gorgeous gold. I've only ever noticed them this particular shade in the early morning, after a long night of sex. Can sex change the color of your eyes? Or is it something way simpler? Did the sex change me and what I notice about Deo?

"Nothing, I just love it when you actually sleep. Even though you're still a scary beast in the morning."

"Deo, we haven't exactly done a whole lot of sleeping." I bite his thumb when it slides too close to my teeth. It's true. We haven't left my bed in three days, but there have been other extra-curricular activities to keep us busy. Very busy. Very deliciously   busy.

I stare up at the popcorn ceiling while Deo traces an invisible line up my arm. I know what he's doing. Next, he'll move on to my collarbone, then my neck, and then—

I roll off of the bed to stop it before it can start, but Deo hooks his arm around my waist and pulls me back to his warm, bare chest. He presses his mouth to the back of my neck and the room starts to go fuzzy.

"Where do you think you're going?" he growls. Deo's hand grazes up my thigh.

"Come on, let me up. Rocko and Marigold came back from their honeymoon last night; you know I've got to go to the shop before him to set up. I don't want him stressing on his first day back." The words are supposed to sound tough and confident, but they come out on a little gasp when his fingers creep higher than my upper thigh. I want to be able to sashay away from Deo, but he knows me too well, and he's doing every single thing he can to ensure I get back in bed with him, wrapped tight in his arms, my brain nothing but a blob of over-sexed jelly.

His fingers are doing things that actually make me weak in the knees with excited craziness, but his words are kicked-back and calm.

"First of all, doll, they honeymooned at an ashram, so I doubt anything could stress him out. He's probably still got a contact high. Second, he'd understand if I told him you were late because we had to thread the needle." I clamp my fingers over his wrist, push his hand away, and bite my bottom lip hard. I need to focus, or I'll fall into his amazing net of sexiness and exchange my job, my degree, my life for endless hours of mind-blowing sex with this irresistible slacker.

Which I realize, with a stab of humiliating horror, does not bother my independent soul the way it should. Am I becoming some love-sick romantic? This is worse than I thought.

I mull over his last words and blink, before his euphemism clicks. "Seriously, can't you just say 'fuck'?" I let the rough word crash over the dewy romance of this morning and enjoy the little frown Deo exhibits when he's confronted with unsettling lack of subtlety before I flip over and kiss him quickly on the lips. He tries to lunge at me, and manages to pull me back down, but I roll out of his embrace and hop off the bed.

"Are you going surfing this morning?" I take in his long, lean body and have to wrestle down the crazy-strong urge to jump right back into bed with him. He's stretched out in the bed's dead center, sheets wrapped around some of him, while other parts are gorgeously displayed. He has his arms behind his head and is grinning like he's got a secret.

"Nope." His smile lures me in and makes me ask my next question, eyes narrowed. I'm not huge on surprises, and Deo's are always the kind that shock me in every way. After the furniture store date and subsequent sex-cation, I don't know if I'm ready for any more shenanigans from him.

It occurs to me that I should try to keep him close, so I make sure my voice stays nonchalant when I ask him. "Okay, so what are you up to? Want to come to the shop with me?"

Usually Deo jumps at a chance to spend the day bumming around Rocko's with me, but he shakes his head, his smile so huge, a tiny twinge of panic surges through me. What is this all about? "I can't, I've got a few things to take care of."

I pull my eyebrows together. "Oh really? Like what *things*?" I try to make my voice sound light, and casual, but I can't disguise the tone that screams *what the hell?* Deo tends to get crazy ideas and just...run wild with them. Sometimes a little too wild.

Deo laughs, and I realize that he knows exactly how nervous he's making me and is enjoying it thoroughly. "Like...things." He stretches his arms back and every bulging muscle silently invites me to press my body against his. I decline the invitations through gritted teeth. This boy and his addictive sex will be the death of my productivity. It's so damn tempting to just bury my workload and fall into him. Just for one more day.

And those thoughts are exactly why I need this distance, this safe space away from his irresistible allure. Deo is too wild, too unpredictable, too crazy when I'm trying to take things slow and plot my life out.

Still, I wonder what the hell he's up to.

I hate this. I hate that I don't have a leg to stand on in this case, when all I want to do is scream at him about keeping shit from me. But I can't. Still, I thought we'd sort of made a silent pact that things would be different the other night when he came home with me and then took up semi-permanent residence in   my   bed.

I inhale deeply and push the air back out in one loud, long whoosh. Deo raises a dark eyebrow and glances at me out of the corner of his eye, smiling in this adorably indulgent way that makes me furious and light-headed at the same time. He notices my dramatics, but he doesn't comment. Instead, he climbs out of bed and puts his pants on, the zip of his zipper indicating that the conversation is over.

I wish that I was above using my womanly charms to get information, but in this case, I'm not. I cross the room and wrap my arms around him from behind. I let my fingernails rake across his chest and bump gently over the ripples of his abs. I watch as his breathing picks up and, when he looks at me over his shoulder, he lets his eyes half-close in that sexy way that lets me know just how much I'm turning him on.

"Whit," he says, turning around to face me and putting a few inches of space between us, I know so he can clear his head. Fail. "You are damn sexy, but I'm not telling you where I'm going."

I push my bottom lip out into my best pout, my last ditch effort to sexually extort this information.

"I'll tell you later. Tonight even. You'll love it. Promise. Don't be a big, nervous grizzly about this." Deo kisses my pouty bottom lip and chuckles as he snatches his shirt off of the floor.

"I get first shower!" I yell, dashing into the bathroom before he can duck in.

I'm dabbing on my dark red lipstick after the quick shower that washed off the last of Deo's smell from my skin. I ignored the little part of me that sighed sadly when the smell of my body wash replaced the scent of him. Something small and bright and heart-stoppingly distinct catches my eye in the reflection of the hallway mirror.

I turn around to make sure it isn't a mirage.

Sure enough, next to Deo's Vans are the dress pants that he kicked off hastily, when we barely made it in the front door after the wedding, but before we fell into my bed for an extended stay. And next to the pants is a tiny red box that must have fallen out of his pocket. I cross the room and pick it up and run my thumb over the soft velvet. My heart is thumping so ferociously in my chest, it wouldn't surprise me if Deo could hear the steady pounding over the sound the shower and his passionately off-key rendition of Otis Redding's "Try a Little Tenderness."

The room feels like it's tilted off its axis, and I grip the wall to keep from sliding to the side. I don't want to open it. I know what's in it.

The croak of the old hinges reverberates through the entire apartment, and my fingers shake slightly, making the box flutter in my hand. It's bad. It's really bad.

Inside is a gorgeous, vintage-looking sapphire ring. It's something that, if this were a time far in the future and things were completely settled and I were ready to get married, I would drool over and lust after and drop major hints about. It's something so beautiful and perfect, it's as if it were hand-picked for me by someone who knows me inside and out. It's unique and breath-taking and so, so...wrong.

I snap the box shut, hiding that perfect ring that twists my guts and stare at the red velvet box. When I blink, I'm furious over the sting of tears that threaten to smudge my eye-makeup. I just wanted things to be normal. Not rushed, not heart-crushing. Normal. He can't even give me a few days to breathe, a few weeks to get back into our groove, a few months to feel out where this is going. My fist locks hard around the velvet.

I can't believe Deo thinks this is a good idea. I can't believe he thinks we're *there* without even talking to me, after everything we just went through. I thought he'd respect the boundaries we clearly need to establish to keep this relationship from taking over our lives, but he obviously thinks he can barge through every closed door, no matter how much I value my privacy.

I set the box down with a thud on the small table and back away with my limbs stiff, like it's a ticking bomb, ready to explode and ruin everything. Just like the one that took Wakefield away.

I manage the tears and lock my heart against his voice, singing those romantic words through the wall of the apartment we just started sharing again. I want to march into the bathroom and demand answers. I want to order him the hell out so I can think without his smell and laugh and crazy sexy self screwing with my judgment. I want to throw him on the bed and have my way with him, because he still turns me on so completely it's scary, even when I'm furious at him. All I know right now is that I can't be here when Deo gets out of the shower. I grab my purse and keys and bolt out the door.

Rocko's tattoo gun is already buzzing away when I push through the door of the shop.

"Morning, kiddo!" he yells cheerfully.

"You're here already." I stop, confused, wondering if Deo threw my world off so completely, he'd even made me lose my handle on the most basic of things. Like time. "Why?"

"Well, I missed you, too, darling. Had a special appointment." He nods at the guy whose arm he is tattooing.

"Okay." I'm trying really hard not to be annoyed. I wanted a few more minutes of quiet. A few more chances to collect my thoughts and push the rising panic away. But I'm pissed at Deo, not Rocko. I have to remind myself of that. "How's Marigold?"

Rocko stops tattooing for a minute and smiles a dazed, proud smile.

"Marigold." He pauses and shakes his head like he can't come up with the words to describe exactly what he's feeling. "That woman is amazing."

And that sentiment and the look on his face—that pure happiness, makes me want to run home and crawl back into bed with Deo.

"Good." I nod. "I'm gonna go to the bank, then. Get some change. Or something."

"Whit, come see this before you go." Rocko waves me over to see what he's working on. I set my purse down and sigh.

The man who's being tattooed looks a little older than me, or maybe just a little more tired and worn. His skin is deeply tanned and small lines fan out from the creases of his eyes. Still, he's smiling and talking with Rocko like he's completely at ease, and, you know, not being stabbed repeatedly by the tiny needle of the tattoo gun. Rocko pauses for a second so I can see what's being inked on the guy's arm.

"What's up?" I smile at Rocko's client to prove I'm not a total ogre. "Whit." I extend my hand to introduce myself, and he shakes with his left, since he's trying to hold his freshly inked right arm steady.

"Eric. Eric Brown. Pleasure to meet you." His eyes are a nice, clear green and his smile makes him look so much younger, I make up my mind that the lines around his eyes are definitely more about stress than age.

"Take a look at this." Rocko's voice is soft, not like he's proud of the precise font or color contrast or design in general. This isn't Rocko sharing his skills, but I'm not quite sure what it is instead.

I look over at the fresh ink on this man's arm.

It's intricate lettering, wrapping around his forearm that reads, *"Here I am. Send me."*

"Nice." I wonder if Rocko is thinking about the tattoo I designed for Deo. Well, the tattoo I designed that Deo wound up getting, anyway. I decide to put all of my mental powers towards going more than fifteen minutes without thinking about Deo if that's possible. I direct my next question at Eric, whose smile puts me at ease. "What's the significance?"

Rocko knows I'm a sucker for this part of the job. It's like my own version of US Weekly. I love hearing the stories behind the ink.

"It's Isaiah, 6:8." His eyes are clear and open, letting me know it's okay to ask. So I do.

"Isaiah 6:8?" I don't bother to wrack my brain, because I wouldn't be able to use all the fingers on one hand to count the number of Bible verses I can even recognize. "I'm not familiar."

I haven't been to church or cracked a Bible open in years. My parents still go twice a week, but after I hit double-digits in age, they couldn't drag me with them.

"Isaiah 6:8, "Then I heard the voice of the Lord saying, 'Whom shall I send? And who will go for us? And I said, "Here am I. Send me!"'" Eric recites in a voice that's ringed with conviction and just the shadow of a hint of sadness.

"Oh, okay." Call me dense, but I don't get it. "I'm not super religious, but it's nice."

Eric chuckles and eyes the ink fondly. "Honestly? Neither am I, but it's fitting."

"Nice job." It's a clean tattoo, and the language is direct and powerful. I get the feeling there's something more they expect me to notice about it, but if there is, I don't get it. It reminds me of Deo and the words tattooed on his ribs. And I sigh when I realize, with that one thought, I've proven beyond a doubt I am a miserable failure at keeping that boy out of my brain for even a tiny sliver of time. "Especially for coming in so early."

"It was worth it to come in early for. Explain it to her." Rocko and Eric exchange a Look, and I feel the slow sludge of panic creep through my veins. Explain *what*?

"I'm in the military, and after each tour that I make it home safely for, I get another tat." Eric glances at the words on his arm, and, suddenly, they don't look sharp and clear. I feel the burn of rage that always comes when tears threaten. I'm sure as hell not crying for the second time today. What the hell is with me lately? Eric's voice helps me pull my shit together and focus on anything other than the tears that are clawing at my ducts. "This is number three."

"Three?" I try not to choke on the word. Three tours he's made it back from. Three times he'd escaped. I full-on glare at Rocko for doing this to me. For dragging me over here and into this. Especially after the morning I had. If I cry now, it will be from pure, scathing pissed-off anger.

"Yep, I guess you could call it war paint." Eric's smile is defiant. He sounds proud, like he's spitting in the face of what has to be one of the scariest situations any person could ever have to face.

My head spins, my legs feel like rubber, and I have to sit down, or I'll crumple in a heap on the floor. I pretty much fall into the swivel chair next to Rocko and Eric and rub my temples, which are tightening like I'm about to suffer from the clamp of a serious migraine.

"You okay, kid?" Rocko's voice is low and worried, but it's like barbs pressing against my already aching skull. Like he didn't know what this was going to do to me. Like this wasn't part of a plan. I don't even have the strength to glare or scowl, because I'm worn the hell out. "Yeah. Just…" But I'm not okay. I grip the seat of the chair until my fingernails bore into the cloth and my knuckles turn white and I lock my feet back around the base to keep from tilting off the seat. Because even though my chair is completely still, the room is spinning.

The world is spinning.

And it has been since the day Wakefield died.

Because of me.

And just when I thought things were slowing down, that I wasn't so miserably dizzy and could maybe stand on my own and start picking up the pieces, Deo buys an incredibly perfect, stupid, screw-up-my-world-completely ring.

"My brother was in the service," I blurt out. My words hang harsh and blunt in the air for a few breaths.

"That's what I heard." Eric doesn't sound impressed or unimpressed, reverent or flippant, excited or bored. He sounds like he just heard a fact that he understands. I manage to lift my pounding head and make eye contact with him, locking on those clear green eyes that have lost the crinkle from his smile, because his mouth is fixed in a straight, tight line. I expect him to look away, but he doesn't. He stares right into me. I want to break his stare and shoot daggers at Rocko with my eyes, but I can't. Because there's something in Eric's eyes that tells me he knows heartache and loss. Maybe even more than I do. And, as painful as it is to see that, I can't look away. Because for the first time in months, I feel like someone gets it.

"He didn't make it," I finally say. The relief that unfurls in me at being able to say those words without having to deal with someone's misguided pity or discomfort is so freeing, I feel the iron clamps of my migraine loosening. I lose my death-grip on the chair and drop my feet back to the floor, taking slow, deep breaths, before I say the words I still can't quite believe are true, forever now. "He never came home."

Rocko stands up and pretends to be busy across the shop. This *was* a set up. But the fire of my rage has long since died out. I focus on Eric, calmed by his even, quiet presence.

My fingers hover over the still-raw design on his arm, and I swallow hard before I make myself ask, so I can know the truth. So I can stop ignoring any grief other than my own. "So what's the tattoo mean?"

"It sort of has a double meaning. The first is that, in the military, we do a lot of things that civilians may think are

impossible. And we just say, 'send me.' Because that's the job."
Eric's shrug is an unconcerned tip of his shoulders, a modest,
honest statement about what he and people like him do, like it's
nothing particularly heinous or horrifying or amazing.

I'm having a hard time wrapping my head around 'the job,' as
Eric describes the terrifying, life-on-the-line thing he does as his
day-to-day. How can one word describe what he does overseas,
in the line of fire, but also describe what I do when I'm here,
organizing Rocko's portfolios or paying his vendors? I want to
know more. I want him to tell me, because Wakefield can't, and I
need someone to explain it to me from the inside. "And what's
the   second?"

He inhales sharply, and his hands fist for a few beats. "I've
lost brothers, too. Not biological ones, like you, but brothers still.
There isn't a single guy in my squad that wouldn't lay down his
life for one of the others. We'd all say, 'send me,' if we had the
choice. I'd sink for anyone of those guys." The clear green of his
eyes is sharp and fierce with his determined words. He means
every single thing he says, and his conviction shakes me to my
core.

I.   Can't.   Breathe.

Eric is the kind of man you would wish you had by your side
in a war. Eric is the guy who survives, the guy who gets it all on a
level some people will never comprehend. I wish he'd been in
Wakefield's unit, because maybe he could have protected my
brother or taught him. There was never a guy less cut out for

service than my little brother. I try to explain the truth about him that crashes through me, weighted with stinging regret.

"Wakefield, my brother, he wasn't like that. Around me, because he was comfortable, he was so funny. I'm talking hilarious. But if he didn't know you? People were always shocked when he finally loosened up. Because until he trusted you, he was so quiet. Shy. He didn't like to take risks. My brother always made all these graphs and lists before he decided to do anything, ever. And he didn't even want to be there." The honest words slice like razors out of my mouth. They shake and whisper, because I'm too ashamed to give them any more volume. "He only enlisted because he wanted the cash for school. Because he wanted me to not have to worry and be able to use our parents' savings. He was really nervous to go at all."

Eric puts one big, tanned hand over mine and pats my hand slowly. He tries to smile, but stops when I give him a look that lets him know he doesn't have to go easy on me or sugarcoat a single damn thing.

"Maybe. Maybe it started that way. But I promise you, by the time he finished basic and was shipped overseas, he wasn't the same kid brother you knew. He'd changed, even if you never got to see that side of him. Lots of people are quiet going in. That doesn't mean they aren't brave. There's a saying that 'courage doesn't always roar.' He was there, doing a job for a bigger cause. And I bet when he went down, he was doing something he was proud of. Something that meant something."

His eyes are locked on mine, and I know he believes what he's saying with his whole being. I just don't know if I believe what he's saying.

"Something worth dying for?" It's blunt, and awful, but I can't help it. I need to know. The truth. All of it.

His laugh is short and resigned. He's not laughing at me, and he's not laughing because he thinks any of this is funny. I think he's laughing because I'm asking questions that don't really have the kind of mystery-solving answers I'm looking for.

The answer to the question I asked is something I've always known, because I was lucky enough to know every beautiful, strong, courageous part of my brother. Even the parts that were just waiting to be tapped into. Just waiting for an opportunity to go from potential to absolute.

Eric's words confirm what my heart and brain realize all at once, and, deep down, have always known.

"We all die, sweetheart. You've just got to live your life with enough meaning while you're still here to make it all worthwhile. I bet your brother knew that, even if he wasn't ready to go."

Rocko comes back over, slathers Eric's arm in the new organic tattoo butter Marigold has concocted and insists we use in the shop now, and winks at me. I breathe in the tangy, almost-minty smell of the balm that will heal those brave words on this smart-as-hell man's arm, and feel a deep sense of something strange.

Something I last felt with Wakefield, just before he left. We were lying in the backyard, catching fireflies on our fingers.

"Remember doing this as kids? At Nana's?" he asked, smiling at me through the overlong blades of summer grass growing high and fast behind our house.

"Yep." I watched as the little bug roamed up and down my finger, tickling my skin with its legs, its bright back flashing with a pure gold light. "I used to wish we could keep them forever. You remember?"

"I remember jars of dead fireflies, if that's what you're asking." His brown eyes, the same shape and color as mine, focused on the bug on my finger. "You're shit at letting go, you know that?"

I gave his hand a quick squeeze with my free hand. "I'm getting better." I flicked my fingers and we watched the bug blink away. "See. I let go."

"Yeah. But you didn't want to. You didn't let it go freely. In your evil heart, you wanted that lightening bug's soul." His grin was goofy. Brotherly. Annoying. Something I didn't realize I'd never see again after that night.

"But I *did* let it go," I argued, pinching his shoulder. "You act like I'm some evil queen stealing the forest creatures' essence to use in my demented potions."

"I don't think you're truly happy for that little guy. You gotta try to be, though. Try to be happy it gets to be free. Free to live its life. Free to have wild sex with other lightening bugs.

Maybe it will be in a lightening bug orgy. Or maybe it will get smashed in someone's screen door. But that's life, you know? You gotta let it live, Whit, whatever hand it's dealt." The goofy smile faded, and I watched it disappear. But I didn't savor it the way I should have. I didn't know.

That night, I'd been thinking he was talking about himself. About the fun he'd never have if he got killed. It chilled me right to my marrow, and I just didn't let myself think about it. But now, today, after talking to Eric, I think Wake was talking about me. About how I wanted things to go according to some stupid plan. Always. The reason he was going overseas was because I had a plan in my head I just couldn't deviate from. And I thought I was leaving that plan by coming here when Wakefield died, but I was only adopting a new plan. Just as rigid. Just as self-centered.

He was right. I was always letting go in the shallowest way possible.

All this time I was driving fast and determined to a goal I never had any intention of sinking into. I was racing like a fiend from one thing to the next, skimming over all my feelings because I was too afraid to sink in and commit to anything. Isn't that exactly what Eric said he'd do for his guys? He said he'd 'sink' for any one of them.

Not race. Not swim. Not float.

Sink.

The scariest thing.

To stay in one place. To throw all your weight at something and let go.

I've never been good at it. Sinking. Even the word terrifies me.

And, I realize, sinking is the only thing that can possibly free me from my endless attempt to tread water.

"Sonofabitch," I say, as soon as Eric has hugged us both goodbye and left the shop.

"What?" Rocko doesn't even bother to pretend to look guilty. "I just thought you might be able to use some perspective."

"That was a set up," I accuse, but my words don't have any malice. I'm just stating the facts.

Rocko's gaze is soft, hopeful, exhausted. He's worn out with worry. Over me. I was too busy fighting every single person who attempted to help me to even realize just how much I was wearing out the people I love the most. "No, it really wasn't. Eric is an old friend. Used to live next door to me until he got shipped off. He's back in town and wanted to get some ink before he went back to base in some god-awful Southern state. He told me the story behind the tat, and, well, I just thought it might help..."

And it did.

Me spending my life miserable, torturing myself with the guilt that is eating me alive, isn't going to bring Wake back. No matter what I do, nothing will.

I'm holding on to something, even though I keep telling

myself I let it go the day they buried my brother's empty coffin.

But what I'm doing is selfish. It's a waste of my life, and it's a waste of my memories of Wake and the courageous way he lived right up to the part where he didn't live anymore. I refuse to tread in the shallows of my own grief and guilt. It's made me so exhausted, I can hardly think straight. It's time to take a deep breath and sink into the love and goodness that scares the ever-living hell out of me. I have to make my life count for something, or I'll be treading through this pain like a coward until   I   drop.

"Rocko, you don't have another client until noon. You have time for one more?" I know exactly what I want.

Rocko raises his eyebrows and I plop into his chair.

-Nineteen-
Deo

"So go find her." Cohen brings out the Everclear, and he clips two shot glasses on the custom coffee table that used to be some kind of architect's file cabinet. Whit would love it. I got it for a decent price because I agreed to let the guy who designed it decorate and do a shoot at my place. He took most of the crap back with him, but he let me buy the table for cost, plus he painted the entire interior. Which is cool, though I never really thought I'd be into a fire-engine red living room.

It's growing on me. Along with home ownership. And business ownership. I'm a fully-minted adult.

Who's about to throw back a shot from a glass that reads: "Mean People Suck: Nice People Swallow."

I push that shot glass towards Cohen and turn the other one toward me. It has a vintage picture of a girl on it with the words: "I can never remember which is better: Safe? Or Sorry?" It reminds me of Whit, and my throat suddenly burns for that damn drink.

"Can't," I tell Cohen. "It's a big, complicated clusterfuck, and I really need to get pretty damn wasted so I can just forget." Cohen hesitates, pulling the bottle closer to his chest. "Cohen, it's this or karaoke. I'm dead serious. And I will sing Culture Club."

Cohen unscrews the cap, but doesn't pour. "Culture Club? Isn't that a little 80s for you, man?"

"I am my mother's son. Dude, c'mon. Do you really want me to hurt you? Because, so help me God, I will make you cry. In public. And you'll have to be the designated driver to boot." My threats finally loosen his rigid reluctance, and he pours a stingy shot.

"Should I be precious and tell you you're taking a step too far?" He pours himself way more than he should, but the fear of my karaoke makes sensible people do crazy things.

"Nah. I promise, no nudity tonight. No puke, either. The designer guy left those little shaggy rugs on the bathroom floor, and they'd be a bitch to clean up. See me being all adult?" Cohen raises one eyebrow at me like he doubts my adulthood, but he offers me a salute with his glass.

"A toast?" He prompts me to lift glass. "To you, man. For making the most incredible fucking changes to your entire life, but somehow managing to stay the same immature douchebag best friend I've known since third grade. Seriously, I'm proud of everything you've done, man."

"Couldn't have done it without you. You may be my lamer, less handsome, stupider side-kick, but you're the wind beneath my damn wings." We clink glasses and let the fierce liquid burn a straight path from our tracheae to our intestines. "One more, brother."

"As long as you don't sing any Bette Middler." He holds the bottle back, and I give him the Boy Scout salute. Or maybe it's the Girl Scout salute? I'm not very Scouty, but whichever it is, it gets Cohen to tip the bottle one more time, and the singe of his quick alcohol buzz makes him more generous this time around.

"To better days coming." He pushes his glass my way.

I rub my thumb over the image of the girl on the glass with the witty wit. Like my Whit. Well, not technically mine anymore. But always mine, anyway. "Better and better," I say with absolutely no conviction.

I convince him that a trilogy of shots is the only way to seal our good luck fate, so three it is, and then he's collapsed on my microsuede couch that Teddi, my designer, called 'cowardly middle-class blah,' but Mrs. Rodriguez called 'easy as hell to clean.' Plus that, Teddi wanted me to think about a couch that had no arms and was a blue so painful to look at, neon wasn't a bright enough word to describe it. Cohen is snuggling my microsuede armrest and drooling, which is all good, 'cause I got Scotchguard protection, like the responsible adult I now am.

"You gonna puke, man? Because I really do owe you for New Year's. Why do you always let me talk you into this shit? Three shots was just stupid." I lean back in my LaZBoy. I can't even repeat the evil things Teddi said about my comfy-as-hell recliner, because my brain might tell my sperm, who might tell my future children and corrupt them. That's how hateful his words were. Over what is, arguably, the world's most comfortable chair. My grandfather, who has a Purple Heart and a mean upper right cut, told me to tell Teddi to fuck himself and the clear plastic chair he wants everyone to sit on. Since Teddi can only grow a millimeter mustache and voluntarily wore a bowtie the entire time he was at my house, Grandpa's advice wins out, no questions.

Cohen burps and groans. "Because without you, I'm too boring."

"Is this because I made fun of you for working in the furniture store. Because that was shitty of me, man. I was living with my grandpa like a slob. I had no idea how the hustle worked, okay? So forget all that crap. I bow down before your years of hard labor." I rock back and forth in my chair and wish I had some pistachios.

Cohen rolls onto his back and puts one foot on the floor. I'm sorry because I know for a fact his entire world is spinning, and it's my fault for encouraging him to press his luck with that third shot. His voice is slightly slurred already. "No. No. I'm glad you work now. I am. But you're still you, and what you do is make life livable. You make life real."

"Life's real without my bullshit," I object, wondering if getting up to make a pot of coffee is jumping the gun. I do take a second to be impressed as hell with myself for having a coffee pot. This is all kinds of responsible of me. On the one hand. On the other, I'm getting stumbling drunk on a random Tuesday night. "Whit knows that. Which is why she ran off. I'm fuck-buddy material as far as she's concerned."

Cohen's moan is long and nauseous-sounding. "Call her."

I shake my head. "No way. You know the sayings, man. If you love her, let her go. Can't keep a wild thing in a cage. Freedom is as freedom does."

"You talk out of your ass so much, I don't know how you can stand yourself. Quit. Being. A. Pussy. Call her." Cohen clutches his stomach.

I take the large decorative bowl off the fancy coffee table, spill the wax pears out of it, and hold it out to him. "Puke, man."

"Can't make it to the bathroom," he mutters, eyes closed tight.

"I owe you this. Puke right here." I hold the bamboo bowl next to him and look the other way.

He takes it in his hands and sits up with a grimace. "You're my best friend. And I love you. Excuse me while I go to your bathroom and attempt not to puke on those weird hairy rugs you have in there. While I'm gone, call that girl. Call her. You're in love with her, asshole. Call her."

Cohen tries to put the bowl back on the table, but misses by a few inches, and it drops to the floor with a loud thwack that leaves a huge crack down the center. He totters down the hall, knocks a black-and-white print of some random door with graffiti on it off the wall and staggers into the bathroom. I'm not adult enough to resist feeling a burst of evil glee when I imagine Teddi's fury at all his decorations getting broken by a pair of immature punks.

I slide my phone out of my pocket and flip to the last picture I took of Whit, smiling sleepily at me, her head cushioned on her pillow, her dark eyes heavy-lidded and so sexy, it tugs low in my gut.

I'm kind of bummed, because, if it was all going to end with Whit, I wish I'd at least been able to make my case for why she should give me a real chance. I planned to show her all the cool shit I'd done with my life, all the slow, torturous changes I'd made while kicking and screaming like a stubborn little shit-headed toddler.

Then I realize that I pretty much have to call her, because we've come full circle. Here I am, on this big day in my life, drunk off my ass and thinking about her. I'm going to call her this one last time, and tell her good-bye, and then I'm going to erase her contact information from my phone and think of her wistfully.

Like an adult.

Only she never picks up her phone, so it's pretty anti-climactic. I get up and find Cohen sleeping in my bathroom, the contents of his stomach safely ejected half in my toilet, half on my shaggy little rugs. I get some silk-covered pillow off my couch and this soft-ass blanket made of some kind of fabric

Teddi bored me to tears telling me all about, and cover him up like I know his mom would want me to.

I check the locks on my doors, adjust my thermostat, and get into my big, empty bed, where I pretend the sheets still have a Whit-like scent. I go to bed thinking about how much more being responsible would rock if Whit was here to help with the transition. And have wild sex with me. Because, sadly, my biggest goal in getting my own place and this big ass bed was to woo Whit into living with me so I could get her in the sack anytime I wanted.

But it wasn't just about the sex, though the sex blows my mind. I also wanted to have her around. Her over-loud laugh. Her bearish morning greetings. Her -thrashing/snuggling night-time presence. I miss her. I miss the way she always pushed me, always made me think, always made me work harder. I feel like I hadn't ever been able to repay her for all that, and just when I was finally in a position to do it, she found the ring box.

Damn my romantic old coot of a grandfather.

I expect the liquor to make me crash for the night. But I only sleep for a few fitful hours. When my eyes crack open, the palest, coolest grey-color is just cracking on the horizon. It's still more night than day, but I'm wide awake. And there's a message on my phone from Whit.

"Deo. Call me. Now."

My hand crushes around my phone. She sent the message almost three hours ago. I'm out of bed and into my shorts in a few quick seconds. I grab my hoodie, yank it over my head, and rush to the front door barefoot, only turning around to make sure Cohen is alright. His snores give me the go-ahead to race to my Jeep, and I'm pulling out when she picks up the phone. "Where are you?" I demand before she can say a word. I'm at the end of my road, not sure which way to turn, so freaked out I almost feel pissed-off.

"Bed," she mumbles. "Deo? I got your call, and I... Can you meet me at the beach?"

"Are you okay?" Her voice sounds pretty normal, and my heart clicks into a slower pace.

Her voice is steady and clearer. "Yes. Sorry if my text freaked you out. I'll...I'll explain everything when we're at the beach. Okay?"

As soon as I know she's alright, it's all calm breathing, slowed driving speeds, and this instant, perfect relief, like the rest of the world could be facing a hostile zombie takeover, but if Whit is cool, it's all gonna be okay.

"Okay. I'll see you there." The last thing I want to do is disconnect, but I can't exactly heavy breathe into the phone til we get to the beach, so I just let her go and trust that she'll be there when I pull in.

I park in the lot and wait for her LeBaron to pull in. When it does, I'm already out of my Jeep and to her driver-side door, too damn happy to see her to care about the fact that I look like a total pathetic pushover. I don't trust that everything's alright until she steps out of the car and into my arms. Because, even if we're officially over after this meeting, I want to hold her one more time.

Her hair smells fantastic, grapefruit sweet. I press my lips to the waves and wrap my arms tight around her shoulders and love the way she rubs her face against my chest. I inhale, and the two best smells in my world get trapped in my lungs: the salty, cool sting of the ocean in the morning and sweet, morning-sweaty smell of Whit. I get to pretend, for a minute, that we're in my bed and I just woke up to that combination smell because she's settled down with me.

I drag the hug out for a little longer than is probably strictly kosher. How long is normal for someone you're worried enough to speed like a maniac at dawn to rescue, but aren't dating anymore, though you'd totally be fuck-buddies with her, except that you'd complicate things by secretly wanting to be exclusive because you're a jealous bastard? Yeah, it's kind of complicated.

Whit looks up at me, and I wonder if I'm transferring all my gooey missing-her-so-bad nonsense, because, under any other circumstances, I'd swear she was looking at me with lovey eyes. But this is Whit. My hardcore girl. She didn't do lovey eyes much when we were all mad in love. So, I'm either sliding into delusions, or the Everclear is still bending my brain.

"Um. Should we go sit? Like on the beach? If you want?" It's not like Whit to sound so unsure of herself. She's usually a bossy little brute leading me around by the nose.

I wonder what's making her so damn nervous, but I'm glad she wants to chill with me. I take her hand in mine and we head down to the cool sand. We sit side by side, and when she pulls her hood up to combat the chill of the still-grey dawn, I put my arm around her shoulders and rub a hand along the side of her to warm her up.

"Why are you doing this?" she asks, her eyes trained on the lightening horizon.

"Because you look cold. I thought Pennsylvania was, like, almost in Canada. Aren't you used to being cold?" I rub harder, purposefully misinterpreting her question.

She turns and looks at me, her eyes wide and totally serious. "No jokes. Not now. Why are you here?"

"Because you told me you needed me." It's more elaborate and a fucking million times simpler than that. I want to tell her that no matter where I am or what I'm doing, I'm always waiting for her. I'm always going to be there when she needs me, even if I know she doesn't want anything that's going to last long.

She swivels her entire body, and I redirect mine, so we're facing each other instead of the choppy waves. "I'm...I shouldn't have walked out on you, that day at my place. When we..."

"Had marathon sex? And you found the ring?" Her eyes go perfectly round and I take both her hands in mine. "No jokes, right? I felt like you stabbed me right in the heart, Whit. But I love that about you. That you're fierce as hell. And fearless. And strong. So I know why you had to kick me to the curb. I get it. Because I'm a shit-ton better than I was, but I'm still nowhere near good enough for you."

Her mouth opens and shuts and she swallows hard enough that I hear the gulping sound. She breaks my hold on her hands and wipes her eyes with the ragged cuff of her sleeve. "Every single thing you just said is so wrong."

I go still. Stone still. Ice statue still. Han Solo in carbonite still. And my rational adult heart gives a little thrum of hope.

She licks her lips and sniffles. "You, um, you totally over-estimate me, Deo. I'm not even remotely any of what you said. I'm a coward. I run away when things get hard. I push people out of my life like a stupid maniac. And, that day? I came home to make things right with you. And when you weren't there, I wanted to go find you, but I didn't. Because I'm gutless. I'm completely gutless."

I want to correct all the stupid bullshit she's yammering about, like how not awesome she is, but one part of her speech races in front of all the other parts and gives me a crazy rush Everclear couldn't begin to compete with. "Wait. Slow down, doll. You wanted to find me?"

She nods and bites her lips, first the top, then the bottom. "Yes. And apologize. And tell you...that...tell you that I..."

The wind whips wildly, blowing her hair in her face. She lifts her hand to tuck the dark strands behind her ear, and I catch her wrist, looking at the tattoo on the left side, under her pinkie.

"What's this?" I'm looking at the delicate anchor, still healing, and meet her eyes. "What's it for? What's it mean?"

She shakes her head, and I interrupt before she can brush it off.

I rip my hoodie off and point to the words on my ribs. Her words. "*This is part of me now.* You know how many times this goes through my head? But, you know what? I don't know if I should have gotten it." I'm half-disappointed, because the look of naked lust that slackened her features when I ripped my shirt off suddenly disappears and is replaced by guilt. "I should have tweaked it, because I knew what I wanted it to say that day. I wanted it to say, *You're a part of me now.*"

She puts her ice-cold fingers on my skin, and my teeth chatter. "Deo—"

"Don't." I grab her fingers and squeeze them. "If there's someone else, tell me. If this is some kind of symbolic thing because you're moving on, tell me. What you and I had was the most intense thing I've ever felt, but if it's over for you, just kick me hard enough so I'll remember the pain and stay out of your way." The hope that had picked up a few minutes before crashes down with a weight that buckles me. She'll tell me, it will be closure, and I'll do my thing and try to fill the hollow I know she'll leave behind with something else. Probably a lot of Everclear and karaoke.

All jokes aside, I feel like she really did kick me. In the junk and the kidneys. Like a heart-break ninja. Fuck my life.

She pulls her hands from mine and holds my face hard, forcing me to look her in the eye. "Shut up. Shut the hell up for a single second, Deo! Stop interrupting me. Stop and listen." I do. I stare at her gorgeous, sweet face and hold my damn breath. "I love you."

"What?" Confusion takes my brain in two beefy hands and shakes it like a rattle. "You what?"

Suddenly, surreally, her lips are hot and sweet on mine. "You. You, Deo. I love you." She crawls onto my lap, her body pressed hot and eager against mine, her hands running from my shoulder-blades down my back.

The words out of her mouth, her kisses, her body grinding hot and sweet and frantic against mine, all make my brain gun it and then stall. I pull back and her mouth runs along my jaw in wet, sloppy-sweet kisses that roam to my neck and leave me hard.

My fingers run back into her hair. "You love me?"

"You," she repeats dazedly, before her mouth finds that spot behind my ear that has me squeezing her ass and pulling her closer against me.

"The tattoo?" My question seems like it snaps her back to reality for a second. "It's cool if it was about someone else, Whit." It's not, but I'm ready to keep running with this whole making amends, being in love thing.

"You. You, you, you, Deo!" Her voice catches in the gusts of wind that toss her hair and competes with the waves for volume. "You made me want to sink."

I turn her hand and trace my fingers lightly over the still-tender flesh. "Sink? Is that a good thing?"

She hooks her hands around my neck and presses her forehead to mine. "Yes. I'm going to sink into what I feel for you. I'm going to sink into the good times and the scary shit. I'm going to sink with you, because I'm tired of drifting and treading, never committing to anything. I want to sink with you." Her fingers trace the lines on my ribs while mine cover her anchor.

"I love you, Whit." The words feel good ripped raw and free from my heart and throat. I crush her to my chest and kiss her hair and forehead, and the only thought that's clear in my brain is *mine*. She's mine. All mine. She's part of me now.

Or not really now.

She's been part of me for a long time.

And I want to have hot, crazy, nasty sex with her right on the beach. But the sun is an orange sliver over the dark, choppy waves, and it's getting fatter every second, which means that people will start driving by and maybe even coming for their morning jogs and shell combing expeditions. Also, I want her in my bed, because that's one of the benefits of this whole responsible thing: pleasuring your lady on a big ole mattress with sheets that would make sheiks weep with their silky smoothness. And we have matters of the heart to round off before I can take care of the need in my pants.

So I scoop her up, tromp across the sand, and drop her in my Jeep. She looks disappointed, which figures, since she has no clue what kind of sexual deviance is in her near future, and she starts to protest about the Lebaron, but I shush her, because this day is only going to become exponentially cooler, beginning with a stop by the reason I decided to trade my long-collected booty for the clapboard eyesore of a 70s dump I bought.

We drive along the road that leads to a small private beach and pull outside what's basically a biggish shed. Her look is pure, gorgeous confusion. So gorgeous, I let my Deo New World Order plans take a backseat while I maul her for a few passionate minutes. When she's good and breathless, I get my hard-on under control and lead her to my headquarters.

"What is this?" she asks, trying her best to not look totally underwhelmed since, I guess, that stupid happiness is radiating off my face.

"Behold." I swing the doors open and she smiles like she just recognized an old friend. "I officially got my business license in the mail yesterday. Beckett Boards."

"Deo. You can make surfboards?" She runs a hand over a few that line the walls.

"I shaped boards for a few years with some of my father's friends. I've been doing them for my friends for years, and I started coming up with some custom stuff that earned me a little punk cult following. So I figured I'd get my shit in order and get my business license. So, here I am." Now that I flung the doors open on my place for Whit to see, it looks a hell of a lot more like a shed with a couple of okay boards than a business.

Until she turns to look at me, her eyes shiny with a pride that makes me feel like the biggest badass in the world.

"I cannot believe you're doing this." She throws her arms around me and crushes the air out of my lungs. "Deo. How do you always wind up being even more freaking amazing than I remembered?"

"It's the Deo effect." I keep my voice cool, but I'm feeling every kind of choked up. I'm also probably on the cusp of some very hot action, but it gets railroaded by the little clipping tacked to my corkboard.

"What's that?" She walks over and tears the clipping from its tack with shaky hands, and I feel the clammy uncertainty that accompanies the dread of realizing you fucked up.

The awesome promise of the day starts to crumble fast under my feet. "I, uh, maybe I should have, uh, asked you—"

"You did this for Wakefield?" Whit is not a crier, but those big brown eyes are filling fast. "You did this for my brother?"

"Well, yeah. I owe him, you know." I take the clipping out of her hand and tack it back up, and she turns her head to look at it.

"How do you owe it to Wakefield?" Her eyebrows net together as she puzzles this problem.

I slide my hands under her elbows and pull her close. "Because he led you here. And I found you. And I started to think about how he made you live large, because he couldn't. And it bummed me out. All you told me about him, you know? He never got to meet that girl, the one who changed everything for him. And he never got to surf. And here I am, sitting around like a fucking lump, able to do all the shit Wakefield couldn't. And I thought, fuck that, you know? He *can* do shit. And I can help. So, every time a kid gets a custom board, it's because of him. That way he's still changing shit. He's still part of all this."

She looks over my shoulder at the clipping. "The boy? Who is he?"

"Some punk." I look back at the kid with a mop of dark hair, his black eyes squinted because of his gap-toothed smile. "His name is Hudson Alma, and he's a little prick. The kid kissed the reporter's ass because she was hot, then he didn't even thank me for the board, and made me change five hundred details. He was bossing my ass around like he owned the joint. To top it all off, I paddled out with him to do a test run, and the jerkoff showed my ass up. Bad. That little shit will probably become a surfing god someday. He's arrogant enough. You know, and good enough." When I look at Whit, she's shaking her head.

Her laugh is half a sob. "There's something wrong with you." She wraps her arms around my waist with an anaconda grip. "And I love it. I love every damn thing about you. Wakefield would have flipped out over this. Thank you. So much." Her voice gets sandpaper rough, and she puts her head on my chest. "Thank you for everything."

"Wait! This isn't it." I lead her out of the shop, and we walk past the Jeep, along the sandy path clotted with beach grass and noisy with the beat of the waves. The house looks sadder now that I'm trying to imagine it through Whit's eyes, with a dilapidated fence half-falling down around the weed-clogged yard and its loose shingles and faded paint. I lead her to the chipped, peeling door and slide my key in. The house smells like mildew, new paint, and the slightest whiff of vomit. Cohen must have woken up and dragged himself to the couch, where he's snoring so loud, the cherry-red walls vibrate.

"You have a house?" she breathes, looking around the tiny beach cottage. "Are you renting?"

I shake my head. "All mine. Pretty sexy, right? I was kinda hoping you could hang here. With me." I'm careful to keep it cool. It isn't exactly an engagement ring, and she did just tell me she loved me, but I'm not about to set her running again.

Her hand tightens around mine. I have no idea if that jerk of her fingers is from panic or excitement. So, before I can get an answer I may not like, I drag her to the bedroom.

The rest of the house is pretty moderately furnished, but the bedroom is all colossal excess, focused primarily around the enormous bed I got her into the day before Mom and Rocko's wedding. It's warm and dark and inviting in this room, and I pull her in with every intention of seducing her into every crook and corner of my life again.

"Deo," she whispers as I click the door shut.

For one second, we stare at each other across the space of a few inches. Then she rushes the gap and her lips cover mine.

"Whit." I pull back and work her sweatshirt over her head. She's wearing a thin t-shirt with nothing else underneath. I tug that up too, and she hooks her thumbs under the bottom of my hoodie and rips it off in one jerky movement. I press her cotton shorts down her hips, and Whit Conrad is officially standing in all her naked glory in my bedroom.

Score.

She pushes me down on the bed with one eager pounce and seals her mouth over mine, sliding her hand down my shorts to press her hand against my hard-on. I arch into her, my hands on her hips, pressing up and down her back, running over her hair, and gripping her shoulders.

"I want you. I've wanted you for weeks," she says between clenched teeth, her hands clawing at the waistband of my half-unzipped shorts. I drag my hands away from her body for a quick second, just so I can kick the rest of my clothes off. She presses down on me, hot and so wet it's pure torture. "I love you. I love you so much, Deo."

"I love you, Whit." I sit up and pull her close, our mouths fierce and fast, like we're trying to make up for all the time we wasted like two morons. I knock the drawer out of my side-table getting a condom. She tears it out of my hands and then the package and grasps down, takes my painfully hard dick in her small hand, rolls the condom on, and fits me against her, pushing down with one hot, tight thrust of her hips.

The focus in the room blinks in and out, and I dig my fingers into the soft skin of her thighs, kissing her until her quick, gasping moans transfer into my mouth. She's whimpering, her mouth suddenly still and pulled tight.

I brace one hand on the center of her back and lean her against my arm, lifting and pumping into her with quicker, deeper thrusts until her body starts to tighten, like a slowly twisted spring that finally, in one shattering, quaking release, explodes against me.

Her skin is under my hands, her taste is in my mouth, her smell on my skin, the slick heat of her body is wrapped around the rigid length of mine, and it all crashes into me, so much, too much, and everything I wanted. For one perfect, incredible pulse, Whit and I are twined together, anchored to each other, sunk into a love so deep and incredible, neither one of us has a chance in hell of pushing back out of it. I'm part of her now. She's part of me. And we've each traveled the lengths of our own crazy, impossibly tangled paths that seemed to be driving us in opposite directions, but circled us back into each other's waiting arms.

Epilogue

"Are you sure you can't come?" I ask. I'm aware that the boat looks a little worn, but Whit knows I'd never ask her to come if it wasn't one hundred percent safe. She trusts me to take care of her because I always do. And I love doing it.

Her dark hair comes out of the loose braid that's lying over her shoulder with the rising wind. "You know I can't. My finals are in three weeks, and you might need longer than that. Plus, even if you could get me back in time, I'd miss too much school. And you'd never let me get any studying done."

"I could totally do flashcards with you after I eat you out. You know you study better when you're relaxed." Her blush goes root-deep. "Come on. How could you say no to this adventure?"

Her smile curls on her lips and goes right to her eyes. "This is your adventure. And I'll be right here waiting for you when you get back."

"With the wheelbarrow?" I put a hand behind her neck and rub my thumb along her jaw. She presses her face against my palm.

Her brown eyes narrow slightly. "You really think we'll need a wheelbarrow for all your treasure?"

"Probably three or five. We may need to hire some day laborers to transport all our mad loot." I reach for her hand and run my finger over the anchor tattoo, then bump along her knuckles and brush the sapphire ring I put on her finger three weeks after she moved into my beach shack.

I guess a wiser guy would have waited so she wouldn't spook again. But the fair was only around for that one week, and I wasn't about to wait a whole year for my next chance. And I needed a ferris wheel, because I was hell-bent on starting everything with Whit on a lucky note. Nothing could have been luckier than starting things the same way my grandparents did, and the cotton candy, root beer, Cracker Jack magic landed me with a deliciously hot, extremely turned-on fiancé. Awesome all around.

She rubs her fingers over the anchor on my hand, identical to hers. "Aren't you scared I'll only want you for your money?"

I pull her close. "Nah. You loved me when I was a poor surfboard shaper. I know you don't care about my money. It was always my huge cock, and I've accepted that."

She laughs, so loud and happy, it twists my gut, because I know I'm going to miss that laugh like crazy.

"You're so conceited, it's probably dangerous." She says that, but she's kissing me with that wild kick of passion that lets me know we're definitely going to christen my bunk again before Cohen gets here and we set sail.

"Speaking of my huge package, my mom got a box together for you so you won't sink into a depression when you don't have access to my penis." I lead her onto the boat, equipped with a decent amount of used gear for treasure hunting. Business has been alright for me, and Cohen's credit is immaculate, so we were able to get the bulk of what we needed together in time to follow my father's insider lead on a fairly promising dive. I'm excited. Not that I think we'll actually hit the mother-load, but I'm doing it. I'm going on the dive for treasure that was always just a pipe-dream before.

Whit opens the box and smiles. I try to peek, but she crushes the box to her chest. "Girl secrets," she says.

I catch sight of the cover of a book with a grey tie on it, a bottle of lube, and a sparkly purple vibrator. Thanks for keeping my girl happy while I'm gone, Mom.

"Come on over here and share some of your girl secrets with me before I go on my long trip out to sea." I pull her on top of me and enjoy the press of her sweet, warm body has me whispering the words that make her moan and wiggle out of her clothes.

A while later, she's in my arms, relaxed and satisfied. "You sure you don't want to come? I'll let you be captain."

"Mmm. Tempting." She kisses me softly. "I'm proud of you for doing this, Deo. But it's your thing. I'll be here when you get back."

"You sure?" I slide our hands, palm to palm, and thread my fingers through hers, so our anchors are aligned. "I sometimes have this crazy fear I'll get back and you'll have drifted away."

"Nah." She presses her lips over our two thumbs, twined one over the other. "I'm sunk too deep into you to ever drift away."

I feel the beat of her heart against my chest, and I swear my heart answers hers in time. And I know, in that second, that our love is so deep and strong, years of sinking fast and fierce won't even scratch the surface of the lengths we'll go to keep it that way.

Acknowledgments

Thanks to Katie Medvegy for knowing all the things. Like, how to spell Eleanor.

Thank you to Abbi Glines, who cheer-leaded us to the finish like a champ.

Thank you to Todd Maloy for our gorgeous cover.

Thanks to The Black Keys for writing amazing and inspiring music.

Thanks to all of the awesome bloggers and readers who support us and help spread the word about our books. We love you for respecting what we do and sharing what we all love.

Thanks to our families, who let us get all tangled up in fictional worlds for hours....days...weeks...months. We love you so much.

And..

Thanks to all the writers out there who make us cry, swoon, and want to throw books at the wall from sweet frustration. Keep on keeping on and pushing every boundary set up for you, because you are inspiring us every single day.

About the Authors

Liz Reinhardt was born and raised in the idyllic beauty of northwest NJ. A move to the subtropics of coastal Georgia with her daughter and husband left her with a newly realized taste for the beach and a bloated sunscreen budget. Right alongside these new loves is her old, steadfast affection and longing for bagels and the fast-talking foul mouths of her youth.

She loves Raisinettes, even if they aren't really candy, the Oxford comma, movies that are hilarious or feature zombies, any and all books, but especially romance (the smarter and hotter, the better), the sound of her daughter's incessantly wise and entertaining chatter, and watching her husband work on cars in the driveway.

You can read her blog at www.elizabethreinhardt.blogspot.com, like her on Facebook, or email her at lizreinhardtwrites@gmail.com.

****

Steph Campbell is a So Cal Native, happily married mother to four evil geniuses, a nail polish addict and YA Junkie. When she isn't reading, writing or wiping someone's nose, you can usually find her baking something.

Other Novels Currently Available by Steph Campbell are:

DELICATE (Contemporary YA) (July 2012)

GROUNDING QUINN (Contemporary YA Mature) (June 2011)

BEAUTIFUL THINGS NEVER LAST (New Adult)
MY HEART FOR YOURS - co-written with Jolene Perry (New Adult Romance) (May 2012)
A TOAST TO THE GOOD TIMES (with Liz Reinhardt) (New Adult)

Steph blogs at http://stephcampbell.blogspot.com/
Stop by and say hello!
https://www.facebook.com/stephcampbellwrites
Twitter: stephcampbell_

Made in the USA
Charleston, SC
06 March 2013